I0544934

SNOOKER'S LEGACY

PAUL SHADINGER

A MATT PRESTON NOVEL

SNOOKER'S LEGACY
Copyright © 2019 Paul Shadinger
All Rights Reserved

ISBN: 978-1-7337215-0-9

All rights reserved. This book or any portions thereof
cannot be reproduced or used in any manner without the
express written permission of the author except for the use
of brief quotations in a book review.

No part of this book may be reproduced, or stored in a re-
trieval system, or transmitted in any form or by any means,
electronic, mechanical, photocopying, recording, or otherwise.

Edited by: Jessica West
Cover Design by: Kevin G. Summers
Formatting by: Kevin G. Summers
Professional Photograph by: Arisa Collective

PLEASE NOTE

Snooker's Legacy is a work of fiction. This means that all names, characters, places, organizations, companies, brands, clubs, businesses, streets and incidents are the product of the author's imagination or are used fictitiously. Because this is a work of fiction, timelines and facts do not have to add up. Since this novel is made up, any resemblance to any actual events, locals, entities, or persons, living or dead, is entirely coincidental.

If you continue to have ANY issues with this novel, I would invite you to reread the first line of the first paragraph. Thank you.

Matt and I would like to thank you for your interest in this novel and Matt's other adventures which are all available on Amazon.com.

Paul Shadinger
April 2019

ALSO BY PAUL SHADINGER

Fiction

Houseboat (2016)
Code Name: Crescent (2017)
The Gypsy Queen (2018)
Quick, Quick, Slow (2018)

A Matt Preston Novel

DEDICATION

As always, I would like to dedicate this book to every one of you who read my novels, and yet continue to encourage me to keep writing. Without a doubt, none of my novels would exist without your words of inspiration, encouragement and support. Positive words are truly food to any author, and I cannot begin to describe the number of banquets so many of you have provided. Thank you all for your wonderful comments and encouragement. Without you, Matt and the crew would not be here.

This book is also dedicated to my wife, Sandy. Over the years she's seen things in my writing I never saw. It was through her encouragement I've been able to keep writing. I cannot underestimate the importance she's had in so many ways. Truly, without her, Matt Preston and the rest of the cast would still be locked in the bowels of my computer.

Finally, this book is dedicated to our beloved little guy, Max. From the moment that little blond fluff of fur crawled up in Sandy's lap and fell asleep, he has been one of our constant companions. We recently had to put him down and it was perhaps even more difficult to do than when we put Brenna down. As I mentioned before, our pets give us unconditional love and all they ask from us is when they are in pain, and there is no longer any quality of life, we do the right thing and release them from that pain.

Somewhere, over the rainbow, Buttons, Brenna, Pepper and Max are playing and waiting for us to show up. Until then, I will always love all of you and miss you so. If only we could be the person our pets think we are. I do believe the world would be a far better place if we were.

Paul Shadinger
North Fort Myers, Florida
(2019)

TABLE OF CONTENTS

CHAPTER ONE

Tuesday.

Poker night.

I glared over the table at the punk parked across from me and thought, *Unshaven, unkempt, heavily tattooed arms, ball-cap on backward and a foul mouth—just about everything I despise about today's youth.* I hadn't started the evening in a foul mood, but this idiot was doing his best to put me in a poor frame of mind.

Looking around the poker table, I counted eight players that night, nine counting myself, and of those players, two were white. The rest were black, which made no difference to me. The punk was the only other Caucasian there. I knew him, Fred, from before and I was ashamed we were the same race.

Four of the players were members of a jazz band led by another player who went by the nickname Tubs. Some players were also former professional basketball players. Back in the day, before he started his jazz band, Tubs used to play pro-basketball. Many fans to this day say he was the finest player the sport has ever seen. His given name is William Tate, but he's called Tubs because besides being the leader, he plays the drums in his jazz group ensemble. The group has released several cd's, and several times I've even been lucky enough to play piano with the group. I had the time of my life.

Tubs' buddy on the left of Fred was Earl. Earl was a massive man. I mean like scary large. I forget the pro NFL football team he played for, but when Earl played ball, they nicknamed him The Duke of Earl, Duke of Defense. Some broadcasters often joked that he could gather the entire other team in his arms then toss out players until he found the one with the ball then throw him on the ground.

Tubs had dealt the cards, and it was Fred's turn to bet. Fred sat there for the longest time, contemplating his cards, until finally Earl reached over, snatched Fred's ball cap off his head and tossed it onto the floor. "Ain't your mama never taught you nuthin'?" Earl's voice was deep and when he spoke, you felt his words in your chest.

Two players snickered while Fred glared at him. "What'd ya do that for?"

"You wear a hat or a cap outside, but take it off inside. Now, you gonna bid, fold, or what?"

Fred snarled back, "Listen, boy, you fat, dumb, ignorant n…" and that's as far as Fred got. Earl reached over, grabbed the front of Fred's wrinkled sweatshirt, and snatched him one handed—with no effort—from his chair. When Earl yanked Fred across the table, the whole room lurched and dropped from under me. With no warning, the room was gone.

In an instant, I was awake.

Henry the pilot was swearing. I glanced over and noticed he was looking at me. Via our headsets, he said, "Sorry about that, Matt. Rough air caught me totally off guard. I'm lookin' for a different altitude to get out of this mess. Now, go back to sleep."

I thought to myself, *Are you shitting me? Henry, I'm awake now!* You cannot wake up when a plane drops out from under you, then just go back to sleep. I'm not that fond of flying anyway and now I was on an adrenalin high like I'd never experienced. Sleep was a long way away in my foreseeable future.

I tried to remember the dream I was having, but I could only recall it involving a punk named Fred whom I'd had a run in with a few months ago at our poker game, and another player who is the bass player from my friend's jazz ensemble. At the last game, Fred had called one of the black players the "N" word and got himself thrown through a doorway, without the door being open. I wasn't there, but I'd heard about it and wished I could have seen it myself.

Now that I was awake, I tried to find a more comfortable posture to ease some of the aches and pains left over from my last adventure. Settling into a new position, I mulled over the various things I needed to take care of in Seattle. One important thing was getting over to the Olympic Peninsula and seeing my old army buddy Walter and his wife Thein.

Walter and I had just finished a mission where we were helping a friend over in the Middle East. I'd received several severe beatings during our time over there and I was still recovering. Thus the reason for trying to find a new arrangement for the ole body to ease some of the leftover aches and pains.

I hadn't seen Walter since we'd parted company over in Azerbaijan and he'd gone with some hostages we'd rescued while we were all trying to escape from Nakhchivan. They had to leave me behind because of my physical condition but promised they would return to get me. Walter thought he'd stashed me in a safe place, however eventually I realized it was necessary for me to escape. I wanted to see Walter and find out how he was doing since his return and I wanted to see my dogs. Thein and Walter were taking care of my two dogs and I eventually wanted them back. Probably not this visit, but soon.

Gazing out of the plane's front window, I also remembered the pilot, Henry, had asked if I'd give him a few minutes after we landed since he wanted to talk about something. He wouldn't give me a clue and I was curious.

Through the headphones I heard Henry ask for landing instructions into Seattle's Boeing Airfield. Shortly thereafter, we started our descent into Seattle, down through the clouds. At what I felt was the last possible moment, the clouds parted. The tower instructed Henry to park on an isolated area of the tarmac, after which a Jeep drove out and took us back to the terminal. At one end was a little café. Once we were inside, we found a table near the rear.

The cafe was a greasy spoon, and it reeked of old grease from countless hamburgers and tons of French fries. I was grateful the back door was open since there was a light breeze moving through the room, which helped a little with the smell. The place wasn't perfect, but it was acceptable. Looking outside at the overcast skies, I noted several advantages of living in Florida. Our coffee arrived. I added some half-and-half and leaned back in my chair. "What's on your mind, Mr. Walbourn? What can I do for you?"

Henry smiled. "Remember, you Matt, me Henry? I thought we were past the mister part."

I chuckled.

"Don't know if you knew this, Matt, but I'm eligible to retire any time now."

"Really? I'd no idea. You seem awfully young to consider retirement. You must be a lot older than you look. Is retirement what you really want?"

"Not exactly. I'm eligible, but I know what I want to do. However, first I need to ask you something. Matt, I don't want to offend you, but the problem is I don't know exactly know to start this conversation."

"Shoot, dude. As long as you don't ask me any kinky questions, everything else is fair game."

Henry smiled slightly at my little joke.

"Please don't think me rude," he began, and I nodded. "I don't know exactly your total net worth, and I don't care, but I know you have money. I understand when you helped your software friend find the lady friend of his, he gave you part of his company and because you advised me to do it, I bought stock in his company. I know how well I've done with that stock, and I can only imagine how you have fared. I also overheard the Admiral remark one time that you were richer than God!" Henry smiled, but I didn't react to the comment.

Life had been good to me. Investments and inheritance provided me with an excellent standard of living and this financial freedom gave me the time and opportunity, along with some valuable skills Uncle Sam taught me to help friends with various projects.

"The reason I bring all this up is I wanted you to understand why I've come to you. I want to start a business and I want you involved. The situation is this—I can get my hands on three planes the government will soon sell, probably within the next 45 days. One of them is that plane sitting out there on the tarmac. By the way, it's the one we used when I got you out of Nakhchivan. So, I know you're aware what that plane can do." That was an understatement. That plane had saved both of our lives over in the Middle East.

"It would be very difficult for a civilian to purchase a plane like that," he continued. "A person would have to know exactly what to order to duplicate the three planes I want to purchase. The government has a policy on how long they keep a plane. It's based on either engine hours or flight time. The planes have been well maintained and if they were civilian ones, there's no way someone would sell them.

"However, I know how to bid and who to bid through. That means I can get the planes much cheaper than the average person trying to purchase them. I also know five other pilots like me. They have enough time in the service and they are eligible to retire. If we purchase the planes, I can get enough government contracts to keep the three planes busy all the time and that doesn't count civilian work we can pick up. The six of us would keep flying for the government, but in our free time, we would fly for our new company. If this works out like I expect it to, in six months, we may have to purchase another two planes which are coming up for sale and look for additional pilots." Henry reached into an inside pocket of his jacket and pulled out an envelope.

"That's a proforma—or a budget, if you will—for the company I want to start showing best-case scenario and worst-case scenario. I'd ask you please look it over. Will you do that for me?"

"Are you asking me to finance the whole thing?" Not that it would be a problem, but I wanted to know what I was getting into.

"Oh God, no… I'm sorry if I gave you that impression. Three of us are putting up a substantial portion of the money and we wanted to offer you a fourth of the business for your investment. I also overheard the Admiral saying something about how he was tiring of you borrowing a plane all the time and I thought this would help you out." Henry grinned at me and I had to laugh. My friend the Admiral was giving me a hard time because I'd asked to borrow one of his planes several times. The Admiral's whole name is Johnathan Apple Orchard. And yes, I guess his parents had a sense of humor. Orchard was Henry's boss, and he was also a good friend of mine. Over the years, I'd done favors for John and I'd just finished with one over in the Middle East.

Henry continued. "The truth is, we also need and want you involved because of your credit standing. We're not bad credit risks, but with what your credit status must be, our little company would look a lot healthier on paper." He smiled at me and I winked back.

6

"All the numbers are there. Matt, this'd be like having three of your own planes and perhaps eventually five planes. All six pilots would know you'd come first when you wanted a plane."

I held up my hand to object to the one point I disagreed with so far. "No, Henry. I appreciate what you're offering, but if all of you are busy, then I can wait. Business always comes first. Business has to come first. Agreed?" I waited until he nodded. "If I need to go that quickly, I'll fly commercial. Don't promise something that could hurt the business."

"Will you look over the proposal?"

"Henry, after what you did for me over in... wherever the hell we were, I'd finance a rubber band powered plane for you. I don't know if I ever thanked you properly, but your magic button saved my ass. Then you came and found me and got me in your plane. I don't know how you got us out of that place, but I'll always be grateful to you. Is that plane over there a normal military plane?"

When Henry and I had parted company over in Nakhchivan after he had ferried me to our jump off spot, he'd given me what looked like a fat coin. Actually, it was a homing device and once squeezed, it sent out a signal. Henry had a receiver which would locate the device and he could find me. I'd used the device and Henry had flown into the country without permission, landed on a deserted road, found me all beaten up and trapped in a Jeep, and rescued me. To say I was grateful was putting it mildly.

Henry grinned at me and shook his head. "Not really. Orchard and I drew up the specs for that sucker and also the other two I want to get my hands on. There are very few planes made like that where regular people can get their hands on them. I knew we would get away, I only hoped you'd still be in one piece after we escaped. I know I didn't give you a lot of time to get into your seat."

His comment reminded me of something I'd wanted to ask for a long time. "When you came and rescued me over in Nakhchivan, who got that plane airborne? You were still closing the hatch and getting me into my seat, but somehow the plane took off. Who or how?"

"Lois."

My mouth dropped open.

Henry noticed how flabbergasted I was. "Didn't you know Lois was the top pilot in her class? She is qualified to fly just about every plane in the U.S. fleet."

I shook my head. If I thought my current lady friend Lois was interesting before, she was getting more fascinating by the moment now.

"She and I have also flown on a few missions together for the Admiral."

"I'm stunned. Who knew Lois could fly an airplane? Okay, Henry, when do you need an answer? How much time do I have to think about your proposal?"

"This plane we are on right now will be decommissioned the end of the month. If I had this plane now, I'd have a couple of charters waiting to go. And there are another two planes I want to purchase that are on the same schedule. If we're going to get them, we need to place a bid as soon as possible. Even though I have first right of refusal on all three, there are other buyers out there interested. I don't mean to put pressure on you, but I'm sure you see that time is short."

"I think my answer will be positive, but I'd like to look this over first. I'll have an answer for you in... umm, two days. Fair?"

"I can live with that. Now, what all are you planning to do on this trip home?"

"Among other things, Senator Albert Bradson has requested to see me. I don't know what that's all about. And I hope to find time to make a final motorcycle trip. It's time to sell my toy. Don't want to, but it's time. It's just getting too dangerous to ride anymore. Too many very stupid people on the road now days. Besides, at my age, it takes too long to heal if I get hurt. Look at me, I'm still trying to recover from the beatings I received while helping Walter and others.

"I also want to get over to the Olympic Peninsula and see Walter and his wife. My dogs are over there with him and I want to spend some time with them. I have a rather long list of things I need to do, then I want to know where I can find you. I'll want to go to D.C. and see Lois. I miss her, and I need to talk to her. Our time together in Fort Myers left me wanting more. And now you tell me she's an ace pilot. That gal is really something."

"Matt, you don't know the half of it. I'm sure you know how much Orchard relies on her. She has even helped get me out of a few scrapes. You are a lucky man. When you want to go see Lois, give me a couple days' warning and I'll make arrangements to get you there. It sounds like you'll be busy?"

"Yeah, I'll keep out of trouble." I extended my hand and Henry took it in both of his.

"Try to have a good time with all of your errands. You've earned it. I'd ask a favor, however—please don't forget about me."

"Henry, after what you did for me, there's no way I'd forget you. I don't mean to beat a dead horse, but I'm so grateful that you came and rescued me. I like the sound of your entire offer. I'll admit, I'm tired of begging the Admiral every time I need a plane. I promised you I'd let you know my answer in two days, and I will."

I'd already decided to become part of the business, but I still wanted to mull it over. I wanted to make sure there was nothing at the other end of this deal that might bite me on the butt. Lately, it seems my butt has been bitten too many times and I don't have enough left back there for another ass chewing.

9

CHAPTER TWO

I walked out to my truck but as I started it, I noticed an envelope tucked under the driver's side windshield wiper. I retrieved the envelope and opened it. Inside I found a terse letter demanding I come to the Security/Operations office with the letter.

Oh great! I thought. *Just what I need, more crap in my life to deal with.* Ever since my visit to the Middle East, I've noticed I had little or no patience. I was a lot shorter tempered than I used to be, and the happy-go-lucky guy I once was seemed to be missing. I knew part of it was from the physical abuse I'd received over in the Middle East, but some of it seemed to come from a change in my attitude about life. Regardless of the cause, I didn't like myself very much.

I asked a few people where to find the security office and finally found the location. I thrust the note I'd found on my truck at the lady behind the counter. She told me to take a seat. In a few minutes, a man in a uniform came out and told me to follow him. He led me into a small room then pointed at a chair, indicating I should sit. I sat, noticing his nametag, R. A. Peterson, attached to a too tight shirt stretched across a good-sized stomach. The way he wore his hair and the uniform that was too small for him, he reminded me of a high school athlete gone to seed. The hair was close cropped; his face was round and when he talked, his jowls wobbled. With no preamble, he demanded, "How come your truck's been in our lot for so long?"

I sat quietly for a moment, wondering how I wanted to handle this with the least amount of problem or involvement of others. I didn't feel I'd done anything wrong and for sure I didn't care for his attitude. "I believe I was parked in the LONG TERM lot." To myself I thought, *Besides it ain't your parking lot.*

He nodded.

"Then I don't understand the problem."

"We rarely have vehicles parked there for that length of time."

"I saw no signs regarding permissible length of stay."

My comment went unheeded. "Actually, your truck's been sitting there so long, someone has stolen the license plate. Do you have any proof the truck is yours?"

"Yes, but the registration is out in the glove box. Do you want me to go get it?"

"No. Stay there. I don't want you leaving the office. By the way, where were you for so long?"

I reached inside my coat pocket and handed over the credentials Admiral Orchard had given me when I was searching for an international computer hacker named The Gypsy Queen. The credentials said I was a member of a top secret organization.

Officer Peterson picked the creds up and looked them over. "What are these?"

So many smart-assed comments came to mind, but I held my tongue. "Basically, those are my reasons for leaving my truck in your parking lot for so long."

"I don't understand."

"Not to be rude, but you really don't need to understand. But, to resolve your issue, I've been away on a mission overseas. A top secret mission overseas. The key word in that sentence is 'secret'. That's also the reason I still look a little worse for wear. What you have in your hands are my credentials from the organization I work for. Normally, nobody gets to see those. My mission and the organization are top secret, as are the identities of its members."

"How do I know these credentials are real?" He shook the creds in his hands at me.

The comment stunned me. "Are you having me on? You really don't mean you think I'd hand you something like those credentials without being able to prove it?"

"So, prove it."

Taken aback by his pugnacious request, I wondered how I could resolve this without things turning into an even bigger brouhaha. How was I going to prove to this individual what I was telling him was true? His uniform gave me an idea, and I fished out my cell phone and called Jeff L. Davenport, a childhood friend and the Commissioner of the Seattle Police Department. Jeff picked it up on the second ring. "Matt, what's happening?"

"I'm here at Boeing Field and I'm trying to pick up my truck. I'm with some wanna-be officer in the Security office and he's giving me a ration of shit. Besides my truck's license plate being missing, he wants to know why my truck was there so long in the parking lot. I tried to explain the reason is secret, but he won't buy it. I even showed him my cred pack, and he is accusing me of it being fake. Any ideas on what to do?"

"Where are you exactly?"

"In an office called Security/Operations at the north end of Boeing Field. The cat's name is—"

"Hand your phone to him," Jeff interrupted.

I extended the phone towards R.A. Peterson. "Here, this is Seattle Police Commissioner Davenport. He'd like to speak to you."

R.A. took the phone and with an insolent tone of voice, said, "Yeah what do you want?" I could hear a buzzing in the phone. Finally, he sneered. "Look, fellow, I have no idea who you are and frankly I don't give a shit. You could be the dogcatcher for all I know. Just because this guy hands me some bogus identification and then calls somebody on the phone who could be anyone off the street for all I know, I'm supposed to get all gooey. I don't know who you are and you're wasting my time. Good bye."

R.A. hung up and tossed me the phone.

I shook my head. "Peterson, that was not a wise move. Who's your boss?"

"None of your business. I'm asking the questions here! I don't know what's going on, but I'm calling the Seattle police and turning you over to them. I'll let them sort this out."

"You just had the top cop in Seattle on the phone."

"Yeah, right!" R.A. popped off and he reached for the phone sitting on his desk. As he picked up the handset to dial a number, I heard a siren in the distance, approaching the terminal. The siren stopped as a squad car pulled up in front of the building.

"Ahh, I see my ride is here," I remarked. I could hear a commotion out in the lobby and with little fanfare, the door flew open and there stood an older person dressed in a uniform much like the one Peterson was wearing.

"What the hell is going on?" the man shouted. "And why are the police here?"

"Are you his boss?" I asked.

"Yes, why?" The fellow looked at R.A. and asked again, "Peterson, please explain what's happening?"

R.A. boasted. "This is the fellow who owns the pickup with the missing plates you were wondering about. You know, the one that's been sitting in the long-term parking for so long. The police are here to take him in."

"And what did he tell you?" the older man asked.

"You won't believe this! He gave me some cock and bull story about being a spy or something and that he'd been on a top secret mission. Then he flashed fake federal credentials at me."

The two uniformed Seattle police officers entered from the outer office and asked the older guard to please step aside. When the senior officer asked why, one of the officers responded, "We're here to escort a R. A. Peterson to see Commissioner Davenport. It seems that Peterson was rude and disrespectful. However, the main reason we're here is because he's holding a federal agent against his will." That wasn't exactly true, but I wasn't going to correct my allies.

One of the police officers turned and looked at me; we knew each other. He smiled as he nodded. "Hello Mr. Preston. What's the problem here?"

"It seems my truck has overstayed its welcome in the long-term parking lot and now that I wish to leave, they won't believe I know the Chief or that I've been on an overseas government mission."

The officer informed the two guards, "This is Matt Preston. I know this gentleman and he's also a personal friend of the Chief. I believe he's got something to do with a top secret agency back in D.C. After that, I really don't want to know more." The officer pointed at Peterson. "You've infuriated the Chief and I've been instructed to bring you in, in handcuffs if I must. I don't know what you said to the chief, but he is one furious individual now. And nobody on the force likes it when the Chief is upset. Let's go. Are you coming along peacefully, because I'd just love to cuff you?"

Peterson looked at me with horror stamped on his face. "You were, ah… you were telling the truth."

I nodded. I grinned at him. I know, I am so bad sometimes.

"What am I going to do?"

I continued grinning at him as I told him, "You're going with my friends here to meet one of my friends. I told you it was Chief Davenport on the phone, but you wouldn't listen."

The Seattle officer asked again, "Are you coming with us or do I have get physical with you?"

As an answer, Peterson stood and headed for the doorway followed by his boss. The Seattle police officer turned. "You're free to go, Mr. Preston. I'm sorry for any inconvenience this may have caused you. Have a good day."

"And you as well officer. Be gentle with ol' R.A. there. He's having a terrible day. And I'm sure when the chief is done with him, it'll be a lot worse."

The officer's laugh sounded like a growl as he left the office.

Peterson's boss turned to leave, but paused and turned to face me. "May I see your parking stub?" I handed it to him and he wrote *Paid* across the front and signed his name. "It's the least I could do. Sorry about the confusion."

"Thanks. I hope you have a better day."

His smile was more grimace than a smile. Neither he nor Peterson were going to have a good day.

CHAPTER THREE

I returned to my truck and fired it up, waiting a moment for it to warm up. After being parked for so long outside, the interior was really cold and damp. I remembered Senator Bradson asked to see me while I was in town, and I wondered if he might be in Seattle now. I dug my cell phone out of my pocket and called the private number I had for Albert. The phone rang three times and went to voice mail. I hung up and tried his cell phone. He answered it right away. "Albert. It's Matt."

"Hello, Matt! Where are you?"

"I just got into Seattle. I'm still at Boeing Field, had a slight problem picking up my vehicle but everything's okay now. Where are you?"

"I'm in Seattle too. I'm just getting out of a meeting. Any chance we can meet at Mouse's condo... say, in about an hour?"

"That works. See you then."

When I was on my last mission over to the Middle East, Mouse had supplied me with several interesting weapons. The basement of his condo building contained enough armament to outfit a small army. I'd never known a person so well connected. I counted myself lucky to call him a good friend.

Seeing both Mouse and Albert worked out well since I needed to thank Mouse for his help on that mission and I wanted to apologize to Bradson for the trouble he got into for trying to keep track of its status. Senator Albert Bradson also owes a lot to Mouse for his help in getting elected to the U.S. Senate. I don't know what Mouse's involvement really was, but I know without Mouse's help, Albert probably wouldn't have been elected.

I arrived at Mouse's condo building a little early. His building was seventy something floors tall and named The Olympus. I knew it didn't matter if I was early; Mouse would be happy to see me. I pulled up under The Olympus portico and as the valet opened my door, he exclaimed, "Good afternoon, Mr. Preston. So good to see you again."

I'd only seen this fellow once, maybe twice, but he remembered my name. Impressive. "Good afternoon. You have me at a disadvantage. I'm sorry but I don't remember your name."

"Wells, sir. Marshall Wells." The name still didn't ring a bell, but I didn't tell him that.

Marshall got in my truck and drove off. I turned and walked into the building where the concierge also greeted me by name, and we stepped over to an elevator marked Private. He pushed a button, the door opened, and I stepped aboard. I noticed there were just two buttons on the inner panel: one marked Penthouse and the other marked Lobby. I pushed Penthouse.

When the door opened, Mouse was standing there with his arms outstretched. "Matt." He stood there for a moment, looking at my face. It looked a lot better than it did a few weeks ago, but it still showed signs of the beatings I'd received. "Oh, Matt. I'm so sorry you had such problems over in Nakhchivan. I still see signs of your difficulties. I heard all about what happened from Ilox and Orchard. What you did really impressed Ilox and our relationship is much better than before you went over. I know it doesn't help you much, but many people are grateful for what you did."

I didn't feel I'd done much since most of the time, I was tied up and being thumped on by the bad guys. I don't mean to be flip about the whole affair, but I never discovered who the players were during my visit. Other than one person I knew from stateside, everybody was new. I mentioned to Mouse I felt I didn't do that much, and he assured me because of my presence, everyone was concentrating on me, which allowed the rest of my party free to move about with a lot fewer problems than would have otherwise been possible.

Mouse pulled me into the front room and called out for Jade, his wife. She came running into the room and when she saw my face, she stopped. "Oh, god, Matt, you look awful."

"Thanks, Jade. Boy, you look like you've gained quite a bit of weight."

She blushed and hung her head. When she looked up, she had the cutest grin on her face. "I'm sorry, that was rude of me. I didn't mean for it to come out that way. I meant, I feel awful you had to go through what you did. You look wonderful and I'm so happy to see you. Do I get a hug now?"

I held out my arms, and she ran and jumped up. I held her against me and kissed both cheeks. She trapped my face with her hands and gave me a proper kiss. I told her to stop it because Mouse was there. "I don't care!" he told us. We snickered.

I heard a noise in the foyer and Mouse excused himself. When he returned, Washington State Senator Albert Bradson accompanied him. If central casting in Hollywood needed someone to play the part of a senator, Albert would be first choice. Silvering at the temples, a great haircut, a tanned, handsome face, an obviously expensive suit, shined shoes, and a perfectly tied tie, Bradson looked the epitome of a United States Senator. Albert stepped up and gave me a sturdy embrace. "Good to see you, Matt. You had us all worried."

"Glad to be back, Albert. There were moments I wondered if I would make it back."

Bradson looked at my face. "Damn, Matt, you look terrible. Are you still in a lot of pain?"

I shook my head. "Actually, I feel better today than I have in quite some time. I'm healing, slowly."

Mouse led the three of us back to his study. Two walls of the study were tall windows that looked south and west. One view was of Mount Rainer and the other was looking out across Puget Sound with the Olympic Mountains off in the distance. One of the other walls was a bookcase that went from floor to ceiling. The last wall had a centered gas fireplace. The furniture was leather, heavy and gave the room a masculine feeling and I was sure everything felt comfortable to use and it all looked expensive.

Jade asked us all what we wanted to drink, and we all agreed on coffee. When she returned, she had a pot with cups and cream and sugar on a tray. Each of us poured a cup and fixed it the way we wanted. Albert and Mouse removed their suit jackets, unbuttoned their collars, and loosened their ties. I was lucky since I wasn't wearing a suit or tie. We all settled into the large, overstuffed chairs gathered in front of the glowing gas fireplace. I took a sip of my coffee, looked at Albert, and asked, "Okay, what's the problem?"

Albert responded, "Before we get started, I have an update on Senator Buck Markel." Before I'd gone over to the Middle East to help Walter and Ilox, someone had shot and killed two Seattle motorcycle officers in an alley while they were protecting Senator Markel. The Captain of Detectives, Sakol Hasaphonhse had questioned Markel. Sakol didn't like the answers he was getting and felt something was amiss. He had relayed his concerns to Jeff L. then Jeff had called me and asked if I would speak to Albert and see if

I could get any more information out of Buck. Buck went missing before I could get to him, alarming everyone.

"You remember when you called me from the plane after you left the Middle East and I told you I thought we had located Buck?"

I nodded.

"We picked him up and have him in isolation right now. When we found him, he was pretty intoxicated. About all we know for sure is Buck is being stalked by a fellow by the name of Tom McKnight, who calls himself El Wislond. We think his middle name is Wislond, but right now, this is all a guess. Buck still won't tell us much about him."

"I'll tell Jeff what you told me the next time we speak. Since my issue with Fred is resolved, it isn't a pressing concern, but I know he still would like to know who murdered his officers. Please keep me informed."

"Will do."

Albert was quiet now as he sat looking at me and then over at Mouse for an even longer time. I could tell something was going on between the two of them and I wondered what it was. Eventually I asked, "What's going on? I feel that both of you want to tell me something but neither knows where to start."

Mouse nodded at Albert. "May I?" Albert nodded, and Mouse began. "When Albert ran for the senate, we wanted you to take care of a problem we thought might become an issue we'd have to deal with later. Of course, at that time, you were in the middle of the Bud Cox situation and couldn't deal with it. As it turned out, the election was just in Washington state and didn't get a lot of national press attention, so we guess that's why the problem never surfaced."

Albert picked up the conversation. "Matt, I know I told you this before, but I want you to know, if I'd seen you were in trouble of not beating the murder rap, I'd have dropped the senate thing in a second and come to your rescue. I know you were unhappy because you felt you were short changed when I sent Krista Sellers in to defend you. I knew how good she was, and I knew you were innocent. There's no way I would have let you go to prison. Please believe me?"

"Albert, I understand at the time it would have been a really bad move on your part to defend me. I believe you when you tell me no matter what, you'd have stepped up to the plate for me. But why are we here? You're in the Senate and I'm not in jail."

Mouse and Albert looked at one another. Some signal passed between the two of them and Mouse muttered, "You tell him."

"Tell me what? What's going on?" I asked, slightly agitated.

Albert held up a hand. "Calm down. Flat out, some people have approached me and are interested in backing me to run for president. I'm in—"

"Stop!" I interrupted. "President? You mean like President of the United States?"

"No, Matt, president of outer Mongolia. *Duh*! Of course, the United States."

Damn, that was a bomb. It took a while before I got my head wrapped around that concept. President Albert Bradson. Shucky darn! A good friend of mine could be The President of the United States. That was way cool! "Okay. Congrats? Is that correct?"

Both men smiled at me.

"I still don't understand what I'm doing here."

Bradson frowned. "There's a small problem I'd like for you to look into for me."

The words *holy shit* ran through my head. I wanted to know what the problem was, but also I really didn't want to know. I didn't know if I was sufficiently recovered from my last adventure to look into something new.

With apprehension, I asked, "Okay Albert, what do you need from me?"

Albert sat for a while, then got up and walked over to the window. It was obvious he was disturbed about something and for a long time, he stood there gazing over Puget Sound. When he finally spoke, his voice was so soft I could hardly hear him. "Matt, in a lot of ways, these are not happy memories. To be honest, it's rather painful. I try to not think about this often."

I tried to make things easier. "Albert, you're among friends. It appears Mouse already knows what you want to tell me, and I'd trust Jade with my life. My friend, with some of the shit I've done in my life, I'm in no position to throw stones or make any judgements on anyone. How about you come back here, sit down, and talk to me. What do you feel is the problem?"

Bradson shrugged his shoulders and ambled back to his chair. "When I was an undergraduate, I was a real nerd. I didn't have a pocket protector, but I might as well have. I had no social graces at all. I could count the dates I'd had on one hand... well, almost. I was nineteen or twenty before I lost my virginity—I didn't have a way with women like some of my buddies did.

"After I graduated, I worked for various government offices, learning different jobs, as well as being in private practice with Richard Silversmith. I returned to school and earned a pair of post-graduate degrees from the university in Kansas. My mom graduated from KU and when dad was there working on his Masters, they met each other. Even though I grew up in Washington state, they always wanted me to attend school at KU.

"Shortly after I got to KU, I met Linda. Linda Ferrara. First week of classes, she was next to me and I was smitten from the start. My god, Matt, she was cute and sexy as all get out. A total free spirit." As Albert told me the story, I could see from the look on his face he still had fond memories of the girl. "She'd flirt with me and she loved to embarrass me. One time, she asked me how come I never asked her out. I told her because of my age, I didn't think she was interested in me that way. I was at least ten years older than her. She said if I didn't ask her out, how would I know what she'd do. So, I asked her out, and she giggled and told me she'd think about it. Later, when class broke up, she handed me a note with her phone number and address. At the top of the note, she'd written, 'Friday, pick me up at seven p.m.'

"I was on cloud nine. I picked her up and we went to some movie. I don't remember what the movie was. I was focused on her. We got back to her place, and she kissed my cheek and thanked me for a fun evening. Two weeks later, in class, she asked me if she'd scared me. I asked her what she meant. She said because I'd never asked her out a second time. I asked her if she'd go out with me and she told me to pick her up Saturday at seven. This time, we went to a concert, then had a bite to eat at a restaurant on the way home. I took her home. She kissed me on my lips and went inside.

"I debated all week if I should ask her out again. On Thursday, I screwed up the courage and I asked. She smiled, 'Well, Al, you're getting better at asking me out. How about you pick me up at seven on Saturday evening?' This date, we just walked around, and we talked. After a couple of hours, she asked me if I'd like to return to her place and have sex with her. Just like that, did I want to have sex with her. I think I even stuttered when I told her sure. We went back to her place, and I spent the night. For a young man who had limited sexual experiences, it was the most amazing night of my life up to that point. I don't want to drag this out, but she was insatiable. We'd finish and after a while, she would do things to get me interested in doing it again. It was an experience I'd never had before.

"Late Sunday morning, I crawled back to my room and passed out. Matt, you need to understand, for an inexperienced young man like me, nothing had ever happened for me to compare it with. Up to that point, I'd always been uncomfortable around women, and my experience with sex was seriously limited. However, Linda was wonderful. For the next couple of weeks, I repeatedly asked her out, but she always had an excuse. I asked her if I had done something wrong the last time we'd had sex and she said I was wonderful and told me to stop worrying.

"Then one day, she told me to pick her up at seven on Friday night. Even though Linda belonged to a sorority, she rented a house with two other girls. When I showed up at the house, I met one of her roommates. After the roommate left, Linda excused herself from the room. When she returned, she was naked. She extended her hand, motioning for me to come to her bedroom, and informed me we would be alone for most of the weekend and she wanted to have sex. It was the same as last time. She was at me all night long." Albert was blushing.

"Another couple of weeks went by and then she told me when to come by again. I did and this time, she met me at the door in a bathrobe. She took me by the hand and led me back to her bedroom. Same thing, we went at it all night long. I thought I really cared for her. I thought I was in love but later I realized it was just a case of lust. She had me over one more time with the same results.

"Later the next week, I happened to run into Maggie, the roommate I'd met, at the Student Union. I asked her if she had a few minutes. We talked, and I asked her why Linda would only see me occasionally. Maggie was very uncomfortable with my questions and told me she didn't know if she should be the one to be telling me what was going on. I begged her to tell me. Eventually she told me Linda was seeing some guy she'd been with for over a year. Maggie added that Linda was also seeing a couple of other guys besides me, and she was having sex with them as well. It crushed me. I know I cried, and Maggie told me the evening I first met her, she and Linda had argued about me. Maggie was ashamed she told me, but she added she liked me and felt sorry about the way Linda was treating me and felt she needed to disclose what was happening.

"The next time I saw Linda, I asked her about the guy she was seeing. She told me it didn't matter. She seemed to feel she could go with the guy and still have sex with me from time to time. I told her I loved her and what she wanted was unacceptable for me. She told me if I couldn't handle it, then for me to fuck off and it was my loss. Her exact words.

"Shortly afterwards, Maggie and I started to date, and things between us got serious quickly. We'd been dating for a short time when I ran into Linda at the house when I was picking Maggie up. Linda informed me she was pregnant, and I told her congratulations. She advised me it was my baby and asked me what I was going to do about it. I asked her how she could be so sure since she was screwing other guys besides me. Linda told me women knew things like that and it was the way things timed out. It was me. I told her that wasn't the way things worked, but I'd think about it. I was kind of shocked that she could be so sure that the child was mine.

"I talked it over with Maggie and she told me Linda's boyfriend was a loser. He'd dropped out of school and was dealing drugs to make a living. Maggie assured me that there was no way Linda's baby was mine, but that Linda was hoping I'd step up and give her money for the baby. Linda knew my parents had money, and she thought it might work. The next time I saw Linda, I told her I didn't believe it was my child and to go away and leave me alone. I'll admit I felt bad, so I arranged for her to receive five thousand dollars, but I never saw Linda again. Later, I heard she had a baby boy, and she'd already arranged for an immediate adoption of the child."

The room was still. Everyone seemed too embarrassed to move or speak. My coffee was cold, and I noticed Jade had tears in her eyes. I felt bad myself. I'd guessed what Albert wanted me to do, but I wanted to hear him say it. Softly, I asked, "What do you want me to do, Albert?"

He took a deep breath and there was a soft sob in it. "Not a day goes by but I don't wonder if it might have been my son. Maggie tells me it was very doubtful. You want to know what I want? Well, I would like for you to see if you can find Linda and perhaps even the child. When I ran for the senate, it didn't matter all that much. The media didn't know about Linda and even if they found out, nobody was going to try to track down something that happened years ago in Lawrence, Kansas.

"I know running for the presidency will be a different ball game. They will check me out every which way. They'll be looking for my kindergarten teacher to interview and see if I colored between the lines. There were several of our classmates who knew about Linda and me, and I'm sure somebody knew Linda ended up pregnant. Matt, to put my mind at rest, I need to know if the child was mine. I told you one reason, however, another is I can't afford to have something like that crop up in the middle of a tight campaign and bite me on the butt."

"Is Linda still alive?"

"I have no idea."

"What about the boyfriend?"

"I looked into what happened to him after I became a senator. I found out they arrested and tried him for killing an undercover DEA agent for which he received a life's sentence. While he was in prison, he got involved in a breakout attempt and guards shot and killed him. I tried quietly to find out what happened to Linda, but I was afraid people would ask questions, wondering why I was so curious, if I pushed it."

"Do you know where the baby was born?" I asked.

"I assumed at some hospital in Lawrence. Even though I'd given her some money to take care of things, she did nothing. There's a small clinic on campus and I heard Linda waited until the last minute and then went to the clinic when she went into labor. I don't know what hospital they took her to."

I asked Albert for Linda's last name, which he provided. I also got the boyfriend's name. Nobody knew what the baby's name was and since the new parents promptly adopted him, it didn't matter anyhow. I told him I felt I was being sent on a fool's errand. If the press, or someone knew no more than what Albert had just told me, how would they fare getting information about this incident.

Mouse had been very quiet all through Albert's confession. I looked at him. "How important do you think this is?"

He shrugged. "If Albert makes a run for the presidency, and if Linda's still alive and saw he was running, who knows what she might do. I'd like to know where she is and what her status is before we start the campaign. As Albert said, this is not something we want to come out and bite us on the butt. If we could find Linda, we might find out if she knows where the kid is. If Linda comes forward, it's his word against hers as to who the father is. And without the baby to prove it one way or another, who knows. Any way you look at it, the media would have a field day with that bombshell. It would be best if we could have as much info on this as possible and have it contained."

I sat for a long time, staring off into space with my fingers tented in front of my face. I felt Albert would make a good president, or at least as good as any of the rest we've had over the years. Finally, I nodded and told them I'd look into it for Albert. Mouse offered me a credit card to travel on and I thanked him but said I'd rather be on my own. I explained if the media got wind of what I was doing, if something came up and the media accused me of wrongdoing, I could claim I was doing it all on my own. Any card I was using would be mine and nobody could prove I was working for somebody. Albert would be clean. Both men agreed that was best.

I looked over at Jade. "What do you think of all this?"

"Why are you asking me?"

"Jade don't play the innocent with me. I know better. I know how sharp you are, and I know you're Mouse's right hand. I respect your judgment, and Mouse and Albert do too since they wanted you to be here and listen to Albert's story. I ask you again, what do you think of what he told us? Your opinion regarding any danger of fallout should that info get out."

She blushed slightly. "I'm sorry for what Albert went through. I'm sure it was painful for him. A first love, especially one like that, can be a real sorrow." Directing her question at Albert, she continued. "Isn't your wife's name Maggie?"

Albert smiled and nodded.

"Same person?"

Albert nodded again.

"So, in a way," she said gently, "it turned out for the best?"

Albert had a big smile on his face.

"If for no other reason than to find out what happened to both Linda and the baby, that will help Albert feel better about things. I think Matt should see what he can do. Of course, the more information we have, the better off we are if this somehow blows up in our faces.

"I agree with the idea that Matt is the best to look into this. Matt seems to have a lot of luck when it comes to investigating things. When I was kidnapped, I thought I would die and there was no way anybody would ever find me up at that

29

cabin in the mountains. When Matt walked through the door into the front room, he reached deity status with me. You all know how I feel about him. I'm living proof that a person can love two people. Mouse, I love you more than life, and Matt, I love you as much. If there's any possibility of solving this, I think Matt's your best bet."

Looking at the three of them, I shook my head. I totally disagreed. Without a lot of hope, I told them, "Tell you what, kids, I'll look into this. I'd like to have a chat with Maggie before I do anything else. Albert, I'd like for you to ask her if she'd share with me everything that happened with Linda when you two were back in school.

"However, there are some things I need to do first, but along the way, I'll keep checking it out. We have almost thirty months before there's an election and I promise to have some kind of answer by the end of this summer. But remember, I'm starting with nothing."

Everyone agreed.

We spent more time covering different ideas. It was obvious by Albert's mood that telling us his tale had taken a lot out of him. His answers were just one or two words and it appeared his memories were on playback for him. When Albert headed for the elevator, he stopped and looked at me. "Matt, if I hear any more about Markel, I'll let you know."

"Thanks. It's mainly for Chief Davenport now. He wants to know who took out his two officers."

I felt we had reached an impasse with everything else and I suggested we call things done and I made preparations to leave. I told them I'd be in touch.

Riding the elevator down, I was annoyed with myself because I hadn't been more forceful regarding taking up what I considered to be a Don Quixote quest. Exiting the lobby, I found my truck waiting under the portico with the driver's door opened. "Thanks, Mr. Wells."

The valet smiled. "Please, it's Marshall. Have a nice evening, Mr. Preston."

"If you're Marshall, then I'm Matt. Okay?"

"Drive carefully, Matt. The idiots are out in force tonight."

I snorted as I climbed into my truck and drove off into the night.

Driving away, I thought about how once again I found myself getting into the stupidest situations. I wanted to tell Albert I wasn't up to dealing with any problems right now. My body was still trying to recover from my last adventure and mentally, I wasn't in any kind of mood to solve anyone's problems. But when a friend needs a favor, you help them.

Right?

When will I ever learn?

Right now, I'd have to say, never!

CHAPTER FOUR

A few days after my meeting with Albert and Mouse, I returned to have my initial chat with Maggie Bradson at The Olympus. This time, Jade took us to a different area of their condo. The décor said this was obviously her area. The room had several black lacquered pieces of furniture with Asian prints and drawings on the walls. One wall was a bank of windows that also looked over Puget Sound. Being seventy-five stories in the air, the room was naturally still, but the room felt stifled; it was too quiet. However, the room was simple but very tasteful and I thought it was just like Jade; elegant and sophisticated.

Jade, Maggie and I were the only ones present and Jade motioned for us to join her. The two of them sat down on a couch and I was directed to sit in a strange looking chair. Due to my size, it didn't look like it would be comfortable. I was pleasantly surprised when I finally settled in. From the moment we were seated, I watched Maggie fidget. I assumed it was because she wasn't happy about being questioned about her past. Since she was friends with Jade, I thought having a woman present might make it easier for her to open up about the past. I assumed it was a good way to set things up, but the way Maggie kept squirming, I decided it would be best to find out exactly why she was so upset.

"Maggie, would you rather do this a different time? I can see you're not happy being here. I thought having Jade here might help you relax. Would you rather she leaves? What can I do to make this easier?"

Without answering, Maggie stood and walked over to the window. She stood for a long time, examining Puget Sound from seventy-five stories up. I found it interesting both she and Albert had done the same thing as they stalled for time. I'd waited Albert out and I knew it was best to wait for her to tell us what was on her mind. When she was ready, she'd tell us.

We'd met before, but I never really had an opportunity to check her out. Now, looking her over, I noted what a handsome woman she was. I guessed her to be in her mid-forties. She was tall and elegant with dark auburn hair which she wore short. Her eyes were round, and I'd noticed they were hazel colored. She wore big round glasses which seemed to magnify her eyes. Today, she was wearing a short, light blue skirt with a long, dark blue jacket over a semi-transparent white blouse. Through the blouse, you could see a fancy dark blue bra which showed off her well-formed figure. A lovely woman who was both chic and extremely sexy all at the same time.

She turned back to face us with arms folded across her chest. She dropped her head, took a deep breath, and returned to the couch. I asked her again what I could do to make this easier for her. She shook her head. "Nothing. It's okay. Al said you had questions, and I needed to talk to you about everything. Let's get this done. What do you want to know?"

I paused, trying to figure out what her issues were, but I didn't want to upset her any more than she already appeared to be. "Somehow, I'm getting the feeling something is wrong. I feel perhaps you're not comfortable with his decision to run for president?"

The way she glared at me, I realized I was correct, and I also wondered if I would even get an answer. When she replied, her voice was tinged with anger. "If that's what he wants to do, I can't stop him."

"Bullshit, Maggie! You know better than that. Something as important as running for president has to be a two-way street. You need to be fully onboard with what Albert is trying to do. Come on, you're not that naïve. Would you like to explain in more detail what is your issue?"

I noticed tears on her cheeks now and I wondered what was going on. Jade leaned over and took one of Maggie's hands in hers. "What's wrong, Maggie? Why are you so upset? What is it about Albert running that has upset you?"

Maggie pulled her hand away from Jade and her voice was a snarl. "This!" she snapped as she moved her hand in a circle, gesturing toward Jade and me. "Basically, I don't want to have to answer a bunch of questions. From you two… or anybody. Answering a bunch of questions sucks! It just rots my socks that I have to dig up the painful memories associated with what happened back then and I don't care to relive unpleasant old memories. But I know I'll have to. I don't want my life examined and then have to explain past decisions or have to justify them. Nobody lives a perfect life, me included. And now it starts." Maggie pointed at me. "Please don't take this personally, but first you and Jade, then who knows what. I'm so angry and frustrated by this. I know if I told Albert I didn't want him to run, he'd drop out, and that isn't fair either. But is having my life exposed fair? You're just unlucky enough to be the ones to feel my wrath about this whole thing."

"Is Albert aware of how you feel?" Jade asked.

Her laugh was sharp. "Oh yeah. He's upset, very upset! But he still really doesn't know precisely how I feel.

35

He was so angry when I first told him, he didn't want to listen. However, I think that having to talk with you is worse than having to talk with Al. Anyway, he begged me to have this conversation with you, so here I am. What do you want to know?"

I leaned back and tented my fingers in front of my face. It was something I'd often seen Mouse do and when I realized what I was doing, I almost laughed out loud. It made me feel like I was more in charge of the meeting, however. There was one thing that kept nagging at me. I didn't know exactly what it was, but I kept getting the feeling that Maggie wasn't telling us something. I could understand part of her anger regarding having her life torn apart, but it felt like she was too angry for what she said was the reason.

"Maggie, the first thing I wanted to discuss with you, ah… well… tell me about Linda and Albert back in your days at the university. We're trying to figure out if there is danger ahead if things about Linda leaked out."

She smiled and shook her head. "I'll explain everything, but I need for you to understand something about me. When I first got to school, I was grass green. My parents sheltered me as a child. I was so naïve that when I purchased my first pack of cigarettes, I thought I was living on the edge. It was the most sinful thing I could ever imagine doing and I thought for sure I was on the highway to hell. Even though I wasn't all that sophisticated, the one thing I soon realized was that Linda, that bitch, was playing Al for a fool. It just made my socks rot to see what she was doing to him. After I told Albert what Linda was doing, the two of us talked, I mean like really talked, and I discovered what a nice guy he was, or is. Even though he was ten years older than me, we fit together like two peas in a pod.

"Shortly after Albert stopped seeing Linda, she dropped out of school. She later told Albert she was pregnant with his child. The stupid thing is, she'd marked on her calendar the days she had her period. Her periods were extremely regular, so regular that Robyn and I were jealous because Linda knew exactly when they would start. I could count the days she marked on her calendar and from my math, it didn't look like it was possible for the child to have been Albert's. The window was too small, and I thought it was a little too convenient. I never told Albert I'd looked at Linda's calendar, but he told me several times he didn't believe her, and I agreed. We both felt she was after him because he had the deepest pockets of all the guys she'd slept with, and the bum she was almost living with didn't have two pennies to rub together. It was all about the drugs with him."

"Where was the child born?"

"I know Albert gave her five thousand dollars for an abortion, but she waited too long, and she ended up going to the campus wellness center when she went into labor. From there, I think they sent her to a hospital, but I don't know which one. There were only two in Lawrence then, so it can't be that difficult to find out where."

"Boy or girl?"

"I heard it was a boy. She had adoption papers all in place so that as soon as the baby was born, they took him away."

"Any idea who the adoptive parents were?"

"No, we were no longer on speaking terms. She was angry because I started seeing Albert. I didn't pay much attention since Albert and I were dating, and I was trying my best to help him get over Linda. She had him so hooked on sex, he'd do anything for her. I tried to take her place." Maggie blushed. "Like I was so experienced. Albert was only the second man I slept with. I guess we were both good for each other in that way."

"Why do you say that?"

"You know how inexperienced I was and even though Al was in his early thirties, he wasn't all that sophisticated in… well, you know, that area. When we met, he'd seen a

37

few ladies over the years, but nothing serious. He'd mainly been working on his career. He'd returned to school to get a degree in government management.

"I know you know how they met, and I never could figure out why she took after him the way she did. It was like shooting fish in a barrel. It would just rot your socks to see the way he mooned around after her. After a while, it made me sick, and since he'd never really had a sexually active relationship before, he was hooked. Later, when we started dating, as I tried to help him get over her, we got hooked on each other." Maggie was still red because of her revelations.

"What about your roommate, Robyn?"

"What about her?"

"Was she close to Linda? And do you know what her last name is now, assuming she's gotten married?"

"Meenen, Robyn Meenen, was her maiden name. I know she got married, but I don't know what her name is now. In the beginning when we moved in together, we were all good friends. When I saw what Linda was doing to Al, it upset me and we had a fight. Robyn also told Linda she felt what she was doing was wrong, and that ended their friendship. Robyn and I continued to be friends, but Linda pulled away from us once she was preggers and moved out."

"Do you think Linda would try to make problems for Albert if he ran for office?"

Maggie sat for a long time, watching out the window as the clouds floated past. Finally, she turned. "I don't know. Part of me says yes, but I think she really cared for Albert in a way, and because of that, I don't think she'd create problems. But in all honesty, I really don't know what she would do."

"You didn't stay in touch with Robyn?"

"No. But I can check with my old sorority and see if they have an address for her. I think I heard Robyn is a veterinarian in some little hick town in Arkansas. The Alumni

Association keeps records of alumni addresses. I know the secretary. Since Linda didn't graduate, I doubt if they have any records on her. But do you want me to check?"

"Please do it. I think I need to talk to both of them."

"When I get back home, I'll contact my friend."

"And may I make a suggestion?" I asked.

A flicker of fear showed in Maggie's eye. "What?"

"Sit down with Albert and have a talk. I mean have a real 'come to Jesus' meeting. Be honest about your feelings. Maggie, if you don't let him understand now how you feel about things, down the road at some press conference, some hot-shot reporter will sense the same things I did. They will ask questions and they will not be as gentle on you as I was. I feel even now you're holding back..." Maggie opened her mouth to speak, but I held up my hand. "No. That wasn't my point. If you think you hated answering *my* questions, there are reporters who will reduce you to pudding. You'll be do-ing Albert more harm than good if you don't talk to him now.

"The problem I'm having right now is Albert trusts me. He expects me to tell him what happened today. Both what you told us and what you didn't tell us. He expects me to share my feelings with him. But you are also a friend and I don't want to do that to you. Whatever is going on needs to come from you. So, how about you suck it up and have a talk with Albert? I mean a real talk. Share with him your feelings and also whatever you may not be sharing with Jade and me. If you don't tell him, Maggie, eventually I have to tell him what transpired here today. It's better coming from you than from me."

Maggie frowned as she asked, "Why is it so hard for me to do that?"

"My ol' pappy had a saying. 'whenever you have to make a decision, whatever's the hardest thing to do is usually the right thing to do.' It seems to fit really well today. Think about it."

I stood as Jade escorted Maggie to the elevator and down to The Olympus' lobby, making sure she got safely to her limo. When Jade returned, she disappeared in the back of their condo. A few seconds later, she returned with Mouse. I noticed this was one of those rare times since I'd known him he didn't have a suit jacket on; his vest was unbuttoned and his had tie was untied, just hanging around his neck. Something was up! Mouse indicated I should sit. "Can I get you anything?" he inquired.

"Yes, Scotch and ice. A lot of Scotch, a kiss of water and a little ice. Just that. I need it." Jade returned shortly with a drink in hand. I took as large a sip as possible and I was pleased to find she had made it quite stout. I set the glass on a coaster, leaned back and, tenting my fingers in front of my face, I looked at my diminutive friend. "Mouse, we have a problem."

Surprise was clear on his face. "What's the matter?"

"Maggie doesn't want Albert to run for office."

"I thought it might happen, but what makes you think that?"

"She told me."

"If she was unhappy with our little Q & A session to-day, I shudder to think what she'd do in a real press conference. Unless she changes her mind, Albert doesn't stand a chance. They'll use her to shred him."

Mouse looked over at Jade. "Do you agree Maggie isn't on board?"

She nodded. "Yes. Even before Matt asked questions, I felt there was something wrong. I agree that a real press conference would turn out poorly. Matt promised not to say anything to Albert, but until Maggie changes her attitude, I would release nothing to the press about his plans to run for office."

I added, "And I can't shake the feeling that there's something else Maggie isn't sharing with us. When I said something, she wanted to defend herself and I didn't want to hear it. She seems angry about something, or frightened. She's too angry, I feel, for it only to be that she doesn't want her life upset by his candidacy. It's just a feeling I have and..."

Jade's eyes got wide. "Umm..."

"What?" I asked.

"I got that same feeling. I thought it was just me and I was ignoring it. But if you felt the same way, I wonder what she's not telling us..."

Mouse said, "I don't understand. What did Maggie say that makes you feel she isn't telling the truth?"

"It's nothing she said, or that she isn't telling us the truth," I corrected him. "It's more like she isn't telling us the whole truth. Or that something is going on and she's afraid it might get out. As I remember, she told us at the start of our conversation, 'I don't want my life examined and then have to explain past decisions or have to justify them. Nobody lives a perfect life, me included.' Jade and I never thought to follow up and ask her what she meant with her comment. But obviously there's something out there we don't know about and it looks like she's frightened it will come out."

Jade's mouth dropped open. "Oh my god," she exclaimed.

"What?" I asked.

"I think I know what's going on."

"Well?"

"Maggie's having an affair."

Mouse was reclined in his chair but after hearing Jade's comment, he sat straight up. "No way!" His face showed his disbelief. "Are you kidding? Why do you say that?"

"Darling, a woman can tell when another woman is having an affair. It's that, or she had an affair and she's afraid it will get out. I never thought Maggie would have one, but you never know. Anyway, now that Matt made his comment about Maggie not sharing everything that's going on, and

Matt reminding me of what Maggie said when we first started our chat, I feel like that maybe what's going on."

I've always been impressed with Jade's intelligence. I knew that if Jade felt Maggie was having an affair, Mouse would listen to her and carefully weigh whatever she told him. Mouse walked over to the window and stood for a long time, looking intently out across the view of Puget Sound. It seemed to be the place where people went to ponder over heavy matters. When he turned around, he addressed both of us. "What are we going to do?"

Jade calmly responded, "Nothing. For now. We'll let it be. Maggie needs to talk to Albert and tell him about how she feels regarding his run for office. Perhaps she will see if she is having an affair and continues, it may come out. If it was something in the past, perhaps we can help keep it from becoming common knowledge. Anyway, I think in a day or two, I'll have lunch with Maggie and I'll ask her who it is or was. Perhaps I can point out to her the dangers involved if she is still having the affair and it continues. If I can get her to share with me who she had the affair with, we can see what we can do to help her. She needs to see that if Albert runs for office, things like that probably will get out."

Mouse returned to his chair and flopped down. In all the time I'd known him, I'd never seen him so agitated. Finally, he asked, "What are your plans now, Matt?"

"If Maggie can get me an address for either of her ex-roommates, I'll talk to them. I have the time right now to help Albert. For the three of us and for Albert, I'd like to make sure that the child Linda produced is not related to Albert. As for our feelings about Maggie, I like Jade's idea of having lunch. I also think her way of just asking who she is or was having an affair with is a good idea. Don't ask her if, but who. That will shake her and who knows what we might learn."

"Can you stay for dinner?" Jade asked.

"I'd love to. I have several things I need to discuss with you." I leaned back in my chair and looked out across Puget Sound. Tomorrow, I would like to go over and see Walter and Thein.

While savoring the excellent Scotch, I smiled at the thought of seeing my old friends.

CHAPTER FIVE

I was on my way to see Walter and his wife Thein, and the day was the best kind Western Washington had to offer: flawless. Even though the day was cool, there were blue skies with big fluffy clouds. Puget Sound looked like a mill-pond. The waves hardly patted up onto the shore.

Standing on the top deck of the ferry and smelling the fragrance of salt air with the wind in my hair made me think about my motorcycle for a moment. I knew I'd miss it once I sold it, but I also realized I was doing the right thing; it really was time to sell the bike. At that moment with those thoughts running in my mind, I looked down at the cars pulling onto the ferry and watched a brand new Mercedes S class convertible drive onto the ferry with the top down. Instantly, I knew what I would do to help me get over the sale of the bike. When I got back from seeing Walter, I would order a new S class convertible. Somehow, I knew by making that order, it would make the sale of the bike much easier.

Looking out over the water and remembering where I had been for the past previous weeks, I was happy to be rid of those problems. Besides clearing up Albert's possible issue, my main goal was to figure out what I wanted from a relationship with Lois. I was still one happy camper when

I thought about her. The rest of my life needed some work, though; how to get rid of my car collection and Seattle holdings, and where I wanted to live now.

When the ferry pulled up to the dock on the other side of the Sound, I'd been so far off in my head I had to run down the stairs just to get to my truck in time to drive off. Once I was far enough from the ferry, the traffic thinned out and the drive was pleasant. I drove up to the parking place for Walter's cabin and as usual, it was empty. I don't know why more people don't come over and see the beauty of the forest, but that's okay since it leaves the view all for me.

I'd hiked the trail into Walter's cabin enough times by now, I knew the way without even looking. When I came around the corner of the cabin, I observed Walter lying on his back in the middle of his deck with Thein nestled in his lap. Since they were both nude, it was obvious what they were doing. I quickly turned around but before I could slip away, Max saw me, gave a bark and ran towards me. The commotion woke up Bean who also came running across the deck, barking. It embarrassed neither Walter nor Thein to be discovered making love on their deck; and make no mistake, since it was their deck, I was the intruder.

Thein stood up and walked over. Now that she was standing, I could clearly tell she was expecting another child, which explained why they were making love in the position I'd found them. When she'd come and asked me to help Walter over in the Middle East, she'd neglected to tell me she was pregnant. Now, it was very obvious.

She extended her arms, and I wrapped mine around her body and carefully lifted her for a moment. Gently, I set her down and, still holding her in my arms with her arms around my neck, I kissed her cheek. Several times, she kissed my face, occasionally muttering, "Thank you. Thank you for getting my Walter and bringing him back."

After a while, I became more than just a little self-conscious holding her naked body with Walter standing there. I looked over at him and mouthed the word, "Help!"

Walter snickered, then he said something to Thein in Vietnamese. She giggled and released my neck. I released her. One last time, she reached up with both hands and held my face. "Thank you for getting Walter. I heard you were badly hurt. I see your face still has marks on it. Are you okay now?" I told her I was. "How long are you going to stay?"

"I don't know. At least overnight, and then we'll we see. That's if you want me to."

She nodded then headed off to the cabin. As she walked away, I noticed every part of her was tanned. Evidently the two of them spent a lot of time on their deck, without clothing.

Walter stepped up and wrapped his arms around me, giving me a big hug. I winced due to the tenderness I still felt in my body. Also, it made me uncomfortable to be holding a naked man in my arms, but since it was Walter, I hugged him back. Walter didn't bother to go get dressed. Instead, he motioned for me to sit in one of the comfortable chairs he'd built.

Thien came back out with something wrapped around her lower body holding a large glass of cold water. I thanked her, and she pulled up a chair. She said something to Walter, and he looked over at me. "Thein says I should go put something on. Do you want me to get dressed?"

"I won't tell you what you're wearing is my favorite outfit, but no, I want you both to wear whatever you want. This is your home, not mine. I came over uninvited to talk to about Max, Bennie and Rascal. Like I said, do what you want. I believe Rascal belongs here with little Matt, if the two of you want him here."

"You know if you leave Rascal, little Matt will be so happy? He's been in heaven with three dogs. That would be sweet of you to leave him," Thein told me.

47

Walter spoke up, "Okay, now what about your dogs?"

"May I leave them here for a while longer? I'm working on some issues in Florida. I'm thinking about buying a place there and selling all my stuff in Seattle, but it's still in a planning stage. Since I have to travel back and forth for a while, may I leave the dogs here?" I wanted to tell Walter about my search for Albert's... what was I searching for? But as I considered this, I realized that was something I needed to discuss with Albert first.

"You know you don't have to ask. We all love your dogs and they can stay as long as necessary."

"Thanks."

"Okay, now I have questions," Walter said.

I had to laugh. I was sure Walter was about to burst, he was so full of questions.

"The last I saw you, we'd left you at a hotel in Nakhchivan with instructions for you not to leave, for any reason. Considering your condition, I didn't think you'd be able to go anywhere. Obviously, I was wrong. And, for what it's worth, I want you to know I wasn't happy about leaving you. But at the time, there really weren't any other options, and we had to get the hostages to a place where Ilox could pick them up as quickly as possible. That wasn't as easy as he'd led us to believe it would be, by the way."

That was no great surprise. Considering how everything else had gone on the mission, why should the end go any differently than any of the rest?

Walter continued. "At least Ilox kept his promise and eventually sent people to help get the remaining hostages out of the country. The problem was we found military everywhere, and it took a lot of time to hook up with Ilox's people, then it took two more days to get back to where we left you.

"When we got back to the hotel, you'd disappeared into thin air. There were armed guards everywhere and everybody was really upset. It was a good thing Antranig stayed behind with me and didn't go back with the hostages. When we got back to the hotel where we'd left you, he was able to ask around without raising too many questions. We learned the soldiers discovered where you'd been hiding in the hotel and when they came to get you, you shot and killed a general and his aide. That created a major stink. They were searching for you everywhere, which was partly the reason we had so many problems getting the hostages out of the country. That and the dead general and his aide. We couldn't believe you'd somehow escaped since the last time we saw you there was no way you could even move, or so we thought.

"I felt awful, as if I was deserting you after you'd volunteered to help me. Later, we overheard soldiers talking about a Jeep that someone stole, and I was positive it was you. Especially after I heard someone drove the Jeep off into the desert and an unmarked plane picked up the driver. After that, we couldn't find out a thing and it was like you had evaporated. I was positive you'd been on that plane and gotten away. The main problem was I didn't learn exactly what was going on until I was back with Ilox in Florida and Orchard called us and said it was you who was picked up by the plane. He told us you were safe, but he wouldn't tell us any more than that. Tell me what happened?"

"You may find this hard to believe, but you know about as much as I do. I was so out of it that most of the escape happened in a blur of pain. And the thing that kept me moving was mostly fear." I told Walter about waking up with the general sneaking into my room. I told him how I shot both the aide and the general and I could hear all the military traffic passing under my window and how freaked out I was. I stated at that point I didn't remember being told to stay in the room, but now I think about it, I doubt it would have been a good plan since it took so long for them to come back and get me.

I told him how Henry had provided me with an emergency transponder and told me all I needed to do was get away from town to a location where Henry could land, activate the transponder, and he would find me. I described how he found me in the clump of trees and how I vaguely remember being trapped in the Jeep and Henry helping me back to the plane. I continued telling him how I kind of remember getting into a plane, but I vividly remember thinking we would crash. One time when we were trying to get away I looked out the window and saw a plane crash behind us. I told him how pleased I was to find Lois on board. "When I woke up and finally realized what was going on, I was in a hospital in Germany and Orchard was there. He told me you and Antranig had safely escaped, but nothing more. What happened?"

"I found out that Ilox didn't tell us everything. One thing I found out was he does have a lot of pull with certain agencies of the U.S. government. Somehow, Antranig got word to his father we were in trouble and we needed rescuing, quickly. They sent a plane to get us, but I don't know who the plane belonged to. About all I ever learned was the pilot was American, and the plane was amazing in what it could do. The pilot had us meet him southeast of town where he landed the damn thing on a freeway. When he landed, there weren't any cars around. But as he took off, there were two military vehicles with their lights on coming straight for us. Somehow, he got the plane off the ground at the last minute. The dude really could fly a plane."

"Was his name Henry? If so, he works for me now."

I know I shouldn't have done it, but the look on Walter's face was priceless. He stuttered a little then finally got it out. "Wait a minute. He works for you? What the hell does that mean?"

"Henry has flown me other places in the past. I met him when I was looking for The Gypsy Queen and Orchard loaned me a plane. Henry flew Lois back to Washington after we spent time together and when he got back, he made me a business proposition and asked me if I wanted to invest and be part owner in a company he was putting together which would own three surplus government planes. Said he had half a dozen pilots lined up."

"Sorry, Matt, I don't remember the guy's name."

"If it wasn't Henry, I'm pretty sure the fellow who flew you out now works for my company."

"Matt, you are one crazy fucker!"

"Why thanks, Walter, I love you too."

Thein excused herself and said she would make dinner. Walter asked if he should drag out the pipe and I told him I hadn't smoked since the last time I was with him. I teased him he was a bad influence on me.

For the next couple of hours, we discussed what had happened over in Nakhchivan. I covered in more detail everything that had gone down with McNaulty. I told him what Orchard had said about the beatings I got and how they probably had saved my life. I ended with, "If I ever see him again, I swear I will flatten him. I don't care what the reasons were for slapping me around."

"I'm sorry you had to deal with that. I feel partly responsible. I'll never be able to thank you enough for coming over and getting involved. I think it took all four of us to get things done. While McNaulty and his boys were dealing with you, that took the pressure off the three of us and people stopped looking for us. We could get a lot done, but I didn't know you were taking a beating while things were happening. Thanks, but please don't do anything like that again."

Thein told us dinner was ready, and we ate on the deck looking out over the Olympic mountains. I had to give Walter credit, the location for his little home was amazing. He really had an eye for putting a house with nature where they both seemed to meld seamlessly.

Dinner was wonderful. I believe if Thein was my wife, I'd be over 300 pounds in less than a year. Even when I was full, I had an extra helping. Normally, I didn't eat Vietnamese food anymore. It's not a racist thing. There are things about me and my life I never want to share with people. And most of the time, my military service is one. People may know I served, but I don't like to speak of it or any details of my time in Southeast Asia.

I ate Vietnamese food the whole time I was in Vietnam. Every day, every meal. I didn't dare eat American food because if I did, I was afraid I'd smell like American food. When you were out on patrol or on a mission, you had to smell Asian. I didn't dare take a chance. Have you ever smelled a person after they ate garlic? Drank wine with the meal? Or perhaps eaten onions? You know, you can smell like your food. And in enclosed spaces, it comes out of your pores and the fragrance is even stronger. I wanted no one to smell me or know I was there. So, I ate their food.

I've heard some Japanese women don't like having oral sex with American men. They say Americans taste different because of all the meat we eat. Our diets affect the taste of our semen. In the same vein, it's said having oral sex with women who observe a strict vegetarian diet tastes much different than women who eat meat; especially red meat. Since Nicki and I had done nothing in a sexual way, I can't say if it's true. Anyway, as for Vietnamese food, it is what it is. Old habits die hard, but when I'm with Thein and Walter, I'll eat it. She makes things taste so good, I forget my prejudice.

After dinner, I sprawled out in the comfortable chair on the deck with Beanie curled up in my lap. As I stroked her, from time to time she would give a happy grunt. Dad was holding and petting her, and life was good. Walter came out with two beers dripping cold water from them along with his pipe. He told me he kept the beer under the cabin in a stream fed by glacial runoff. The beer was ice cold.

Walter fired up the pipe and handed it over. "Take two puffs. That is all I will let you have."

I had to laugh. "So, when did you become my father?"

"I know where the seeds came from. An old friend smuggled them in from someplace he wouldn't tell me. I planted both seeds, they sprouted and produced a nice harvest. And you get to sample a couple tokes."

Since Walter rarely smoked anymore, what he had would last him a long time. I told him since he'd warned me about the potency of his harvest, I needed to discuss something with him before I smoked any. I told him about Albert without mentioning any names. I told him it was a guy running for political office. I covered the story about Linda and her attempts to saddle Albert with the baby. He understood why having something like that in his past could be a real danger if the media ever got wind of it.

"What are you going to do?" Walter asked.

"I don't know and that's one reason I'm over here. I was hoping you might have a suggestion or two."

"Do you think there might be a birth certificate?"

"Dunno. Well, wait a minute. Since there was an adoption, there may be a birth certificate, but I'd guess it would show the adopted parents as the child's real parents. However, whatever the deal is, they usually seal those records. Even if there's a real certificate, I don't think I'll have much luck getting a look at it."

"What about your federal creds that Orchard provided you with?"

I smacked my forehead. "Damn, I totally forget I have those sometimes. I can sure try using those. Maggie said she would check her sorority and see what they have in the way of alumni records. One problem with that idea might be, I understand Linda never graduated."

"Anything I can do to help?" Walter inquired.

53

"Yes, stay up here on your mountain top and keep it safe for me to come and unload from time to time."

"Done."

I asked about little Matt and Walter told me he was over in Seattle visiting his aunt with the Rascal. Now I understood why I'd found them on the deck the way I had. I told Walter about my problems with the city and my properties downtown. Because of that, now I had to do something with my car collection. I didn't think selling them would be a problem. However, over time, I had collected several MGB's. There were several cars that were complete, but there were many I'd purchased as donor cars. When I sold that lot, it would be buyer takes all. There was no way I would let the collection be sold item by item. I went on telling Walter how unhappy I was with the way Seattle was going. "It ain't the city I grew up in. Traffic is a nightmare. Prices are getting stupid. All the touchstones from my youth are gone. It just isn't the place I want to live full time. I'll have a condo at Mouse's building, but that's all."

"Where will you go?"

"I don't know. Still working on that."

"Here, try this." Walter extended the pipe. It had been a long time since I'd partaken since I really didn't care for it anymore. But I was in a strange mood and I thought it might help. I took a puff. Oh, my god. It tasted fantastic, and it was some powerful smoke. Walter told me the next day, I took a second puff, but I don't remember. However, I do remember talking about Lois to Walter and Thein.

~ ~ ~ ~ ~

The next morning over breakfast, Walter kept thanking me for coming to help him over in the Middle East. I finally had to tell him to give it a rest. I knew I had to help. He made me understand he considered any obligation I might have thought still existed would be considered paid in full. I was not to come and bail him out again. I told him, "Yeah, yeah." But I know he knew better. Our paths go too far back not to feel certain obligations.

As I got ready to leave, he stepped up and wrapped his arms around me. I checked to see if his wrap was on and if it properly covered him. I gave him a big hug. Thien came up and motioned for me to bend down. I bent down and wrapped my arms around her. With her arms about my neck, she looked into my eyes. Tears flowed down her cheeks. "Once again, you've saved Walter. Words do not cover how I feel. I love you, Matt Preston. And now you need to go find love, settle down, and be happy like Walter and me. Be good to yourself. You are a fantastic person. Get this Lois person and bring her here. I need to see if she is good enough for you." She winked then gave me a kiss far from chaste. I hugged her as hard as I dared.

~ ~ ~ ~ ~

Walking back to my truck, I thought about Walter and the way his life turned out. He'd really lucked out. Even though his life hadn't started out all that well with an abusive father and all, the fates sure favored him now. A wife who adored him, a great family, a peaceful home in the mountains and some careful investments I'd made for him. Walter had a lot of positive things in his life. He deserved to be happy, and it made me glad.

Actually, it gave me hope I might have a chance for that kind of happiness.

CHAPTER SIX

I just missed the ferry heading back to the other side of Puget Sound. I really didn't mind, though, because stuck there watching the boat sail away gave me some time to think. The last time I'd spoken with Art, the older gentleman who helped me out with my car collection and rebuilding the old MG, he'd mentioned he thought he knew of a fellow down in Portland who was interested in them. Getting rid of all the half-built cars, the parts I had, and the couple of totally restored cars would be a huge load off my mind. I had a few friends who were interested in my cars. Thinking about my antique cars reminded me of Snooker down in North Fort Myers. The last time I'd visited him, he told me of a small collection he owned and said he wanted me to look at them. I wanted to see him again and check out his collection.

The last time I'd looked at my text messages, I noticed I had a text from the Tronscosos. They owned a dance studio in Fort Myers. Someone killed the previous owner in the studio. Besides helping with the investigation into the owner's murder, I provided the kids with advice on how to go about purchasing the studio from the previous owner's estate. There were also several purveyors who didn't want to help them get the business straightened out, and I'd stepped in and shown them the error in their thinking. Promising the purveyors I'd guarantee they would get their money didn't hurt matters either. I called the dance studio. "Hello. E&R Dance Studio. Elora speaking. How may I help you?"

"Hello, Elora. This is Matt Preston."

"Oh, Mr. Preston. Thank you for calling me back."

"Gee, and here I really thought we had progressed to Matt and Elora. What's with the Mr. Preston stuff?"

Elora giggled. "I'm sorry, force of habit. But thanks for calling back. Are you in Fort Myers right now?"

"Not right now. But there's a good chance I might be in a few days. Why?"

"When you get back, Ramiro and I would like to talk to you. Could you please call us and we'll see what we can arrange?"

"I'll call you when I'm headed your way. Like I said, it should be in a few days."

We said our goodbyes and hung up.

When I put my phone away, I noticed I'd missed a call and a text. I checked the call and saw it was from Maggie Bradson. My return call to Maggie went to voice mail and I left her a message. "Maggie, this is Matt Preston. I see you called, and I missed it. This is my return call. Tag, you're it! Call me, please."

The text was from Tom Frost, also known as Snooker. His nick name has nothing to do with the game Snooker; it came because of his abilities with a pool stick and getting you to play for money. It you ever played him for money, you'd been Snookered! Ol' Tom would muff a shot and hit a ball so it just missed falling in the cup, and you'd think you could beat this guy. Then Mr. Frost would hold school and give a lesson on how to play pool. He was truly a legend. I took a chance and called him. The phone rang twice. "Hello. This is Tom Frost. May I help you?"

"Snooker, this is Matt Preston."

"Matt! How wonderful to hear your voice. Where are you?"

"I'm up in Seattle. But I think I might be down your way in a few days. Would it be convenient to see you?"

"If you come to Fort Myers and don't see me, I'll be really hurt."

"Okay. I'll let you know my schedule as things happen."

"Remember, I still have part of a bottle of superb Scotch with your name on it. I'm looking forward to seeing you."

While I'd been chatting with Snooker, I'd felt my phone vibrate in my hand. Checking what had caused it, I saw Maggie had called me back. I was getting popular in my old age. I returned Maggie's call. "Hi, it's Matt. Sorry I missed your call."

"Matt, thanks for calling back. I've left messages with my friend at the alumni office. She's on vacation for three weeks. I'm sorry, but for now, I can't help you with any addresses. Sorry I'm not more help. Will that work?"

"Not a problem. I have things I need to take care of. When you get the info, call me and let me know what you find out. Thanks for the update."

We said our goodbyes, and I figured this was the cosmos's way of telling me I should to go visit Lois. I looked up Henry's contact number on my phone and called. He picked it up on the second ring. "Matt, what can I do for you?"

"How come this connection sounds so weird?"

"I'm on the plane and I'm talking to you over my on-board STAT system."

"Ah. Where are you?"

"Getting ready to touch down in San Fran. Why?"

"Where are you headed after that?"

"Well, Orchard needs this plane and I'm supposed to get back to D.C. Where do you want to go, Matt?"

"Surprise! D.C."

"You're still in Seattle, right?"

"Yeah."

"Give me three hours and I'll pick you up at Boeing Field."

"This won't get you in trouble with the Admiral, will it?"

"Don't sweat it. Just be ready to roll when I get there."

"Deal!"

Next, I called Lois. She must have known it was me because she answered, "Hi, lover. You know I want you?"

"So, if I showed up in D.C., you might have time for me?"

The excitement in her voice was clear. Without giving me a chance to answer her, she rattled off, "You're kidding! Really? Yes! When?"

"Henry will pick me up at Boeing Field in about three hours and then I'm on my way. Do you want me to come to your office or do you want me to go to your place and wait?"

"I don't want the Admiral to know you're in town. For now, I want you all to myself. Go to my place. If I'm not there, I'll make arrangements for you to get in."

~ ~ ~ ~ ~

I was standing at the end of the tarmac when I saw Henry's plane pass overhead. The plane banked and touched down with very little noise. As soon as the plane stopped rolling, a fuel truck was pulling up beside one wing. The hatch opened, and Henry stepped out. For some reason, a handshake seemed too formal between the two of us and when he spread his arms, I stepped up to him and we embraced. I clapped him on the back and thanked him for picking me up.

"You have got to be kidding!" he said. "I'm delighted to have the company."

"We need to talk."

"Oh shit, this sounds serious." Henry scowled.

"Yeah, I found out you've been two-timing on me."

Henry laughed. "We can talk about it. Go sit in the copilot's seat. I'll be right there. I needed to talk to you, anyway."

The fuel truck pulled away, and I heard the hatch bang shut. Henry slipped into his seat and started his pre-flight check. Once the flight list was checked, he fired up the engines, and we rolled. They cleared us for take-off and the plane exploded off the runway and into the air. A sharp bank and we headed for D.C.

I pulled the boom down on my headset so I could talk to Henry. "You said you wanted to chat with me about something. What can I do for you?"

"Have you decided about our business?"

"That's what I wanted to talk to you about. I want in. I've had a talk with my bankers and I've arranged a line of credit for you. I'm having a company created so when you purchase a plane, register it in the corporation. When we land, I'll give you the name and number of the banker you want to contact. The bank expects to hear from you."

"Matt, I don't know what to say."

"Nothing. Without you, I wouldn't be here. There's nothing I wouldn't do for you."

"You need to stop that. You needed help, and I was there to help."

"Yeah, but at what a risk to you? I didn't expect you to come back and risk your life for me. I heard you cut it so close there were tire tracks on top of one of the armored cars that were trying to blow us out of the sky as you flew over them. Don't you think you were cutting it a bit close?"

"Like I said, you need to stop that. We're here and we're both safe. Anyway, partner, are you still headed for Florida, eventually?"

"Yeah, why?"

"Look, even though I only have access to three planes at the moment, we need a home office, a base of operations, and especially hanger space for repairs. I've done some investigation, and I discovered Florida has some of the best rates on hanger space around the country, especially the southwest Florida area. Your little airport in Fort Myers is perfect fo us. Their market prices haven't caught up yet with the majority of the country. Since you'll be down there, would you mind looking around and seeing what you find?"

"Sure. I should have some time and I'll check. I'll let you know what I find."

"Great. I know I have the three planes pretty well tied up. I'll have your banker contact the proper people and get the funds transferred. We also have a good shot at one more plane coming on the market in about a month, and I like our chances for a second one just like it. These are larger, and we need something bigger than the three we'll be getting. You look for space. I can't ask for more than that. Okay, sit back and relax. D.C., here we come."

Henry must have been pretty sure I was going to go ahead with the deal since he had a booking already lined up for the plane we are on in D.C. He needed to get there as quickly as possible to pick them up. We landed and as I was walking across the tarmac, four business types went scurrying towards the plane. I also noticed the plane now had an attendant who hadn't been there on the flight from Seattle. The attendant stopped the men before they clambered into the plane. A fuel truck pulled up next to one wing and started filling the plane. Shortly after the truck pulled away, the group of men climbed aboard and once it was buttoned up, the plane taxied toward the main runway. It looked like our business was off and running.

Parked outside the gate was the taxi I'd called to take me to Lois' place. I climbed into a beat-up old cab which stunk like old beer, stinky cigars and barf. I wasn't very impressed with D.C. taxis. I gave the driver Lois' address, and we took off.

The ride took about forty minutes and by the time I'd paid my fare, I was eager to get out of the fetid cab. I stepped into the lobby and looked up Lois' name on the residence's list. I pushed the button next to her name, wondering if perhaps she might be home. I was pleased when she buzzed me into the building.

Stepping off the elevator, I found her waiting in the hallway. Seeing her standing there, expecting my arrival, I realized what a delight she was. My delight and appreciation was because she was interested in me, and that gave me a feeling of pride. In that moment, I felt I was very lucky to have such an attractive woman excited to see me.

Lois threw her arms around my neck and, with a lot of passion, kissed me on my lips. For several reasons, her kiss started waking up... things. Thankfully, somebody came out of their unit or it might have gotten a little embarrassing. Lois and I quickly parted. She grabbed my arm and pulled me into her apartment. Once the door clicked shut, Lois threw her arms around me again and resumed kissing me. Finally, I heard her whisper in my ear, "Please, take me to the bedroom and make love to me."

Those who know me know I hardly ever disobey a beautiful woman, regardless of what they ask me to do.

So, I did exactly what she asked.

~ ~ ~ ~ ~

I spent the next couple of days in total bliss. We ate when we were hungry. We rarely dressed and never left Lois' condo. Dawn of our third day together found us wrapped in each other's arms after a wonderful wake up session. I leaned over and kissed her lips and whispered, "Lois, I'm so in love with you. I missed you so much out in Seattle. I don't know exactly what to do."

"I'm so pleased you came for a visit. To be honest, I wondered if you would come."

"You're crazy. The more we're together, the more I realize how special you are. My life is changing right now. Seattle is different and I'm trying to figure out why. But you're also driving many of those changes." Lois kissed me and reached down between us. I'd heard some people hear bells ringing and when she touched me, I thought for a minute the stories were true. However, it was her phone that was ringing and not my heart. Although I felt happy enough to be ringing.

"Oh shit," she muttered as she reached for it. "Hello." She listened for a while. "John, how the hell did you know Matt was here?" I could hear him laugh over the phone. "Just a minute, I'll ask." She pulled the phone from her ear. "John wants to know if we'll have dinner with him and Jennifer tonight?" I nodded. "Yes, John." She continued to chat with him as she got the time and location where we'd meet. She pushed the end button on her phone and looked at me. "How the hell did he know you were here?"

"I have a suspicion. Henry might have let it slip. He's the only one who knew I was here. Oh, wait... Mouse and Albert know I'm here too."

"Gee, darling, why not take out an ad in the paper and let the world know you're here?" I tickled her, and that turned into something else and that... well, never mind. Later, we eventually got around to taking a shower.

I was drying Lois' well-shaped back and bottom when an ugly thought hit me. "Umm, the restaurant tonight?"

She looked at me over her shoulder. "Yes?"

"Is it fancy?"

"Rather."

"Shit!"

"Why shit?"

"All I have with me are two pairs of jeans, two shirts and a warm sweater. What am I going to wear?" Lois gave me a sly grin. She extended her hand and pulled me back to the spare bedroom. She opened the closet door where I found two garment bags hanging on the pole. "What's this?"

"Open them."

Inside one was a brand-new, custom, double-breasted, dark blue suit with pale chalk pinstripes. Inside the other, a brand-new French-cuff white shirt with two handsome ties around the neck. "Where did this come from?"

"When you were in the hospital over in Germany, after you got out, I thought you might need a place to stay for a while and I hoped you'd stay with me. I didn't know we'd end up in Fort Myers trying to figure out who killed the dance studio owner.

"Anyway, I found out from Walter the name of your tailor and I ordered the suit and shirt and had them shipped here. In the suit pocket are cuff-links and there's a brand-new pair of black shoes on the floor. And I also have new socks and underwear for you."

"Gee, I feel like a kept man. I sure hope I can perform to your satisfaction."

"Baby, if you did any better, I'd be comatose. And in case it worries you I might not be satisfied, when we get home tonight, I'll give you another shot." Her grin was absolutely wicked.

I reached out to grab her, but she ducked out of reach as I watched her darling bottom sway across the room. Calling over her shoulder, she told me, "Get dressed. I don't want to be late."

"Yes, ma'am."

~ ~ ~ ~ ~

Stepping into the lobby of the restaurant, I noticed that over half of the men were dressed in formal wear. I was thrilled to have my new suit. I loved the color and it fit me perfectly. Because of my visit to the hospital after my last adventure, I'd lost several pounds and I could tell it by the way my clothing fit. Lois was wearing a dress that looked like something out of the roaring twenties: black with several rows of fringe. When she walked, the fringe moved in a rather suggestive manner. Or maybe it was just my dirty little mind. Well, maybe suggestive might not be the correct word, but I thought it was sexy.

The maître' d showed us to the table where John and his wife sat. I didn't get to see Jennifer often; it was a pleasure to see her again. The two ladies knew one another. When Jennifer stood, they embraced. I extended my hand to John; he slapped it away and hugged me. Tonight, John was wearing the uniform of a two-star admiral. "Are you really an admiral?"

"Well, my General Schedule rating is equivalent to the rank of either a two-star general or an admiral. Since I spend more of my time involved with navy business than any other, I sometimes wear this uniform. Besides, this way we get a better table."

I chortled, and we sat.

I'd always enjoyed my time with John and this evening was no different. Once during the meal, he leaned over and put his hand on my sleeve. "I have to tell you one more time how pleased I am about your trip over to the Middle East. I'm sorry you had to get roughed up like that, but the way things turned out has cemented so many relationships. However, I don't want you to do anything like that ever again. I'd be crushed to lose your friendship. Okay?"

I smiled and nodded. If I had any choice, there was no way I'd get involved with what happened over there ever again. My face was just now getting to the place where I didn't scare children and make little old ladies shriek.

Later that night, on the way back to Lois' place, she asked me, "When are you going to leave?"

"Oh, want to get rid of me so soon?" That comment got me a rather firm slap on the shoulder. "I was thinking I'd contact Henry and see when he would have a plane in the area and then head on down to Fort Myers. I have two requests to visit people and Henry wants me to line up hanger and warehouse space for our new little business." Speaking of Henry reminded me of something else. "Hey, how come you never told me you had a pilot's license?"

"You never asked." Lois winked.

"Henry said you can fly all sorts of things. He said you were the one who took off when he came and rescued me."

"That's sort of the way it happened. I got the plane moving then he slid into the pilot's chair. He was the one who took over as the plane was lifting off. You didn't see it, but we were playing chicken with two tanks. They were heading towards us side by side and I'll bet there were tire marks across the tops of the turrets where we grazed them."

"Well, thanks for coming for me. And thanks for taking care of me afterwards."

"And when we get back to my place, I want you to take care of me!" Lois gave me a suggestive wink.

"Oh damn, work, work, work. No rest for this old body."

"No! And don't forget it."

~ ~ ~ ~ ~

At first, I thought there was a phone ringing in my dreams, then I realized it was for real. I reached for the phone but I remembered where I was before answering. This was Lois' phone, not mine. I heard her answer. "Hello." I thought she really had a sexy voice when blurred with sleep. I could hear the buzzing of whoever was on the phone. "Really?" Lois responded. "Okay. Give me an hour and I'll be in." I noticed the buzzing was louder now. "Admiral, I'll get there when I get there. Now get off the phone so I can get ready." Lois ended the call.

"What's up, babe?"

"That was John. There's a problem I can't discuss with you, but he needs me in the office as quickly as possible."

"What do you want me to do?"

"Call Henry. Go do what you have to do. If I can get away, you want me to come down and be with you?"

"I assume you're making a joke. Of course, I want you to come down. I wish we were going now... together. We still have to join that mile-high thing you keep babbling on about."

"Babbling? I'll show you babbling, buster." I reached for her but she quickly pulled away. "Stop. Please. I'd much rather stay here with you than help John put out his fires. Having you grab at me makes it all the more difficult." Lois leaned over and kissed me on the lips, and I reached up and took her naked breasts in my hands. I pinched one nipple firmly. She moaned. "Oh, you are a bastard. Now stop. I need to go." I didn't want to stop, but I also knew it was unfair of me to tease her when she needed to get going. I lay in bed and listened to the shower. Images of her wet body danced in my head. I needed to stop thinking about her... like now!

I padded around the apartment, looking for my phone. Once it was in hand, I called the central number for our air service. I left a message on the recording asking somebody to call me back. I'd just kissed Lois goodbye when my phone rang. It was one of our other pilots. "What's up, Matt?"

"Is anybody going to be around D.C. soon?"

"Just a sec." The phone was still for a minute or two. "Still there, Matt?"

"Yeah."

"There's a plane in the area around four this afternoon and it's headed to the Caribbean. Where are you going?"

"I'm trying to get to Fort Myers, Florida."

"That works. Be at the Baltimore/Washington airport at one. Be at the south end and you will see some private planes parked there. The tail number on your plane is N3794N. Talk to you later, Matt."

CHAPTER SEVEN

So far, out of six pilots Henry had arranged to work for us including himself, I'd met three. Today was somebody new. For some reason, I thought they were all males. Nothing was ever said one way or another, so I guess it was part of my stupid male attitude regarding male and female roles. Today, I discovered we had a female pilot working for us. Like I said, makes me no never mind who flies the plane since I trusted Henry completely. If he thought she was good enough to fly for us, so did I.

The flight down to Fort Myers was short. It felt like I'd hardly gotten settled when we were landing. I'd called ahead to Hertz and there was a car waiting for me. I briefly thought if coming to Fort Myers was going to be a habit, perhaps I should look into getting myself a car and leaving it at the airport.

I called Elora Tronscoso at the dance studio. "Elora, this is Matt Preston."

"Matt. Great to hear you voice. Where are you?"

"Just landed in Fort Myers. I was calling to see if it was convenient for me to stop by. You'd said you wanted to see me."

"Yes. Come on over now."

"Be there in five."

I noticed they'd changed the sign out from the previous owner's name and even though the speaker was still hanging over the door, it played more softly than it had the last time I had visited. I parked and went in. Once Elora saw me, she came running up and wrapped her arms around me. I gave her a big hug and kissed her on the cheek. Her husband Ramiro saw me and came up with a big grin on his face. When the previous owner had died, he left a lot of debt that needed to be addressed. I'd counseled the kids on what to do and I'd even spoken to a few of their debtors and promised they would get paid. I was pleased to see the place was clean and looked prosperous. They still had a crummy floor, but I kept that thought to myself. "What can I do for you, Elora?"

"Well, the problem is our bank. We tried to borrow money to have a new floor installed because the floor we have right now is dangerous. The bank turned us down because we are so new and we don't have the credit history they want."

"Let me guess, you want to see me because you'd like for me to go to the bank and see if I can arrange for them to loan the money?"

Elora blushed and Ramiro looked at the floor. Elora looked at me, nodded, and whispered, "Yes."

"Tell you what. How about I loan you kids the money? How much would a new floor cost?"

"Oh Matt, you don't know what you are offering. A good floor is anywhere between thirty and fifty thousand dollars."

The lightbulb when on in my head. "Okay, now I understand why you've done nothing to the old floor yet. I'll loan you the money on one condition."

"What's that?" Ramiro asked.

"I'd like to look around at various floors. It's not that I don't trust you kids, I just want to get a feeling for myself. I promise I won't order anything unless you approve it. I've been around construction most of my life and I'd like to get a good understanding what you need and what's included in the price. Is that fair?"

"Yes. And thank you."

Elora asked, "What interest rate are you going to charge?"

"I'll charge just a minimum, say half a percent. I want to help and this is a way I can do it."

Elora stepped up and wrapped her arms around me. I gently hugged her then stepped back. Looking at Ramiro, I smiled. "Don't get upset. She hugged me first."

"Do you want me to hug you?" Ramiro asked.

"Don't take offense Ramiro, but no. I'm good. I'll be in contact with both of you in a few days."

I knew I'd help them regardless of the price. They'd worked hard to keep the doors open, and I was proud of their hard work. I know how banks can be and for me, a handshake and a promise to repay me was good enough.

I'd just fastened my seat belt when my cell phone vibrated in my pocket. I looked at the display screen and I saw it was Snooker. "Hey, Snook! What's up?" I asked.

"Are you in town?" I told him I was. "Can you swing by the condo around five this afternoon? I'd love to see you." I agreed. "Don't bring any Scotch. Remember I still have what's left of the bottle you brought me last time." I agreed, and we hung up.

It was straight up five when I arrived, and as I was getting out of my car, I heard Snooker blowing his conch shell. I listened to the mournful sound as he blew three strong blasts. Today, I heard other residents calling out their approval. I was sure that'd make Snook happy.

Martha let me in and I walked to the back where Tom was just placing the conch shell on the table. I noticed two glasses of amber liquid on the coffee table and from the color, I assumed it was Scotch. He motioned for me to sit and pointed at which glass was mine. I was right. It was Scotch, and a superb brand to boot—the same one I'd bought for him last time.

As I settled myself in the wicker planter's chair across from Snooker, my cell phone rang. I intended to turn it off, but I noticed the call was from Senator Bradson. I asked Snooker if he minded if I took the call. He motioned for me to go ahead.

"Howdy, Albert." As I said that, I realized the only person I ever heard call him Al was Maggie. For everyone else, it was always Albert. Interesting. "How ya doing and what can I do for you?"

"Hello, Matt. I'm doing fine. Are you somewhere we can talk?"

I stepped out onto the lanai. "Yeah, go ahead."

"Like I told you before, I finally found ol' Buck. He's a hard person to track down. I spoke with him, like you asked. Sorry this took so long. He was hiding out at an old rundown motel in a village in Maryland called Hoadly, a few miles from D.C. When they found him, he was so drunk he didn't even know where he was. Later, I saw him, and after he realized who I was, he didn't want to talk to me. I reminded him of a few things I can't divulge to you, but it helped him decide it was in his best interest to come clean with me.

"Buck knows who shot the four men in the alley. The man calls himself El Wislond." Albert said Buck and Wislond had a long history.

"Buck wouldn't or couldn't tell me any more than that. He's now signed into a hospital, under a fictitious name, and they're monitoring his condition carefully. Whatever it is with this Wislond individual, it scares Buck shitless. He told me the man, El Wislond, said he would murder him. But that Buck would never see him coming and that he could consider himself living on borrowed time."

"Why didn't this Wislond dude do the deed that night in the alley?" I asked.

"This Wislond character told him since Buck had ruined his life, he would kill him, but wouldn't tell him when or where. He wants him to suffer."

"Wislond sounds sadistic. Okay. Thanks for the info. How much of this can I share with Sakol and Chief Davenport?"

"I guess you can tell them everything. Buck didn't tell me not to repeat what he said. I know it worries him. He's positive Wislond will kill him at some point. I got the feeling Buck did something a long time ago to Wislond and he knows his time is short."

"Any chance there's a way to track Wislond down? There has to be a way to get a handle on him."

"Buck asked one agency on his committee to consider this, but they have all drawn a blank."

"Well, thanks for the info. I'll pass it on. I'm sure Sakol will be happy to know he hasn't lost his touch. He was positive something was wrong with ol' Buck's story and it turns out he was right."

"Stay in touch."

"Later."

I called Jeff and filled him in on what I'd learned. I told Jeff to make sure and tell Sakol his bullshit detector was working as great as ever.

After letting Jeff know what was up, I hung up and moved back into the condo to take another sip of Snooker's Scotch.

"I'm sorry about that, Snook. A little piece of old business."

"What was all that about?" he asked.

I told him about our other senator from Washington and the murdered cops and bodyguards and how Albert had just found out this was all connected to something, or someone called Wislond or El Wislond. Snooker had taken a sip from his drink but when I said the name, he coughed and gasped for breath. I patted him on the back a few times and after he caught his breath, I asked him what happened. "What do you know about El Wislond?" he asked, obviously alarmed.

"I guess I could ask the same question. Do you know who Senator Buck Markel is?"

Snooker grimaced. "Oh yeah. I know way too much about Markel. The man is a total asshole."

I explained to Snooker, "A few weeks ago, the senator was on his way to a speaking engagement when his limo and police escort got ambushed when they pulled into an alley. Somebody opened fire, killing everyone but Buck. At first, when Buck was questioned, he claimed he didn't know a thing. Senator Albert Bradson is an old friend and as a favor for another friend, I asked Bradson to look into the situation. The senator just found Buck in an old run-down motel, drunk and babbling about El Wislond. Okay Snooker, now it's your turn."

Snooker stood and painfully limped over to the screened window offering a view of the canal and the river beyond. Eventually, he turned and faced me. "Sorry about that. Some not too pleasant memories there. At one time, they'd stationed me at Fort Bragg, North Carolina. I think I was a staff sergeant at the time and in my squad was a kid named Thomas McKnight. Thomas Wislond McKnight. For some reason, he called himself El Wislond. The kid was a real punk, a total loner. Nobody in the unit liked him. I don't know why he insisted we call him El Wislond, other than it was his middle name and, I guess, a family name.

"Back then, it was First Lieutenant Buck Markel, and he was our company Executive Officer. Buck took it upon himself to make life hell for the McKnight kid. I heard a rumor that McKinght was screwing Buck's sister, don't know for sure that is was true. But any crappy job, poor Tom got it. I knew nobody who pulled more kitchen duty than that unfortunate kid. One time, he got a pass to meet his girlfriend, and they were to be married. The night before McKnight was supposed to leave, Markel pulled it and confined him to quarters. McKnight couldn't even call his girlfriend and tell her the marriage was off. The girlfriend, understandably furious, dumped him.

"When Buck got assigned to Nam, he pulled some strings and had McKnight sent over to his outfit. By that time, Buck was a captain and commanding officer of the company. It didn't seem possible, but he made things even more difficult for McKnight.

"On my own, I did an investigation into McKnight. Much later, by accident, I found out that McKnight had been having sex with Buck's sister. This was after Markel told him to stay away from her. I've always assumed a lot of Buck's vindictiveness was because of what happened to the sister. Buck had good reason to want McKnight to stay away from her. I found out they had expelled McKnight from a number of schools for bullying and fighting and as a youth, he was a first-class punk and eventually ended up in reform school for a while. It appears he eventually fooled many people at the school because they released him. Not a good thing, as it turns out.

"When Markel got out of the service, he practiced law. Later, I heard Ol' Buck moved on from having his own practice and ran for district attorney. As luck would have it, they arrested McKnight for possession of drugs in Buck's district and Markel prosecuted the case. However, during the trial, it was decided that it was doubtful Tom was involved. That didn't matter to Buck. He continued to press on until he eventually got the kid thrown into prison.

"After that, I lost track. As you know, Buck was governor of the state and then a state senator. When they sentenced McKnight, he told Buck he would get even if it was the last thing he ever did. Until this moment, I haven't heard the name Wislond or Tom McKnight for well over twenty years."

"Can you excuse me for a minute?"

Snook motioned for me to go and I stepped out onto his lanai and called Bradson to tell him what I'd just learned. He thanked me and we hung up. Next, I called Jeff again and told him what I'd just found out from Snooker. I suggested Jeff call Albert, but knowing what kind of power a state senator would have, I doubted if Jeff and Sakol could do much to Buck. Still, I wondered what would happen next.

I settled myself once again in the wicker planter's chair across from Snooker. We held up our glasses and touched the rims together. We each took a sip, then Snook set his glass down and pushed himself up out of his chair. Knowing how difficult it was for Snooker to stand, it surprised me when he stood and limped over to the screened window. He stood there a long time, gazing over the river with his hands clasped behind his back. I wondered if he'd forgotten about me.

Turning to face me, he said, "Sorry about that. I was on a trip there. Sometimes, all I have left are years and years of memories. I always felt badly about McKnight, but there was nothing I could do about it. If I had been a top Sergeant, I could have stepped in, but my rank at that time wouldn't allow me to spar with Buck and not end up being court marshalled.

"And some days, when I blow the shell, I think back to how it was and all the friends that are gone now. Occasionally, it really gets to me. Today was one of those days. Going down memory lane with ol' McKnight didn't help things either. I couldn't stand McKnight, but that didn't change how I felt about what Markel did to him. Sister or no sister, what he did was uncalled for and I felt it was an abuse of his power. Anyway, sorry about the side trip there." He grinned at me.

"Not to worry. I'm sure you saw a lot of things over the years which bring back old memories. Anyway, I was wondering why did you want me to come out and see you? Not that I don't enjoy spending time with you. But was there something specific you wanted?"

"Matt, I wanted to thank you again personally for getting involved with Zoe and Stephen. You owed me nothing, but you helped anyway and you were unbelievable. Zoe is so pleased with how it all turned out and I feel responsible for getting you involved. You are everything I'd heard about you and then some."

I held up my hand to stop him. "Stop! This is unnecessary. You've already thanked me. What are friends for if not to help each other? You need to stop now. This is getting embarrassing."

Tom smiled as he nodded. "You are quite the man, Matt Preston. I'd have loved to have served with you."

I know I blushed. "That's a real compliment. There are many people who I wouldn't want to spent time with, but the service doesn't give you that choice." Snook made a sound like laughter. "I would have liked to have served with you too. Conversely, I would not have played you a game of pool, but everything else is fair game."

Snooker guffawed and shook his head.

"Thanks. The other reason I wanted to see you was to ask for your help. I know that Zoe has no interest in my little car collection, and I wondered if you would help her sell it when the time comes?"

I sat for a moment, wondering if I would get myself into another crazy situation, but I knew I couldn't refuse his request. "Sure, I guess I could help her. But that will be a long time from now and maybe she'll change her mind about your cars."

"Thanks again. I knew I could count on you. However, as for changing her mind, I doubt it. Her age group don't feel that same was about cars that we do." Tom looked relived as if I had solved a large problem.

For the next few hours, we relived experiences ranging from back in Nam to our love of automobiles. Martha brought out snacks for us to nibble on as we exchanged stories. I received a refill on my drink, but Tom didn't. He seemed to understand why she didn't refill his glass since he didn't mention it.

Again, Snooker mentioned his small car collection stashed away in a warehouse not too far away, and how he needed to do something about it. "As you can see," he pointed to his feet, "I can't drive anymore, and the cars are just parked out there. I know I need to dispose of them, but I feel if I sold them, it's like admitting defeat. I may be getting older, but I refuse to grow up."

I snorted and told him I had said the same words many times myself. "I've told you I have some cars back in Seattle and I also need to deal with them, but I've put it off for the same reason you have. Look at it this way, Tom, someday, your cars will be famous. They will know your collection as Snooker's Legacy." I was pleased to see he got a good laugh out of that idea. I continued, "I want to see them. Next time I'm down here, we'll go out and look at your cars. Deal?" Snook nodded. "Since I'm spending so much time lately in southwest Florida, I'm also considering finding a place to live."

"I've enjoyed it. There are worse places to end up."

"What do the doctors say about your legs? Any improvement?" I asked.

"Sadly, no. Who knows what they exposed us to over in Nam, and also some other places I served. The list of things wrong with me seems to grow every time I see a doctor. Since there's nothing I can do about it, I choose not to dwell on what's happening in the old body. I'm just taking one day at a time, but I really feel bad about my little collection out there rotting away in that warehouse. What am I going to do? I miss not trading and perhaps getting a car I've always wanted. But even that old excitement has lost a little of its luster. However, there have been a few cars over the years I sure wish I still had."

We both had owned cars we wished we still owned today. We also both had stories regarding woulda, coulda, shoulda, which we swapped. I told him the details about my small collection back in Seattle, about which ones I'd sold and which ones I was in the process of selling. "After those sales go through, I'll be down to just my truck. Oh, and my motorcycle, which I plan on selling just as soon as I return from my last road trip. I'm also in the middle of selling most of my properties back in Seattle which means I won't have a place to keep any old cars. Prices and taxes are getting to be insane. Seattle isn't the place I grew up in anymore." I noticed Snooker chose not to elaborate about his collection and I decided he just didn't want to think about them since he couldn't drive anymore.

We continued to swap old war stories and since we'd both served under similar circumstances overseas, we could relate to each other's tales. He told me about several missions he'd been on which sounded a lot like some of mine. When I told him mine, he nodded in understanding.

We decided the war had been an awful mistake and a lot of great kids had given their all for the wrong reasons. Snooker was feeling very introspective this evening, and I got the feeling he was lonesome for somebody with whom to discuss the old days.

When it was time to leave, Snooker pushed himself out of his chair, and when I grasped his hand to say goodbye, he pulled me to his chest and gave me a hug. "You have made an old man very happy this evening. Thanks."

"Truly, I can say the same. I rarely like to play 're-member when,' but since you and I have traveled many of the same trails, tonight was enjoyable. The next time I'm here, I want you to take me out and show me your collection, Snooker's Legacy."

He smiled and nodded.

"As for Zoe and Stephen, I was glad to help. Make sure I get a wedding announcement."

"Consider it done."

As I drove away, I wondered what he'd been like back in the day. Walter had told me Tom had been hell on wheels as a top Sergeant and he'd have second lieutenants for lunch. If you did your job, he was there for you, but if you were a screw-up, there was no place safe for you to hide. I'd also have loved to see him play pool. Considering the stories I'd heard about his prowess with a pool stick, he must have been something to behold. I was happy I got to meet him when I did and that I could call him a friend.

I could feel the big grin on my face.

CHAPTER EIGHT

I was driving around Page Field looking at various hanger spaces and warehouses, and I saw several possibilities. When I drove around the south end of the airfield, I noticed a warehouse that would be perfect. It had a For Lease sign in the window. I called the number on the sign and a woman's voice answered, "Good afternoon, Tilkens Properties and Leasing. How may I help you?"

I introduced myself and explained I was parked in front of an empty building down by Page Field. "Can you give me any information about it?"

"Gee, Mr. Preston, Mr. Tilkens is out right now showing a property, but if you'll give me your number, I'll have him call you back as soon as he checks in. The one thing I know about that property is there is also hanger space across the road with airfield access and it was part of the warehouse property at one time. I believe both are for lease."

"That's fantastic. It's exactly what I'm looking for."

"I'll have Mr. Tilkens call you as soon as he gets in."

"Thanks. Goodbye."

I'd hardly put my phone back in my pocket when it went off again. I wondered how come I had gotten so popular. Looking at the screen, I noticed it was Maggie. "Hello, Maggie. How are things going?"

"I had a long talk with Albert last night. I did as you said. I told him exactly how I felt and what my issues were. He said exactly what I thought he'd say. He says he won't run."

"How does that make you feel?"

"I feel guilty."

"Let's try this again, how do you feel about that?"

"I guess I want him to run more than I *don't* want it. I know that man and I think he would be an excellent person for the job. I know there are things he'd have to give up to run, so I guess for me to stand in his way would be rather petty. About the only thing I can think of that could bite us on the butt is the affair with Linda and how that turned out. But he wasn't married at the time, so it isn't like he was cheating on me, and who really knows who the father was? I feel I can deal with him running."

"What do you want from me?"

"Will you continue to look into what happened to the baby? And if it looks like you can get a DNA sample, let's have tests run to determine if Al is the father."

"Okay. Have you been able to get me any names and addresses?"

"Yes. My friend found Robyn's current address. Her married name is Bueler. Dr. Robyn Bueler. And her husband's name is Tocs—rhymes with docks except with a T." Maggie gave me her address and added, "Lowell is the name of the town where the clinic is. Robyn lives in Rogers, which is the next town over, and they are all centered around Bentonville, which is the hometown for Walmart. As for Linda, it was as I expected. Because she quit school, they have no information on her."

"Maggie, I'm about done here in Fort Myers for the time being. I'll call you when I get to Arkansas. And thanks for being upfront with Albert. I know it wasn't easy, but in the long run, it really was the right thing to do."

"I know you're right, but it was tough. By the way, Matt, Jade and I had lunch the other day."

I knew where this was headed. "Really, how was lunch?"

"Matt don't play the innocent with me. Jade told me about the conversation the two of you had after I left. And she was correct, I had an affair. I'm ashamed and I know this doesn't make it right, but after Al was elected, I felt neglected. He was always so busy, and I was alone a lot. I'm not making excuses, I'm just telling you how it was. One of his aides and I ended up in a strange situation and one thing led to another and we ended up having sex. The affair was torrid and short. I realized how important Albert was to me and I ended it quickly. The aide moved on and I don't know where he is now. When Albert and I had our talk the other day, I confessed about my affair. Actually, things are better now between us than they have ever been.

"However, talking about the old days and how things were and all, well, things got a little heated, if you know what I mean? He apologized for neglecting me and I apologized for straying. I told him part of the reason I didn't want him to run was I didn't want my indiscretion to come out. Albert told me he needed to take care of things so I never again felt the need to stray." Maggie giggled like a schoolgirl and I was positive she was blushing. Hearing her tell me everything made me feel a lot more comfortable regarding the outcome of him running for office.

I called the main phone number Henry had set up for our little airline company and left a message explaining what I needed. A few minutes later, Henry called me back. "Matt. I'm sorry, but the soonest anybody can get to you is tomorrow afternoon. Do you still want somebody to come and pick you up?"

"Is this going to screw things up for you guys?"

"Don't worry about it. The one thing we're discovering is we have to get the next two planes coming up for auction. Business is growing a little faster than we expected. However, that's a good thing."

"Great, I'll see you tomorrow."

"Ciao."

I dialed Lois. She must have had her phone in her hand because she picked up after the first ring. "Oh Matt, am I glad to hear a friendly voice."

"What's the matter, babe?"

"I can't tell you. But things have been really crappy around here."

"That bad?"

"Worse! But yes, things here are crazy. Anyway, you called?"

"Yeah. I miss you. I wanted to hear your voice."

"Oh, thank you. I'm so pleased you called. What's going on?"

I told her about Maggie finally having a good talk with Albert and their decision. I told her about my trip the next day to Arkansas and how I needed to look for the veterinarian. "I have a name and address, so I should be lucky. When I finish with that, I want to take my farewell bike trip and then sell the bike."

"Oh, Matt, I know how much you love to ride."

"Darling, there are a number of reasons not to ride anymore. You are the number one reason. I don't want to get hurt and not be able to spend time with you. I know I'll miss the bike, but I'm getting to the point where if I hurt myself, it takes way too long to heal. 'Sides, they say there are two kinds of riders. Those who have had an accident and those who are going to have an accident. I have had an amazing string of luck when it comes to riding, so let's not push it."

"I will never tell you what to do. But I'll admit I'm pleased to hear you will give up the bike."

"When I get done, I'm coming back to see you. That's if you want me to."

"You're welcome anytime, you know that!"

"I love you, Lois."

"And I love you. Thanks for calling."

"Are you going to be okay?"

"Yeah, don't worry. It's just the same ol' screwed up world as usual. I'll be fine." We said our goodbyes and hung up.

While I was in Florida and since I had the time, I decided it had been too long since I'd seen my old friend on the Fort Myers police force. When I got to the Municipal Building, I checked in with the desk sergeant. I was in luck, Brian Polk was at his desk. I told the sergeant I knew the way to his desk, and I guess he must have remembered me because he let me wander back on my own. When Brian saw me, he jumped up and stuck out his hand. "Matt. Damn, it's good to see you."

"You have time for a cup of coffee?"

"For you? Always! Come on, I've had enough of this place for today, anyway." We walked two blocks to a little café where a lot of the off-duty police hung out. We caged a table and ordered coffee. "What brings you to Fort Myers?"

I explained about the dance studio and their request to help them arrange for a new floor. I told him about Snooker and my concern regarding his health, and about my visit to the airfield and how I was looking at various vacant buildings in the area. "I found one hanger space and I understand there is a warehouse just across the street that, at one time, went with the hanger."

"Oh yeah, I know all about that."

"How come?"

"The fellow who owned the properties passed away without a will. His only living relatives are two sisters, so they inherited the properties. Matt, the two of them fight like cats and dogs and can't come to an agreement on one damn thing. I know of two separate occasions where officers had to go out and physically restrain them just to keep them from killing one another.

"I know Tilkens personally and he's trying his best to get the buildings leased, but the gals fight over that too. They can't agree on what to charge for the space or even the length of term. It's sad because the fellow who owned it was a nice guy. The sisters never married and all they do is fight. And, get this, they live together in the same house!"

"No shit?"

"You would think they would have moved apart a long time ago. But there are a lot of tales I can tell you about this little burg."

"How are you and Doris doing?"

Polk had asked me to help investigate the murder of the original owner of the Tronscosos' dance studio. I'd interviewed Doris Wentworth for Polk and I found her to be a tall, elegant, intelligent, sexy, striking woman who could be anywhere between mid-forties to early sixties. I've never been great at guessing ages. Later, when Doris and Brian finally met, sparks flew between them from the start. She thought his good looks and buff body very appealing. He was infatuated with her alluring presence as well. The last time I'd seen them together, they could hardly keep their hand off each other.

"Doris is well, thank you."

"I take it the two of you are still an item?"

He nodded. "We live together now. I've put in for retirement and I'll be leaving the force in few months. I can't believe how well the two of us get along. At first, I had a lot of problems with how much money she has. I didn't want her to feel I was just interested in her money. She knows now how I feel about her. It wouldn't matter if she didn't have a dime, I love her. Matt, I hate to leave her in the morning. I think about her all day long and I'm eager to get home. When I get home… well, I won't say more except to thank you for the introduction." The man was actually blushing.

"Brian, with the way you two feel about each other, you would have met sooner or later. You're perfect together and I'm so pleased to see things working out for you."

"How are you and Lois doing?"

"I was just up in D.C. visiting her. I'm not sure how it will turn out. I know I feel things about her I never felt for any other woman. Considering my age, that's saying a lot, and I know what you mean about thinking about her all day long. I'm discovering that relationships ain't easy."

"No shit! I've tired marriage twice and I know being a police officer screwed up the marriages a lot, but still, two times? But I'm willing to try it again with Doris. She's amazing."

"It's how I feel about Lois. I guess we are two rather pathetic individuals."

Brian's laugh was hardy.

We walked back to the station and shook hands. We agreed the next time Lois was in town, we had to have dinner together. "Good luck with your retirement."

"The way Doris keeps me busy and all, I don't know exactly how much retirement there will be."

~ ~ ~ ~ ~

The next day, I arrived at the airport early and drove around looking at the space I wanted to lease for our hanger and warehouse. I parked and as I was walking about the hanger area, my cell went off. "Hello, this is Matt."

"Mr. Preston, this is Tom Tilkens."

"Yes, sir. Funny you would call right now. I'm currently walking around the hanger area."

Tilkens explained exactly what Polk had told me the day before. I asked him to see if the sisters could come up with an amount that would satisfy both. It was obvious the space had been empty for some time. I pointed out to him he might want to mention that to the sisters. They were not only losing rent money, but having the buildings stand vacant wasn't good because of the Florida weather. He promised to call me back in a few days with an update. I thanked him and as I hung up, I saw my plane landing over in front of the terminal. I dropped off my rental and when I climbed on board, I was pleased to see Henry was the pilot. After they fueled us, we headed for Arkansas.

Henry had put the plane on auto-piolet when I felt my cell phone vibrating in my pocket. He showed me how to put my call through the communication system on board the plane so I could talk through the headset I was wearing. "Hello."

"Hello. Matt?"

"Yes."

"This is Elora. How come you sound so strange?"

"Sorry. I'm on a plane. We're on the plane's communication system."

"Oh. Sorry to bother you. Have you found out anything about the floor?"

"Elora, I am sorry. Yes, I would like for you to call…" I gave her the information I'd learned on dance floors and the name of the person I talked with. "You two look over the various kinds of flooring and pick what you want. I have already told them they are to install whatever you want, and I'll pay for it. When I get back, we'll sit down and work out a payment schedule. Will that work?"

"Oh god. Thank you, thank you. You are so wonderful."

"Stop. I'm not wonderful. I want to see you two succeed. And I want more dance lessons. I'll stop by when I get back to Fort Myers. Okay?"

"Thanks, Matt. We really owe you for this one."

"Goodbye."

CHAPTER NINE

The plane's tires chirped as they touched on the tarmac. Henry rolled to the end of the runway and taxied over to a waiting fuel truck. We disembarked and watched the workers fill the tanks. "Any idea how long you'll be here?" Henry asked.

"No, I really don't know. But I doubt if it will be more than a few hours. Do you need to get going?"

"I have some time. I can hang around for a while, but please either text me or call me and let me know as soon as you know what's happening."

"Deal."

My rental car was parked in front of the terminal and I asked the attendant if she knew where the Lowell Veterinarian Clinic was located. "Where's your pet?" she asked as she looked behind me.

"Oh, I don't have one. I like to get my drugs from a vet, they're so much cheaper and much better than the human kind." The look on her face was priceless. She gave me directions, but I could see she was wondering what kind of fruit loop she was dealing with.

The veterinarian center was modern and if I was using this center, I'd feel very comfortable with them. I parked then went inside the lobby. The young lady behind the counter greeted me and asked me how she could help.

"I'd like to see Dr. Bueler, please," I told her.

"May I tell her what this is in reference to?"

I fished out my Federal cred-pack and flashed it. "This is a private matter between the doctor and me."

Her eyes got big, and she muttered as she fled, "Just a moment, sir. I'll get her."

Dr. Bueler returned shortly with the young receptionist hiding behind the her. The doctor was a tall, good looking woman. I'm over six feet tall and we were almost eyeball to eyeball. She looked like she could handle large animals as well as the little ones. She extended her hand; we shook.

"I'm Dr. Bueler. May I help you?"

"My name is Matt Preston, Doctor Bueler. Is there a place where we can chat privately?"

"Yes, Mr. Preston, follow me." The doctor led me into the back of the building and eventually into her office. All the chairs in the room were covered with drug samples and folders and things whose purpose I had no clue about. It was obviously a working office. The walls were covered with pictures of all sorts of different animals, and I liked the general feeling of the place. She shut the door and when she turned to look at me, she had a frown on her face. "What's this about?"

"Doctor, there's nothing for you to worry about. I just have a couple of questions and I'll get out of your hair. Do you remember your roommates from college?"

A puzzled look replaced the frown as she responded, "You mean Maggie and Linda?"

"Yes."

"Do I remember them? Sure. But that was a long time ago. Why do you want to talk about them now?"

"Did you know Maggie's married to the United States Senator from Washington State, Senator Albert Bradson?"

"Yeah. I saw a picture of her husband and her in a Newsweek magazine not too long ago at some celebrity charity function, and boy did she look great. I was always impressed with Maggie and now even more so. Anyway, why's a federal agent asking me about her and Linda?"

"Doctor, what I'm about to share with you I must ask you to keep to yourself for the time being." I waited until she nodded. "Senator Bradson has been approached, and he's considering running for president."

"Of the United Sates?"

I couldn't resist. "No, outer Mongolia." She smiled at my little joke. "I'm sorry, yes, president of the U.S. And one of those individuals backing his run is worried about what Linda Ferrara might have to say about the senator. I've interviewed Maggie, and she told me about the Senator and Linda's affair and her pregnancy when they were in school. Were you aware that Linda told Albert it was his child?"

"Yes. At the time, we were both furious with Linda. I know Maggie and I talked about it and we decided the chances of it being Al's child were slim at best. Linda was stupid to think we'd believe her. She marked on her calendar the days of her menstrual cycle. We knew what days she'd had Al over and when she had her period. It didn't work out so it could have been his baby. But hey, who knows?"

"I understand the child was born at the Wellness Clinic on campus."

"Actually, I believe the child was born in an aid car from the clinic on the way to the hospital."

"Any idea which hospital?"

"I'd assume it was the one closest to campus. But I really don't know for sure. I heard she had a boy. Like I told you, things were tense between Linda and me when she moved out, and we never discussed what happened."

"Do you know anything about Linda after the baby? I know she dropped out of school. Do you know what happened to her after that?"

"Funny you would ask that. I have a client who has two cute dogs. Not that that's weird, but Linda's name came up during the woman's visit. She and I had gone to the university together, and we were in the same sorority. After graduation, we'd lost track of each other until she came in about a year ago. Her husband works for a company that does business with Walmart, and she and her family had to move here. She showed up one day at the center with her dogs. They needed their annual checkup, and she told me she'd heard good things about my center. We got to yacking and playing the old 'do you remember' game. Linda's name came up because my friend had just seen her less than a month before in a casino in Las Vegas. Linda was dealing Blackjack or something. They recognized each other and when Linda took a break, they had a drink together. Linda mentioned nothing special, or at least nothing that my client thought was worth sharing."

"Do you happen to know which casino Linda was working at?"

The doctor sat for a moment, deep in concentration. She shook her head. "No, I don't think she ever mentioned it. We talked about a lot of stuff. One of her dogs had an issue, so of course we spent most of our time discussing what to do about that."

I extended my hand. "Thank you, doctor. You've been very helpful. I'd like to ask you one more question, if I may?"

"Shoot!"

"If the senator was to run for president, what would you think?"

Doctor Bueler was leaning against a table with her arms folded across her chest. She stared at me for a while. I could tell she was working on her answer to my question, so I waited her out. She took a deep breath. "Before I answer your question, I have one for you. Who are you? By that I mean, why are you looking into Al's past? You flashed federal credentials, but you've never exactly explained why you're so interested in what happened with Linda and everything. Please explain your interest in our past?"

"That's fair. Albert and I go a long way back. For years, he was my attorney. I had a run in with the law and they accused me of murdering a young lad. The kid was popular, and this happened just as Albert was running for the senate seat. His office sent in what I considered to be second best and it upset me. Eventually, they found out the real killer, and I was released. Albert later told me that if things hadn't turned out the way they did, he would have sacrificed his run for the senate and defended me. I believe this was true. I tell you this story to show you how close Albert and I are.

"Now, he's asked me if I would look into Linda's claim regarding the baby. This has bothered Albert for a long time, and he wants to know who the child's father is because he feels if there could be a chance it's his, and he gave it up, I think he wants to make it up to the person. Also, if he makes a run for the presidency, he doesn't want something out there which might sink his efforts. When Linda finds out he's running, what would she do?

"The funny thing is, even though Albert and I are friends, we have never discussed a thing in the way of politics over the years. We talk about just about everything else, but that subject never came up. I don't know if we're on the same page about things like that, but I know him as a person, and I feel the person I know would make an excellent president. I'd vote for him. Does that help explain my interest?"

The doctor nodded. "Yes. And I feel the same way. I really don't know where he stands on political stuff, but I agree he has a good heart and he would be more than just some hack politician running for office. Whatever decisions he'd make would be made from the heart and not out of expediency. If he runs and somehow the press finds me, I'll back him all the way. If they ask me about the baby, I'll tell them there is no way it was his and anybody who says different is lying. Does that answer your questions?"

"Yes. Thank you for being so candid. I cannot imagine I'd have more questions, but if I do, may I call you?"

"Of course." Dr. Robyn reached over on top of her desk and picked up a business card. "May I ask you a favor?" I nodded. "Call me from time to time and let me know what you find out about Linda and what happened to the child, if you would."

"Sure. Thanks for your time."

"When you asked to see me, I never dreamt it would be about something from this long ago. Goodbye, Mr. Preston."

"Goodbye, doctor."

I made it as far as the front door when Dr. Bueler came running out of her office. "Mr. Preston, Mr. Preston," she called out. "Hey, I remembered something my friend told me about Linda. When I asked her where Linda was working, she told me she didn't remember the name of the casino, but she mentioned she and her husband had stood outside watching something that had to do with water. I'm sorry, but she said the casino where Linda worked was kitty-corner to the hotel and then she said something about a water feature, but I don't recall exactly what she said about it. I remember I thought at the time it was a strange thing to remember since Vegas doesn't seem to have a lot of water being it's in the dessert. Does that help you at all?"

"Kinda, there aren't that many hotels with a water feature out front. However, it's a start. Good day, doctor."

The reference about waters cut down the number of places she might work. There was a hotel called The Bellagio, and out front was a large man-made lake with lots of water squirting up in the air from nozzles under the surface. They played music and tried to match the music to the squirting water. It makes for a nice show.

After that, a bit closer to town was Caesar's Palace, which was famous because of Evil Knievel and his disastrous jump over their fountain. Then even closer to town was Treasure Island, which held a sea battle a few times a day on a man-made lake they had out front. Also, inside a hotel called The Venetian, they had fake canals similar to those in Venice. It was a start. Now I had to figure out which casino she meant, and which one was kitty-corner.

Driving back to the airport, I mulled over the conversation I'd just had with the doctor. I was a little disappointed with the information I'd received. Yes, I had more to work with than before regarding where I might find Linda, but I was hoping the doctor had known more about who adopted the baby. I know I was just being lazy. In my defense, I still hadn't recovered totally from my last adventure over in the Middle East and I'd hoped this investigation would be over by now. In addition, I really wanted to be able to spend more time with Lois. Sure, I was trying to put my best effort into it, but I'd be lying if I said it was my best effort. There was still more I needed to do for Albert. But for now, I just needed to hurry back to the airport. It was time for Henry to head for Las Vegas.

~ ~ ~ ~ ~

I'd always found Vegas to be a strange place in many ways. There are parts about it I love, and there are parts I find depressing. I'd told Henry to go with the plane since I didn't know how long my stay would take. He told me he wanted to stick around for a few days since he had a friend in town he wanted to see.

I debated renting a car and finally decided if I couldn't walk to where I wanted to go, I'd take a taxi. Because I'd decided Treasure Island was where I would start my investigation, I called ahead from the plane and made reservations for one night at a nearby hotel I knew of until I figured out at which casino Linda worked.

The taxi dropped me off in front of my hotel. I stood on the sidewalk next to The Strip and slowly turned around. As always, it surprised me how much the city had changed since the last time I was there. Thinking back, I guessed it was at least ten years since I'd been here. Parts of the town were unrecognizable. My hotel was called Tropical Isle and located at the far corner from Treasure Island. I figured it was a good place to spend the first night until I asked around.

One thing I don't understand is how people think they will come to Vegas, gamble, and leave a winner. Just look around the city. All of those fabulous hotels didn't happen by accident. This city is a monument built to celebrate losers. Think about it. If the casinos are paying out large amounts of money to winners, they won't be able to build the huge hotels spread out over the city. This city is not built to celebrate winners; this is all about suckers and losers leaving lots and lots of money behind. And that's the part of the city I find depressing.

I walked through the front door of the Tropical Isle and checked in. I didn't care what the room looked like since I hoped it was only for a night. It was a good thing about the room since it was as basic a room as I'd ever seen. I'd had cell phones with screens bigger than the TV. At least there was no temptation to hang around. The next morning, I would start checking hotels that had a water feature out front, so I didn't plan to spend a lot of time in the room anyway.

Treasure Island was a total bust. I must have walked several miles as I circled the casino. Not one casino I checked at had heard of Linda. I had the same luck at Cesar's Palace. I was really getting discouraged. I had a sinking feeling I was on a fool's errand. I was seriously considering bailing for the rest of the day because I was about three-fourths of the way around the Bellagio and having no luck. I decided I'd check one more hotel and if I struck out, I'd try elsewhere tomorrow. The last casino I checked at was in a large hotel called Das Berliner.

Wandering around inside the gambling area, I spotted a person who I thought looked like a pit boss. I asked him if Linda Ferrara worked the casino and he said she did. Success! I could have kissed the gentleman.

I decided to check into the hotel and went to the desk. With a name like Das Berliner, it didn't surprise me to find the female staff dressed in *dirndls* or other Americanized ideas of what German *Fräuleins* would wear. But the males didn't fare much better since they were dressed in *lederhosen* and cute little Alpine hats. The hotel was playing the German motif to the hilt.

At the check-in desk, I asked for a room facing the Bellagio. The young woman behind the desk looked like she'd just stepped off a travel poster for Germany, with blue-eyes, braided blond hair wrapped around her head, and a white blouse with a tightly laced *dirndl*. I received my keycard and went up to my room, knowing I wouldn't accept the first one they offered. As soon as I opened the door, I saw I was correct. Dark and small with a window looking out over massive HVAC units. I went back to the desk and found the gal who had checked me in. "May I help you?"

I handed her the keycard. "The room is unacceptable. If this is best you have, please cancel my room. I'll go down the street to another hotel where I'm sure they have nicer rooms than the one you gave me."

Before the gal could speak, a man dressed in a typical Miesbacher German coat and *lederhosen* stepped up next to her. "My name is Herr Harris. I'm the assistant manager. What seems to be the matter here?"

"I called from my plane on the way in and had reserved a room across the street, but when I saw your hotel, I decided it looked more interesting. I specifically asked the young lady when I checked in for a room with a view of the fountains across the street. What I found was an exciting view of your HVAC system. Please cancel my room, and I'd like a receipt showing I owe you folks nothing."

Herr Harris looked at the computer screen then back at me. "I'm sorry, Mr. Preston, there seems to be a mistake. She gave you the wrong room." The gal stepped aside, and Harris took over. Shortly, he handed me a new keycard and motioned for one of the bell-hops. "Please escort Mr. Preston to his room."

The bellhop looked around and with a puzzled look, he said, "Where's your luggage, sir?"

"This was an unexpected stop for me. I'd made the reservations from my plane on the way here. Whatever I need during my stay, I'll get at one of your shops." I smiled at Herr Harris and I thought he would burst from happiness.

The second room was perfect; it had a small sitting room with a separate bedroom. The bathroom looked large enough to hold a small party, and the shower was big enough for at least three people. I handed the bellhop a ten and told him to make sure Herr Harris knew the room pleased me. From the front window, I had a perfect view of the fountains across the street.

I called down to the main desk anyway and asked for Herr Harris. When he answered, I could detect concern in his voice. "Is everything in order, Mr. Preston?"

"Oh yes, the room is perfect. I was just wondering if you could tell me if Linda Ferrara is working today?"

"One moment sir and I'll find out." It took a little more than just one moment, but he returned soon. "I'm sorry sir, she is not scheduled until tomorrow evening. Is there something one of our other personnel can do for you?"

"No. I'm an old friend and I wanted to surprise her. I'll be here for a few days and I'll look her up tomorrow."

"Very good, sir. May I make reservations for you at one of our restaurants for tonight?"

"I need to make some calls, but I'll let you know. Thanks."

I called Henry's number. "What do you need, Matt?"

"Have you left yet?"

"Umm, no. Why?"

"Would you like to have dinner with me tonight?"

"Sure, but I have a date and…"

"That's great. Bring your date. I'm staying at Das Berliner just across the street from the Bellagio. There are several restaurants here in the hotel and I'll make reservations tonight at Der Bahnhof for three for… "

"How does eight tonight sound?"

"Great, call me from the lobby." I gave him my room number, and we hung up. I called Herr Harris and told him I needed reservations for three people tonight, and the time. I told him we wanted to eat at a restaurant inside the hotel called Der Bahnhof. He told me he'd take care of it.

Another thing I really don't like about Vegas is that the town is not made for single people. Or at least I don't feel it's a good place for singles. I was lonely. I missed Lois, so I called her number, if for no other reason than to hear her voice. She sounded upbeat when she answered. "Hi, lover. What's up?"

"I take it you have caller ID? Or do you answer your phone like that for everybody?"

She giggled. "No, darling, just you. Where are you?"

"Las Vegas and I'm lonesome. Can you get away?"

"Las Vegas, huh? Sounds like fun. I'll call you back in a few minutes."

I called Henry again. "Now what do you want, Matt?" I could hear the smile in his voice, so I knew he was just giving me a hard time.

"Do you have anything coming from D.C. that's headed this way soon?"

"Damn son, you are lucky. We closed on our fourth plane and it'll be headed out for L.A. in just a couple of hours. We have a big charter there. Why?"

"I called and asked Lois to come and stay for a while with me here in Vegas. She's asking the admiral right now if she can get away."

"Let me know as soon as you can. I think we can fit her in. The few minutes it takes to land and drop her off here won't matter. Besides, if we have to, we can strap a parachute on her and push her out over Vegas." He paused, and I remained silent. "The plane will be empty, anyway. We have a charter to Hawaii for some corporate types. Our new plane is a quite a bit larger than the other three and we can carry more passengers. We've had to turn down a number of charters in the past because we didn't have a large enough plane. I think Lois will be thrilled."

I'd just hung up when Lois called me back. "Orchard said yes. All of our fires are out right now, and I can get away for a few days. Let me call the airlines and see when I can get a seat out to Vegas."

"Not to worry. Go home, get what you need, and get over to the Washington-Dulles Airport as soon as you can. The service got a new plane today and they have a charter out in L.A. that's going to Hawaii. They'll drop you off in Vegas. How long before you can get out to Dulles?"

"The faster you let me go, the faster I can get to you. Love you."

"I love you too, and I miss you so much."

"Keep that thought."

I called Henry back and told him Lois was on her way to the plane. "I know her phone number and I'll text her and let her which plane to look for. I'll tell the pilot to expect her."

"Thanks, Henry. See you tonight for dinner."

~ ~ ~ ~ ~

I wandered through the shops in the lower level of the casino until I found a men's shop. They had a nice, tan, light-wool pair of pants they promised would be cuffed in less than an hour. They also had a dark-blue, cashmere blazer that felt like it was made just for me. I found a light blue shirt that was almost long enough for my arms and if I didn't button the sleeves, I could get away with wearing it. The dark brown dress shoes I was wearing fit the outfit, but I still purchase a new pair of socks. Before I'd even paid for my purchase, the pants were ready to go. I asked them to deliver my outfit to my room, and the clerk informed me it would be no problem. I glanced at my watch and saw I still had a few hours to roam around.

When I got back to the room, I showered and shaved. Just when was I dressed and ready to go, the phone in my room rang. Henry was on the other end and told me he was in the lobby. "I'll be right down." When I stepped off the elevator, I spotted Henry and noticed he was with another guy. I stepped up to Henry and extended my hand.

"Hello, Matt." He shook my hand. "This is my date, Roger."

The coin dropped, and I laughed. I couldn't help myself. I was laughing so hard, I had to sit down. I motioned for the two of them to sit. "I'm sorry, Henry. I'm not laughing at you. I'm laughing at me."

"Do you want to cancel tonight?" I could see I'd embarrassed him.

"Oh, god no. Really, I'm sorry if I embarrassed you. I had to laugh. This just caught me so unprepared. It's not every day you find out some hot-shot super spy pilot who has ice water running in his veins, and who saved my sorry ass turns out to be gay. I don't give a shit, Henry."

Henry smiled. "I can tell you don't seem to have a problem with it. Usually you can tell almost right away if people have a problem with it or not. You don't really care one way or the other, do you?"

"It has nothing to do with me. No, I don't care one way or another."

"Too bad more people don't share your attitude. However, I can see why you found it amusing. I thought Lois would have told you I was gay."

"Henry, the subject never came up. And besides, I don't care who you want to sleep with. It doesn't change who you are and what you did for me. It's my fault I thought because of everything you did for me, and the amazing way you can pilot a plane, you were straight. That's my bad! I honestly never gave your sexuality a second thought. And now that I think of it, I've made some rather crude remarks to you over time. For that, I apologize."

"It's because of your remarks I thought you knew I was gay." Henry was starting to laugh along with me. "Do you remember what you said when I got you out of Azerbaijan?" I shook my head. "You were all beat up, hiding in that clump of trees, and you set off the transponder I gave you. Remember, I found you in that Jeep and when I saw how beat-up you were, I said you looked awful. You told me you bet I said that to all the guys I wanted to have sex with. I thought you knew and were teasing me."

I looked at his friend. "Roger?"

He nodded.

"If I have offended you at all by any of my remarks or attitude, I apologize. Don't take this wrong, but I love this guy." I reached out and grabbed Henry's arm. "I should be dead right now. This wonderful man came and saved my crazy ass. This man is more macho than ninety percent of the men I know. And even though I know better, I still assumed macho means straight. I really am sorry."

"No worries," Roger said.

Henry gently slugged my shoulder. "Knock it off. You're embarrassing me."

When I looked at him, I noticed his face was red. "Let's go have dinner." We stood and headed towards the area where various restaurants were located. Henry looked at me and smiled, "Matt, I have a surprise for you."

"What?"

"If I told you, then it wouldn't be a surprise. Right?"

We stopped at the maître 'd's desk. "Sir?"

"Reservations for three under Preston."

"Oh yes, Mr. Preston, your other guest is already at your table."

"Other guest? What are you talking about?"

Henry took my arm and led me after the maître' d. "Come on, Matt. This is part of your surprise."

When we got to the table, Lois was sitting there with a huge grin on her face. I know my chin must have been on my chest. I also found that my eyes had moisture in them. I was so happy to see her.

"How the hell did you do this?" I inquired.

"The flight takes about five hours. But there's a three-hour time difference between D.C. and here. I've been here for a little over half an hour, waiting for you guys to show up."

I sat down, leaned over, and pulled Lois closer to me. I'm not one who goes in for public displays of affection, but I decided this was different. I kissed Lois on the lips, and I could feel her lips tremble. I think she was as affected as I was. When we parted, she put one of her hands in my lap.

She gently squeezed my quickly growing chub, and I leaned over and whispered for her to knock it off.

"I plan on it. Several times." Lois winked at me and whispered, "I love you." I told her I felt the same way.

Dinner was fantastic. The food was top drawer, and the company matched the food. Roger turned out to be a great storyteller and seemed to have lived a life almost as interesting as Henry's. I found it noteworthy that tonight, I could occasionally see gay characteristics from Henry. When we'd been together, there'd been no signs, but tonight he was allowing himself to be what I considered was his true character. I found it refreshing.

After dinner, we had a drink in one of the many bars scattered around the casino. Eventually, Lois leaned over and kissed Henry on the cheek. "I'm sorry, but I think Matt wants me to go upstairs now."

"I do?" I asked.

"Yes, Matt, you do. Like now!"

"Oh!" I got the hint. Sometimes I can be slow, but not this time. Henry also understood what Lois meant and blushed. I said good night to Henry and Roger and told them to behave themselves as she led me off toward the rooms.

I'm pleased to tell you our room was soundproof. Either that or our neighbors were kind enough not to call the main desk and complain. Lois and I proved how much we'd missed each other.

I think I'm really falling for this lady.

Actually, I know I'm falling for her…

CHAPTER TEN

I checked with Herr Harris to see what time Linda would be on duty and he told me, and was also kind enough to tell me which area she'd be working. I took one of my business cards and wrote our room number on the back, then Lois and I wandered down to Linda's section about an hour after she was scheduled to clock in. From Albert and Maggie's description, I thought I might know what she looked like, but having a large name tag on her blouse helped.

Linda was a handsome woman with short blond hair and expressive brown eyes. She was packing a few extra pounds, but she carried them well. I'll be the first to admit I'm in no position to point fingers regarding extra pounds. She dressed in what Das Berliner obviously considered a typical German peasant dress. Her *dirndl* was laced across her bust, causing her low-cut blouse to show generous amounts of cleavage. I was sure many male players concentrated more on her chest than on their cards. Even though Linda was an interesting woman, her face showed she'd lived a hard life. When she spoke, I heard a smoker's rasp and noticed her teeth were capped and didn't fit properly. I wondered if she still smoked.

Linda was dealing Blackjack, so Lois and I sat at her table in chairs next to each other. There was one other played at the table and after a few hands, he got up and left. I smiled my best smile at Linda and asked, "May I ask you about two names?"

"What do you mean?"

"I'd like to talk to you about Robyn and Maggie, your roommates back in college."

I noticed Linda grasped the edge of the table for a moment.

"I don't think this is the time or place, but if you wouldn't mind, I'd like to chat with you later," I told her.

"Who are you?"

I gave her my card. "I'm doing a favor for Albert Bradson. If I can have a little of your time, I'll explain everything."

I noticed a gentleman stepping up to her table. "Linda, is everything okay?"

"Yes, Jim. We were just talking about two people I used to know back in my college days."

"Well, this isn't a social hour. We pay you to deal cards, not to talk."

"Sorry." Linda dealt Lois and I a new hand. As Linda turned over her cards, I noticed her hands were trembling. She busted and gave Lois and I each a matching chip to our bet.

"My room number is on the back. When you're off duty, would you come up and talk to us?" I asked.

"I'll think about it. I'm off at three this morning."

"Thank you." A new couple came up to the table and sat down, which ended our conversation. Lois and I stood and said goodbye. As we passed Jim the pit boss, I stopped for a moment. "Sorry if I got Linda in trouble. We have friends in common and perhaps it wasn't the right time to discuss them."

"It's okay. It looked like you upset Linda by something you said to her. I watch out for my girls. She is one of my best. Actually, she is considered an assistant pit boss. She helps me out a lot with the rest of my crew. I don't like to see my people bothered by customers. Have a good evening, sir." I nodded, and we left.

~ ~ ~ ~ ~ ~

Lois and I fell asleep around four in the morning without Linda showing up. The next morning, when we finally got up and went down for breakfast, I saw Herr Harris behind the desk. After breakfast, I stopped and asked if Linda was working again this evening. He told me she was.

Lois and I went shopping and purchased swimming suits. My suit actually could be worn in the pool. Lois' suit was nothing more than a wish and a promise. I thought it looked sexy as hell and was most eager to see it wet. Lois informed me that the suit wasn't something to wear in the pool but rather something to wear while tanning. I decided it really didn't matter because the fun part was looking at her. I was positive the whole thing would fit in a teacup.

After dinner, we wandered around to the gambling tables. We spotted Linda chatting with her boss and we waited until she went to a table. Lois and I took seats and when Linda realized who we were, she became flustered. Lois and I put out chips, and I told Linda she needed to do something. If she didn't deal, her boss would come over and ask what was wrong. I waited until after we'd played two hands then I asked, "How come you didn't come and see us?"

"Look, I don't want any problems."

"We are not here to make problems. Actually, we are here to make sure that there are no problems. Please consider stopping by our room after you get off duty. Lois will be there, so you won't be alone in the room with me."

"I'm not worried about you. I don't know if I want to deal with my feelings about what happened so long ago. I'll think about it. I'm not saying no, and I'm not saying yes."

"That's fair. Your boss, Jim, is headed this way. Quick, deal us another hand." I know cards are the luck of the draw, but Lois and I both got a twenty-one. Linda had to hit on her fifteen and got an eight. Busted! I decided it was time for the two of us to leave. We stopped in a couple of the bars and listened to various bands. I felt Lois tap me on the shoulder and when I looked at her, she motioned for me to lean over. She whispered in my ear, "Take me back to the room. We have time before Linda shows up, if she will show up."

"What do you want to do?" I asked, knowing exactly what she wanted to do, but trying to play dumb.

"It isn't Blackjack. Get me to the room and I'll show you." As soon as we got to the room, she left a trail of discarded clothing. When she arrived at the bed, I discovered she was wearing my favorite outfit. Lois turned and held out her arms. "Do you get the picture now?" I'd already gotten the idea and did my best to please her.

It was almost four when we heard a timid knock on the door. When I opened the door, Linda was standing in the hall. Before she stepped into the room, she looked both ways up and down the hall. I thought she looked pale, and she seemed frightened. I motioned for her to come in and sit, and I took the chair across from her. I wanted to make her as comfortable as possible. "This is my friend, Lois. Do you mind if she stays while we talk, or would you prefer if she left?"

"She can stay. But I don't understand why you want to talk to me. What's this about? College was a long time ago."

I decided the best way to play this was acting as a government agent checking up on Bradson. I laid my creds on the table. Linda picked them up. I told her, "I'd like to ask that this conversation doesn't leave the room. If the news got out, it could create a lot of problems."

"What news?"

"They have approached Senator Bradson about running for President of the United States."

"Al? President? Damn!"

"Yes. And I wanted to talk to you about the child you had when you were in school." I didn't know what her reaction might be, but I sure didn't expect the one I got.

Tears ran down her face. She moaned and shook her head. "No! No, no, no. I don't want to talk about that."

"Why?"

"It hurts too much. Not a day goes by that I don't think of my little boy. I wonder how he turned out. What he looks like. What you are asking is very painful for me."

"I don't wish to upset you any more than you already are, but was Albert really the father?"

"Why are you asking all of these questions? Why now?"

"I'm trying to help Senator Bradson. Can you tell me if he was the father of your child?"

"Oh shit, I don't know. I doubt it, but I always wished it was his child."

"Why?"

"Look how he turned out. A senator and all, and now possibly running for President. Al was by far the nicest guy I ever slept with. He had good genes."

"You told him it was his."

Lois interrupted, "May I ask a question?" Linda nodded. "Why Albert? What was it about him that made you interested in him? He was at least ten years older than you."

Linda was still for a moment, smiled briefly then started speaking, "I think his age was part of it. Until then, I'd never been with a man as old as Albert. And he was so different than the other boys I had gone with.

"Besides his age, he had a sophistication I found appealing even though he was sort of shy. I just found the combination of his various personality traits interesting. Besides, after the first time we were together, he was like a kid in a candy store. It was cute. I'd never known anyone who was so blown away about making love."

Lois nodded. "Thanks, I think I understand. What did he say when you told him the baby was his?"

"Do we have to talk about this?" Tears continued to roll down her cheeks.

"I'm sorry. I know this is painful. Just a few questions more. Okay?"

She nodded and sniffed, wiping her tears away for the moment.

I proceeded as gently as I could. "You told him it was his child?"

"Yeah, I figured he wouldn't want a child and since I needed money for an abortion, I thought he might give me some."

"But you didn't use the money he gave you for an abortion, did you?"

Her chin was quivering, and the tears came again. Lois went into the bathroom to retrieve the box of tissues.

Linda shook her head as she answered. "When it came time, I couldn't go through with it. By the time I felt I was ready to... well, do something, it was too late. I put the child up for adoption. The head nurse at the Wellness Clinic was friends with the head of the English Department at the University, and he and his wife volunteered to adopt the baby. The professor's name was Doctor Elwood Bickerstaff. They called him Dr. Woody behind his back. I knew who he was because I'd taken two of his classes. His wife, Paula, couldn't have children and they wanted a child so much. I knew they'd take good care of my son.

"Dr. Woody was very British, you know. Never let them see you smile. He'd strut back and forth in front of the class and drone on about some stupid subject nobody gave a crap about. I'm rambling, and I guess you don't care about that part?"

I waited a moment for her to get control of her emotions. "Do you know if the professor is still alive?"

"I know his wife passed away, but I don't know about him. I heard he retired. I believe if he's alive, he may still live in the Lawrence, Kansas area. I've no idea what happened to the baby, however, he would have just turned thirty. I'd guess Doctor Woody would be in his early seventies now?"

"Did you ever get married?" I asked Linda. She shook her head. "If Senator Bradson runs for President, how do you feel about it?"

Linda sat for a long time, looking at the two of us. I waited her out. "I take it your real question is will I make problems for Albert? Will I tell the press he might have been the father of my illegitimate child?" I smiled in encouragement and nodded. "If they asked me if I had a child out of wedlock, I'd say yes. If they asked me if it was Al's, I'd tell them I doubt it. That's the truth. It's all a big maybe, but more no than yes."

"I will try to find your son. I want to get a DNA sample if he'll provide me with one. If I'm successful, do you want me to tell him about you? Do you want to see him?"

I watched more tears flow down Linda's face. As she tried to respond to my question, it took several times. Lois got up and went into the bathroom, returning in a few moments this time with a cold, wet washrag. She handed it to Linda who put it against her face. I sat there and waited. Finally, she pulled the washrag down and looked at me. Her eyes were all red and her face was blotchy. "I'm sorry. It's been a long time now, and I thought I had my emotions under control better than that. It looks like I was fooling myself. I would only want to see him if he wanted to see me. If he's angry about me giving him up, then no, I don't want to see him. I have enough guilt of my own, I don't need to take on any more from him."

"I'll make you a deal. If I find him and we have a chat, I'll see how the conversation is going. I won't bring you up unless I feel he'd be receptive to the idea. And I'll call you and tell you exactly how the conversation went."

Linda waited for a while, and I allowed her to think about my comment. Eventually, she gave me a little grin. "You seem to be a nice person. One problem with working here in Vegas is after a while, you think all people, especially men, are assholes. You forget that some men can be nice people. I think you're being more than fair." She got up and stepped over to the little desk in the room and wrote something on the pad of paper. She tore the paper off and handed it to me. "This is my private number. Not many people have this number. If I don't answer, leave me a message and how to get ahold of you."

I agreed, and we said our goodbyes. I walked her to the door, and she paused for a moment. Finally, she gave a little shrug and extended her hand. I took it in both of mine and assured her everything would be okay. She needed to trust me. With a tear in her eye, she nodded. Once the door shut, Lois came and slipped her arms around my waist. She looked up at me, "You know something, Mr. Preston? I love you."

"What brought that on?"

"The way you handled her."

"You know I'm bummed?"

"Why?"

"I'd hoped this interview would answer more of my questions. It seems to have raised more, though. I'd hoped she would have more information about her baby. I see I'm still not done."

"Perhaps, but you were very gentle and kind with her. It impressed me."

"Any chance of showing me how impressed you were?"

"And what did you have in mind?" Lois asked with a wink.

"Well, come here and let me see just how impressed you were." I tried my best to leer at her and she laughed at me.

I was impressed with the way Lois showed me how impressed she was.

Actually, we tried several times to show one another how impressive we believed the other person was. I still think I was more impressed ...

CHAPTER ELEVEN

The phone in my room rang, and I wondered who it could be. Even though Henry knew what my room number was, there was no way he'd call me at that number. He had my cell number. "Hello. Who is this?" I asked cautiously.

"Mr. Preston? It's Linda, Linda Ferrara."

"Good morning. What's up, Linda?"

"I need to talk to you. Like right away."

"Come on up."

"I can't. Can you come down?"

"Down where?"

"I don't what anyone to see us talking. Management doesn't like it for the dealers to get too friendly with customers. Can you meet me downstairs in the parking garage?"

"Sure. Let me get some clothes on. Where will I find you?"

"Take the garage elevator and get off on the very bottom floor. I'll signal you where I am."

"On my way."

I dressed in a hurry and just as I was walking out the door, Lois stopped me. "What's up?"

"Linda wants to talk, but she needs to do it where the wrong eyes won't see us. I'm meeting her down in the parking garage."

Lois looked at me with a puzzled look on her face. "That seems awfully strange, be careful."

I turned to leave.

"Stop," she called after me. I turned, and she handed me her pistol. "Humor me, please take this with you."

I took the pistol out of her hand and looked at it. Shrugging my shoulders, I slipped it in front under my belt, even though I didn't see the point. Riding down in the elevator, I thought about Linda's reason for meeting me in the basement. In a way, what she said made sense, but now that I thought about it, it did seem odd. If management was watching the employees so closely, they would have already seen her in front of the door to my room in the middle of the night and they'd know she'd entered my room. There were security cameras located everywhere in the ceilings of every hallway and even in the elevator. If anybody was curious, they'd already know she and I had been talking.

I pushed the button for the bottom floor and then the button for the floor right above it. When the elevator stopped, I got off. There was a staircase directly across the hallway from the elevator. I opened the door as silently as possible and slipped down the stairs. I reached the next landing and cautiously opened the door a crack. The elevator was standing open. Two guys were rubbernecking into an empty elevator with drawn guns. Quietly, I pushed the stairway door open the rest of the way, holding Lois' gun pointed at them.

I yelled at them, "Do not turn around. Do not turn around. If either of you start to turn, I will shoot the one who moves." Lately, I'd had enough problems with being ignored when I told people what to do, and I wasn't going to give these two bozos a chance to hurt me. I crossed the short distance and drew closer to them. "Now, drop the guns and place your hands on top of your heads." Neither of them moved. "Do it now, dip shits." I poked one in his back with the barrel of my pistol to let him know I was serious then quickly stepped back again, lowering the barrel of my gun in anticipation of his next move.

Just as I knew he would, he assumed I was still standing directly behind him and spun around. I shot him in the knee for his effort. I knew if I hadn't, he'd have shot me. He dropped to the ground, holding his knee and screaming while his gun dropped to the cement at his feet. The other fellow started to turn. I shouted, "Freeze, dummy! If you keep turning around with that gun in your hand, you'll get what your buddy got. Now, drop it, kick it away from you, and put your hands on top of your head. Last warning." The fellow quickly put his hands on top of his head, but was still holding his pistol in one hand.

I reached out with my toe and kicked the dropped pistol off to the side. Now that the other fellow had placed his hands on his head, I took his weapon from him. He was packing a 44 Magnum BFR 7.5 SS, which is a huge pistol. I'd been told once that BFR stands for Big Fucking Revolver and I believed it. This guy had watched too many Clint Eastwood movies. I slipped Lois' gun back under my belt and took the Magnum. I was so angry at these two who'd tried to set me up, I rapped the pistol sharply against the fellow's head.

"Ow," he said, massaging the tender spot. Why did you do that?"

I poked him. "Hands back on your head. Now!" He quickly put his hands back on top of his head. "Because I felt like it and you pissed me off. I will ask the questions and if I don't like the answers, I may feel the need to thwack your noggin again. I wanted you to know how it felt and that it hurt. I know you don't want me to do it again, but I will if you don't answer me. Do you understand?" I didn't get an answer, so I smacked him again but not as hard as the first time. "When I ask you a question, I expect an answer."

"Yes. I understand, damn it. I understand. Stop hitting me with the gun. Ask your questions."

"Why were you standing here waiting for me with drawn guns?"

Silence. I tapped him on his head again, a little harder this time but not so much so that he'd black out. I noticed a trickle of blood was now running down over his ear. "Remember, I ask, you answer. I can keep doing this until you answer me."

He again had grabbed the side of his head. When he pulled his hand away, he noticed there was blood on it. "Listen, buddy," he snarled, "you can beat me all you want, but if I tell you who sent us down here and he found out, I'd get a lot more than a rap on the head."

"And what makes you think you are any safer with me?" I pulled back the hammer and aimed at the other knee of the fellow on the ground and pulled the trigger. Bad mistake on my part. The roar of the 44 took me by surprise. My ears were ringing and the fellow on the ground was screaming. I poked the other one with the hot barrel. "See what I mean. Now, the next bullet is yours. I'll even let you pick which knee I start with. Or you could tell me who told you to come down here and wait for me." I pulled back the hammer to emphasize my point. "Your choice. For now."

Let's get something straight, I'm not usually this aggressive. But I still have a lot of pent up anger from my last mission in the Middle East. I received a couple of beatings from which I'm still recovering. Patience was never one of my strong suits and I've found since I got back from the Middle East, whatever I had before has vanished. These two clowns caught me at the wrong time in my life.

"Sal," he quickly answered.

"Sal? Who the hell is Sal?"

"Salvatore Zampuchini." The way he said it sounded like he was speaking to a mentally handicapped person.

The name rang a bell, but I couldn't remember why the name was familiar. "And who is Salvatore Zampuchini when he's at home?"

"You're shittin' me?"

"Humor me. Who is Zampuchini?"

"He owns some major casinos on the strip, or at least his organization does."

Now I realized why the name was familiar. Salvatore Zampuchini was perhaps The Don of what I would consider the West Coast Mafia. "Okay, let's say I'm impressed. Why did ol' Sal send you down here to talk to me?"

"We're supposed to take you to him."

"And you felt you needed to meet me with weapons drawn?"

"Well, we wanted you to know we meant business. We didn't want any problems."

"Like you have none now? Tell me, where is this Sal fellow?"

"Here, top floor, in his office."

"Take me there."

"I don't think it's a good idea."

I rapped his head once more and asked, "Do I look like I care what you think? Move!"

"What about Louie?" He nodded towards the man lying next to him.

"What about Louie? He ain't going anywhere."

"Are you just going to leave him here? He'll bleed out shortly."

"Where's security? Don't they have cameras all over the place?"

"Not on this level. This level is off limits to guests. That's why we met you here. We were supposed to subdue you and take you to see Mr. Zampuchini."

"Do you have a cell phone?"

"Yeah, why?"

"When I tell you, call security and tell them to get down here and take care of Louie. And then you are to hang up. Say one more word than that and I'll shoot you. Am I clear?"

He mumbled something which I took to be an affirmative answer. We rode as far up as the elevator would go and my companion told me we had to get on a different elevator. We were going all the way to the top and the elevator we were on didn't service the office floors.

Before we got on the next elevator, I called Lois. I stopped her at hello. "You were right, it was an ambush, but they got ambushed. One of them is still down in the parking garage with two knee caps missing. I'm on my way to the offices on the top floor to see a person named Salvatore Zampuchini. I'm told he's king shit around here. If you don't hear from me in fifteen minutes, I want you to call in the cavalry."

"Done."

I poked my buddy. "What's your name? I can't keep just poking you."

"Guido."

"You're shitting me. Nobody is ever named Guido. That's just in movies. It isn't really Guido."

"No, it's true. My great-grandfather was from the old country. His name was Guido and I'm named after him."

"Okay, Guido, call hotel security and have them go check on Louie." He made the call and as soon as he told them where to go, I motioned for him to hang up. He paused for a moment and I pulled the hammer back on his pistol. "Hang up, now." Guido hung up. "Give me the phone." Guido handed me his phone. I turned it off and popped the back off, removed the battery and the SIM card, and placed them into different pockets.

The elevator door opened to a plush, well-appointed waiting area. They'd decorated the room in neutral tones. The gal behind the desk was stunning. Whoever Sal was, he had excellent taste in receptionists. At least Sal had the sense not to dress the receptionist in fake German clothing. She said something to Guido, but when she saw the gun in my hand, she stopped.

I poked Guido. "Where's Salvatore Zampuchini's office?" He pointed at a door with a polished brass nameplate on it: Salvatore Zampuchini. This must be the place.

I motioned for Guido to step to the door and open it, then to step into the office. When Salvatore saw Guido entering unannounced into his office, he spoke. "What the hell is with you, Guido? You know better than to barge…" When Zampuchini saw me with a pistol in my hand, he stopped. "Who the hell are you?" he snarled.

"You have to be kidding. You send two goons to get me and bring me here and you don't even know who I am?" I retorted.

"Oh. Then you must be Matt Preston."

"Bingo. Guido said you wanted to see me?"

Sal's face was red with anger. "Yeah, and I see now I sent the wrong people to get you," he snapped at me.

"No, you didn't. You really didn't need to send anybody to get me. A simple invitation would have worked." I made sure the door to Zampuchini's office was still open, and I motioned for Guido to stand in a corner of the room. "Turn around and place your face against the corner."

"Why?" Guido whined.

"Because you screwed up and now, you're being punished. Would you rather I shoot your knee out?"

He vigorously shook his head as he turned and faced the corner.

I took the 44 pistol I'd taken from Guido and emptied the bullets, throwing them into the waste paperback basket next to Sal's desk, I set the pistol, its empty chamber still open, on his desk. I pulled Lois' pistol from my belt, making sure Sal saw the gun in my hand. I looked at him and said, "Put both of your hands on top of your desk, now. If you move either hand, I'll shoot you. I don't wish to, but I will. Since I don't represent a risk to you, there's no reason for you to try and get the pistol out of your desk. I think you should have no problem just sitting there."

Placing his hands on his desk, he asked, "How'd you know I had a gun in my desk?"

I closed one eye and frowned at him. "Really? Do you think I'm so stupid I wouldn't know you were armed? Are you telling me you don't have a pistol hidden in your desk?" He shook his head. "That's what I thought. Now, we're all together, why did you want to see me?"

Sal frowned. I could see this was not how he'd expected the interview to go. "Linda Ferrara. Why did you have her in your room? What's your interest in Linda? If you wanted a girl, we can get you a woman."

I looked at Sal in front of me with his hands on the desk. His remark said a lot about his attitude towards women. Actually, I thought his comments fit the stereotype for a person like him. I observed his hands were manicured, his temples were silvering, and his hair was brushed straight back. His large, dark brown eyes were set in a handsome, clean shaven, Mediterranean looking face. His suit was of excellent quality and his white shirt gleamed. He looked like the head of a prosperous large corporation rather than the head of a consortium of casinos. "I have a question," I asked.

"What's that?"

"How come you aren't all dressed up in lederhosen and a Miesbacher jacket? All the rest of the staff is. Except for Guido over there."

Sal stared at me for a moment. "You can't be serious?"

"Why not? I think a little Alpine hat would look good on you." I noticed that one of his eyes seemed to flutter. I must be getting to him.

"I'll ask you again, Mr. Preston, what is your interest in Linda?"

"Sir, meaning no disrespect, but my interest in Ms. Ferrara is none of your business. Actually, my reasons are secret. However, to bring this to a speedy end, I'll explain a bit. I work for a top secret agency back in D.C. and I'm investigating Ms. Ferrara for confidential reasons."

"Why?" His eye seemed to flutter faster, and his face was turning redder.

"I explained that. I can't tell you."

"Listen, buster, Linda is a very valuable employee. She's important in my organization. Even though she works as a dealer, she's a lot more than that. She keeps me informed of what the other dealers are doing, and which ones we need to watch for possible cheating. She is of great value, so I have a right to know what your interest is in her." His face took on a scowl and with a menacing tone, he added, "You don't know who you are messing with here. I want answers and I want them now!"

I snickered and from the look on his face, it was obvious he was not used to being laughed at. "Sal don't play tough guy with me. You don't know the misery I can bring down on your head. If you want to play who has the bigger dick, I'm telling you you've lost before we even start. I'm sorry, but my reasons for being here are on a need to know and right now, you don't need to know. This is all top secret. I'm warning you, ask no more questions."

"Why not?"

"You don't listen well. I've just told you I'm not at liberty to tell you any more than I have. Actually, I may have told you more than I should. You don't need to know who I work for, even though I'm asking you to trust me. I've told you what I can. I assure you I represent no danger to you or your operation or Linda. You have nothing to fear from me."

Zampuchini seemed to accept my statement. "Guido, where's Louie?"

Without turning, he answered. "When Mr. Preston surprised us on the lower level, Louie turned with his gun at the ready. Mr. Preston was armed, and he shot Louie in the knee before Louie shot him."

Sal looked at me with one eye half closed. "Really?" I nodded. "Now I really don't understand, who the hell are you? Why are you running around my hotel with a pistol in hand? How did you know something was up?"

I heard a commotion coming from the lobby behind me and when I looked over my shoulder through the open door, I saw Lois standing in the doorway with my pistol in hand and Henry beside her, also with a drawn weapon. When Sal saw the two of them standing there, he shouted, "What the fuck is going on?"

Lois had our creds in hand, so I retrieved mine from her. I laid it on Zampuchini's desk. "Perhaps his might help. All three of us are federal agents from the same secret organization back in D.C. We came to speak to Linda Ferrara, and we'd have left by now had you not sent your hot shot goons after me. So, we can bring this to an end. If I'm allowed to tell you anything, anything at all, about what's happening, I'll call you." Sal nodded. I had a thought. "By the way, do you know people in Seattle?"

Sal sat for a moment, glaring at me. "Yeah. I have people I know up there. So what?"

"Do you know Mouse?"

I swear the tan drained from Sal's face. "Why? Do you know Mouse?"

"Why don't you call him and ask if he knows me?" I rattled off a private number. As I turned, I told Sal, "We're leaving. Call Mouse." When we got back to our room, the light on top of the phone was flashing, signaling we had a message. It was from Sal requesting I call him immediately. I called.

"This is Preston. You asked me to call."

"Mr. Preston, I've just spoken to Mouse. I'm sorry about this misunderstanding. Please forgive me. I did not understand who you were, or that you knew Mouse. I know this really doesn't compensate for my disrespect, but your room has been comped. Again, allow me to offer profound apologies for any misunderstanding that might have occurred."

"Not to worry, sir. I'll be sure and mention your kind gesture to Mouse. Have a good day, sir."

I'd just hung up when the phone rang again. It was Linda. "Mr. Preston, are you okay?"

"Yes, why?"

"I had no choice about the phone call to you. I didn't want to call you, but Jim insisted. He told me Mr. Zampuchini demanded I call you and demand you come down to the bottom parking lot. He wanted to talk to you. Were you hurt?"

"No. After I thought about your call, it made little sense. If you were worried about being seen with me, it was too late since there are cameras in the hallways. They already knew we were talking. Did you get in any trouble from your visit to my room?"

"No, they said nothing."

"Well, Zampuchini may want to talk to you about our conversation. Just tell him I warned you our conversation was top secret. Tell him I threatened you with prison time if you discussed it. If he still insists, tell him I told you he was to call me. Remind him I have told you to call me and report all conversations the two of you have. I can't explain any better, but he does not want to upset me. Remind him of that. You'll be fine. You have my number and if there's any problem, call me at once. Okay? I have people who can call him and remind him why he needs to leave you alone."

"Yes, sir." We said our goodbyes and hung up.

"Let's get out of here," I told Lois. We went down to the check-out desk. Herr Harris himself was behind the desk. I'm positive his hands had a tremble when he handed me my bill marked paid in full. "The hotel's limo will take you any place you need to go, sir. I hope your stay met with your satisfaction."

"It did. Thanks."

CHAPTER TWELVE

The trip back to Lawrence was uneventful. Well, almost. Lois and I joined a club she'd always expressed an interest in. It's called The Mile-High Club, and if you don't know what it is… well, ask around. Somebody will explain it to you. Actually, we joined it twice.

I'd called ahead for a car and there was one waiting in front of the small regional terminal. Lois needed to keep going since Admiral Orchard needed her back, so she stayed on the plane. We promised each other we would get back together as soon as possible. It would be a lonely couple of weeks. Henry said he'd call me as soon as he found out what was going on regarding any return flights. He also asked me how things were going about getting hanger space. "Thanks for the reminder. I need to call the realtor in Fort Myers and find out if the two goofy sisters ever decided what they wanted to do. Just between the two of us, I don't have good feelings about that whole deal."

"Please let me know when you find out something."

"You'll be the first to know. Have a safe flight."

"Later, Matt!"

~ ~ ~ ~ ~

I decided the best way to find out what happened to the former head of the English Department was to check in with the registrar. Her name was Agnes Brown. Agnes was a tall, slender woman dressed in a skirt and sweater combination that looked good with her white, curly hair. She had deep blue eyes set in a warm, pleasant face. She greeted me with a smile. "Good afternoon. How may I help you?"

"Hello. My name is Matt Preston and I'm trying to find a professor who used to teach here, Dr. Bickerstaff. Dr. Elwood Bickerstaff."

"Oh dear, Dr. Bickerstaff retired several years ago." She turned and addressed the woman behind her. "Blanch, when did Dr. Bickerstaff retire?"

Blanch had bright red hair with a red face to match. She was the exact opposite body type of Agnes. She looked up at the ceiling for a moment, lost in thought. "Humm, at least ten years ago. Why?"

"This gentleman here is trying to find him. Do you know what happened to him?"

"Gee, Aggie, that was even before my time. I've heard his wife Paula passed away, but after he retired, I don't think I ever heard any more about him."

Agnes thought for a minute. "Wait a moment, there's a professor over in the English department who's been there for a long time. It's likely she was here when Dr. Bickerstaff worked here." Agnes pulled a small map of the campus from a desk drawer and pointed out a path to where I needed to go. "Go over to the English Department here and ask for Dr. Audrey Billings. She might know what happened to Dr. Bickerstaff."

I found the office, but it was locked. The door of the next office was partially open, and I knocked on the door-jamb. A firm, female voice said, "Come in."

I opened the door and behind the desk was a rather hefty, heavily tattooed young woman. She looked up. "Yeah, what do you want?"

"I'm looking for Dr. Billings."

"She isn't here."

"I noticed that. Any idea when she might be back?"

"A few days."

"What does that mean? Like two days? A week? Can you give me some idea?"

"Perhaps a week."

"Do you know the date when she is expected?"

"Yeah."

The young woman just sat there looking at me. Eventually I asked, "Would you mind sharing that date with me?"

"You want to know when Audrey is coming back?"

"Yes, please."

"Just a moment." When the young woman stood up and turned her back, it surprised me a pair of pants could stretch that tight. When seated, she looked big; however, standing up, her bottom was immense. I was glad she had her back to me because I knew my face was one of total shock. The woman waddled over to a large calendar on the wall. She stared at the calendar for the longest time then without turning, told me, "She'll be back two weeks from tomorrow."

I thanked her. "Oh! By the way, do you know who Dr. Bickerstaff is?"

"Yeah."

"Do you know where he is?"

"He retired."

"I know that. Do you happen to know if he's still alive?"

"Dunno."

"Then you probably don't know where he might have lived or lives?"

"Nope."

"Well, you've been a big help. Thank you."

"Are you trying to be a smart ass or something?"

"Not at all. Have a good day, miss."

I turned and left. Walking across campus, I chanted to myself, "Shit, shit, shit." What was I going to do for the next two weeks? How come the information was coming so slowly? I wanted to finish with this task and take my motorcycle trip. I had other things to do, things that were better than waiting for some English professor to come back from vacation or whatever. There was Henry's business request, and Snooker wanted me to come and visit again so we could see his cars. I didn't know a soul in Lawrence and I wasn't going to sit around for the next two weeks waiting for Billings to show up. Albert needed answers now. Trudging out to my car, I mentally chanted some new swear words. I was not a happy camper.

Before I started the car, I called Henry. "What's up, Matt?"

"I'm stuck here in Kansas for two weeks. Any chance of catching a plane out of here?"

"Matt, I'm so sorry. Right now, I don't see a thing coming your way."

"Shit! Thanks anyway. It was too much to hope for."

"What are you going to do?"

"I think I'll try to find a regular flight to D.C. Might as well be with Lois for two weeks."

"Have fun."

"I will, if I ever get there." I called Lois and told her what was going on. She asked me what I would do. "If I can get a flight to D.C., can I visit you for a few days?"

"Of course. I'd love to see you. You know that."

"Let me make a few calls and I'll let you know what I find out."

I took my rental car to the airport in Kansas City and caught a flight back to D.C. Standing in line as I passed through the mess they called security, I thought to myself how spoiled I'd become flying with Henry. I'd forgotten about taking my shoes off and my belt. I watched as they took away the knitting needles of the little old lady in front of me. Oh, God help me, please. As Robin Williams once said, "If it's comes down to granny being a terrorist, we are lost."

I was pleased to find a driver holding my name on a placard when I arrived in D.C. The ride to Lois' condo was swift. She met me at the door with a glass of Scotch in one hand and placed her other hand behind my head to pull me close. She gave me the most sizzling of kisses. I knew the next few days would be wonderful.

~ ~ ~ ~ ~

John and I lunched one day with Lois and John's wife, and the four of us had dinner twice. One day, I met Albert for lunch, and we had a nice long chat. He told me how Maggie had confided in him about the affair she'd had. "It wasn't something I would have wanted, of course, but the outcome has been splendid. I feel we are closer than we have ever been. She is totally on board with me running for president."

"Are you concerned that someone might find out about her affair?"

"No. If it were to become public, I'd stonewall it. My comment would be 'No Comment' and if that wasn't good enough, I'd tell them it was none of their business. If she did, or didn't, it's between us and has no bearing on my ability to serve as president. I will not let something like that dictate if I run or not."

We briefly touched on Buck Markel and his problems.

Towards the end of the second week, my cell phone rang. It was Henry. "When are you planning on going back to Kansas?"

"To be honest, I'm having such a wonderful time with Lois, I'd forgotten all about it. I guess I'll head back when you have something headed that way."

"Be at the airport Monday morning. We have a charter from K.C. up to Vancouver and then a new one from Vancouver to Hong Kong. Now that we have the two larger planes, we can handle good-sized charters." That was good news. Henry gave me the tail number to look for and we hung up.

It was either late Friday night or early Saturday morning and I couldn't sleep. As quietly as I could, I got up and slipped out to the front room. I was curled up in an easy chair, gazing out at the night sky when Lois came and found me. She hadn't put on a coverup and even though I was feeling down, I loved the way she looked. "Cute outfit." Damn that girl is sexy.

"Thanks. What's up?" she asked.

"Nothing. Go back to bed."

"Bull shit. Please don't do this. I care about you. You rarely get up in the middle of the night and sit out here in the dark. Now, what's the problem?" She stood in front of my chair with her fists on her hips.

"Lois, this isn't easy for me to talk about, this is hard to admit." I was still for a moment and Lois placed her hand on my shoulder. "You know what I looked like when you and Henry picked me up over in Azerbaijan?" Lois nodded. "Basically, I'm healed physically from the beatings I received, but mentally, I'm still having problems. I find now days I harbor a lot of anger. There are times I feel so hostile. I don't like it."

"Towards me?"

"Oh, god no, not you. It's not at one person, more like just angry in general."

"Considering what you went through, I can understand. I feel it's normal."

"Most of the time, I don't think about what happened. But other times, like tonight, I couldn't stop thinking about things. I felt so helpless. There was nothing I could do to stop things. I could never retaliate like I wanted. I got to hit one guy who was partially responsible for the beatings, but it didn't help as much as I thought it would. I try, but I get so angry. I feel so hostile at the entire world."

"Oh baby, I'm so sorry. Is there anything I can do to help? You know I love you, don't you?"

"Yes, and that helps. Believe me. But I find the happy-go-lucky Matt I used to be is changing. I don't think I'm the carefree person I used to be. You know I'm unhappy with Seattle. I'm pissed about that and I feel bad, but if I'm being honest, I resent Albert asking me to solve his problem. I mean, it's not that big of a deal, and you know I'd do anything to help my friends, but lately I just don't want to get involved. I'm so…"

Lois moved to sit down on my lap and I opened my arms to accept her. Once she settled, she leaned over and gently kissed me on the lips. I kissed her back and the next kiss from her was a little more demanding. She reached over and picked up one of my hands and placed it on her naked breast. Her nipple grew taut, and she gave me another passionate kiss then whispered in my ear, "It's okay. I'm pleased you trust and care enough about me that you can open up to me."

"Honey, I wasn't going to have this conversation. But you asked. I'm in a funk right now and I don't know what to do."

"I have an idea…"

"What?"

Lois kissed me again. "Make love with me."

I laughed. "Darling, don't take this wrong, but for one of the first times in my life, I don't want to. Usually making love with you is the best thing ever, but even that sometimes doesn't take away my anger. I try not to dwell on what happened over there, and most of the time I'm successful, but there are times, like tonight, I'm so angry. I can't even sleep, I'm so upset."

Lois curled up against me. "You know when you feel pain, I feel pain too? I've had relationships in the past, but never anything as intense as what I feel with you. When we're apart, there is a part of me that aches for you. When we're together, I feel total happiness. I love you. I also want you to be happy when you're with me.

"I wish I could reach inside you when you're in pain and heal you. I understand why you're so angry. I imagine that's not something you get over in a few days. However, tonight was a start. Tonight was the first time you've shared with me how you feel. Now, when you're feeling down or blue, it should be easier for you to share those feelings with me. Now, I know a little of what you are dealing with and I hope I can help. Darling, I love you."

Lois stood and gently pulled on my hand. "Come. Come with me and please hold me. I want to feel you against me. Later, if you want to, I would like to feel you in me."

We crawled into bed and she curled up against me. I held her as she ran her hands over my back. Lois seemed to feel the tension leaving my body and after a while, she reached down with one hand and gently took my manhood. The warmth of her hand felt good. After a while, I felt myself growing firm.

Surprise, eventually we made love. Actually, twice that night, but I still found something missing. I was becoming a new Matt, a different Matt. Good or bad? I didn't know, but I could feel things were changing inside me. I knew there would always be room for Lois in my head and my heart, but there was an ugliness inside me that was new, and I didn't like it very much. My sleep was troubled and the next morning, I woke with a slight headache—something else new for me.

The majority of the weekend was good. I won't dwell on any one part, but for the rest of it, Lois tried her best to keep my funk at bay. I was grateful she was so concerned. I could see how special I was to her, and I felt the same way about her.

Some decisions regarding our relationship needed to be made. And soon!

~ ~ ~ ~ ~

The flight to Kansas was fast and uneventful. I don't think I spoke more than a dozen words to Henry and when we got to Lawrence, he stopped me as I walked away from the plane. "Are you okay?" he asked.

"Funny you asked. Lois, and I had a long talk this weekend about what happened over in Azerbaijan and Nakhchivan. I'm finding there're still mental scars left over from that adventure. I'm pissed off a lot more and I get that way a lot easier than I used to. I'm not the happy camper I used to be."

"Can I help?"

"Henry, actually, you have. Inviting me to take part in your new venture and asking me to help with some details makes me feel involved in something again. I look forward to doing things with you and I look forward to seeing you. You've done a lot for me. You've become quite a friend."

"Thanks, Matt. You need to get going since I can only wait around so long for you."

"Thanks, Henry. Thanks for asking if I was okay. That means a lot you'd care enough to ask."

"Remember, I saved your ass. You belong to me. Now, go!" And he pushed me away.

CHAPTER THIRTEEN

I drove out to the university and parked in the visitor's area. While walking across campus, I checked out some of the cute little coeds. Several of them looked at me and I was feeling pretty good about myself. Then I realized that because of the color of my hair and moustache, they were probably wondering what subject I taught. I was obviously too old to be a student, so that would make me a professor, but I didn't really look like one. I was being checked out with speculation, not because I was a hottie. Stuff like that really brought on the funk. Inside me, I was still the same age as those darling young women, but outside showed I was no longer in the spring of my life. I was actually looking at late autumn or early winter. I hated what was happening, but there wasn't a damn thing I could do about it.

With my mind dealing with my aging body, I climbed the stairs to Dr. Billings' office and knocked on the door. "Come in!" a voice snapped.

I opened the door to behold what I thought was the oldest person I'd ever seen. The voice and the woman didn't match. The woman behind the desk looked so frail, I wondered how she could move under her own power. Her skin looked like crepe paper, but her eyes were bright and alive behind granny glasses perched on her nose. Her white hair was curly, and she wore a dress that must have come from the back of a covered wagon. She smiled at me as she looked down her long nose. "I can tell you're not one of my students. If you were, I'd remember someone as handsome as you. How may I help you, big fella?"

"Do you have a few spare moments, ma'am? I'd like to ask you some questions."

She motioned for me to sit in a chair opposite her desk. "Who are you?"

"I'm sorry, ma'am, my name is Matt Preston." I handed her one of my cards. "I'm looking for information about your former boss, Dr. Elwood Bickerstaff. Ma'am, may I ask you some questions?"

"Listen, son, if you 'ma'am' me one more time, I'll have to toss you out of my office. Now what the hell do you want to know about ol' Woody? That man is a prig."

I couldn't help myself and I laughed out loud. "So, how about telling me how you really feel about him?"

Her laugh was no little old lady laugh. Her whole body shook, and her face glowed with happiness. I liked this old gal. "That man was one of the most uptight people I've ever known. Anyway, ask your questions Mr. Preston. However, the deal is for every question you ask, I get to ask one in return. Fair?"

"Deal. Is Dr. Bickerstaff still alive?"

"Yes. Are you married?"

"No, but I have a significant other. Does the doctor live around here?"

"Yes. Do you fool around?"

"No. But if you are asking for yourself, I might be tempted to stray." Her laugh was sharp. "Do you know where the professor lives?"

"Yes. How about you call him Woody? I never thought of him as doctor or professor even though he was my boss. Why do you want to know so much about Woody?"

"Some time ago, he adopted a child that a student had out of wedlock—"

She interrupted. "'Out of wedlock', now that's an archaic term one doesn't hear much anymore. I like that. And yes, he and Paula adopted a boy born to a student 'out of wedlock,' as you put it. I believe the boy is now in his early thirties. And again, why do you want to know so much about Woody?"

"The young woman who had the child accused a fellow student of being the father, but later recanted. There remains the possibility that the child could be his. This gentleman has asked me to look into it. As he has aged, he wonders if the child might have been his and he feels some guilt if it is. He wants to make restitution with the boy if it turns out he is the father."

"Why you?" I showed her my Federal credentials. She picked them up and inspected them closely. "I thought I was fairly knowledgeable of the various government agencies. I've never heard of this organization." She shook my creds at me.

"Because it's top secret. It's on a need to know basis, and not to be rude, but it's best if you don't know about this one."

"Ahh, so you're a spy?"

I had to laugh, and I shook my head. "No ma'am, I am not a spy. I do various things for this agency."

She pointed a finger at me. "Remember, don't ma'am me. Call me Audrey. So, these various things you do are like snooping into Woody's affairs?"

"Not exactly. It's a long and complicated story, and I'm not allowed to share most of it right now with you. Could you give me Woody's address please?"

"On one condition."

"And that is?"

"I can sense there's a lot more to this than you're letting on. I'm asking when you're able, will you come and tell me the whole story? I'm so old that by the time you finish telling me, I'll have forgotten it anyway."

"Pardon me, Dr. Billings, but bullshit. You're not that old. Perhaps in years, but where it counts, between the ears, you're as sharp as most people in their forties. And yes, I promise to come and tell you what's really going on as soon as I'm allowed. I promise you! Deal?" It occurred to me the list of people I would have to contact and explain about Albert, and why I was looking for Linda, was growing at an alarming rate.

The doctor wrote on a piece of paper and handed it to me. I noticed it was an address. "Remember, that's a deal. Now, good day, Mr. Preston. I have a class I need to prepare for. I always like to smoke a joint or two before I teach a class." I'd begun to stand and when she said that, I stopped halfway up. Looking at me, she giggled. "Oh my god, I wish I had a camera. The look on your face is priceless. Take care, Mr. Preston."

"Good day, doctor. I'll make sure and shut your door. That way none of the smoke can get away and you can enjoy it all to yourself." I left her laughing.

I shut the door and walked down the hall. I was getting closer to the answers I was looking for. Exiting the building, I found a big grin on my face as I thought about Dr. Billings. I liked that old gal. I'd have liked to have taken a class from her. Damn, I wish there'd been more instructors like her in school when I attended. Perhaps I might have graduated.

~ ~ ~ ~ ~ ~

Thanks to my GPS, I found Dr. Bickerstaff's home with ease. Pulling up in front of the house, I thought it looked like someone had somehow transported a small English cottage to this lot. I expected to see a little ol' sorceress come out the front door. Even the plantings around the house looked like something out of an English countryside.

I stepped up to the door and rapped my knuckles on it. A very tall, thin man opened the door; he was my height, but he was about two-thirds my weight. He was wearing what I thought was a hunting jacket over a blue checkerboard shirt and a strange green tie with pictures of game birds on it. Elwood had a long skinny neck with an oval head perched on top. His eyes were blue, and his cheeks were fairly red from broken blood vessels. He sported white hair parted down the middle and even though I'd never been to England, he looked like what I imagined an elderly English gentleman should look like. His voice was high and thin with a strong English accent. "Hello. May I help you?"

"Dr. Elwood Bickerstaff?"

"Yes, who are you?"

"My name is Matt Preston. May I have a moment of your time? I'd like to chat with you about your son."

"Callum? Why? Is there something wrong?" Alarm showed on his face.

"No sir, there's nothing wrong. I've been asked by this birth mother to see how he has grown up. She's curious about him. She doesn't want to upset you or him and wanted me to make sure you understood she is only curious. You have nothing to fear."

"Are you some kind of private detective?"

"No sir. I work for a government agency, but it has nothing to do with my visit here today. I'm just here on Linda Ferrara's behalf. Do you have a few moments for us to chat?"

The professor studied me for a long time. Eventually, he stepped back and motioned for me to come in. He led me into a room which I thought might be his office. Two walls were covered with overflowing bookshelves. There was a large old desk in front of one window and it too was piled high with books. If I didn't know what the old gentleman had done back in the day, from the look of the room I'd have guessed that he was a professor. Next to the desk was a wingback chair, also piled high with books. "Sit there." He pointed at the chair. "Just take those books off the chair and put them next to the desk." He motioned where he wanted me to set them. "Would you like tea?" Tea isn't one of my favorites, but I wanted to establish a rapport with the good doctor, so I told him I would. Stepping into the hallway, he called out, "Mrs. Watson. Mrs. Watson." A female answered from somewhere in the house. "Please bring us two cups of tea." He returned to his desk and sat in a large stuffed chair. "Now Mr. ahhh…"

"Preston. Matt Preston."

"Mr. Preston, please tell me again what your interest is in my son, Callum."

I thought about this for a moment and I decided in this case, I should be upfront with the elderly gentleman. I needed a lot of information and I thought being honest with him was the best way to get it. "Sir, what I am about to tell you must stay in this room for now. Please don't repeat any of this conversation for the time being. Will you give me that assurance?"

"Yes. You have certainly piqued my curiosity. What's this all about?"

"When Ms. Ferrara found out she was with child, she told a fellow she had been seeing it was his child. Later, she recanted and said maybe it wasn't true, and that she didn't know if he was the father or not. Now, this gentleman is a United States Senator. He's also been approached to run for President. They have asked me to determine whether or not your son is biologically related to the Senator.

"I don't know how much you've told your son about his birth parents, but I was asked to find out what he knows, mostly to protect him from the prying eyes of the press. As far we know, other than Ms. Ferrara, nobody knows anything about your son. The problem is when she was pregnant, a lot of her friends knew she was expecting. We don't know how many people she might have told that the Senator could have been the father. They have asked me to make sure there will be no surprises along the way for the senator. How much have you told your son?"

Mrs. Watson brought in a tray with two cups and a teapot along with cream and sugar. I put one spoon of sugar in my tea and settled back into my chair. I wouldn't push the professor. I figured I'd get more information if I waited him out rather than trying to pressure him.

"When Callum turned eighteen, Paula—that was my wife—and I sat him down and asked him if he had questions about his birth parents. He said he knew he was adopted, but nothing more than that. We explained how his mother was a student at the university when she got pregnant. She had the child and put it up for adoption. I explained how Paula and I had tried for years to have a child and being able to adopt him was, as far as we were concerned, a godsend.

"He asked us about his father, and we told him there was some question regarding exactly who the father was. We told Callum we'd heard the fellow his mother was living with was killed in some incident while he was in prison. We also told him we weren't sure if that was his birth father or not. As I am sure you can imagine, it was a difficult conversation to have. We tried to be as honest as we could be about his birth parents, but we also didn't want to make them sound like bad people. I knew Linda from one of my classes and I always liked her. She was an excellent student, very bright, and it was a shame she didn't finish school."

"Did Callum seem like he ever wanted meet his birth mother?"

"He's never said one way or the other."

"How do you feel about him meeting his birth mother?"

The professor leaned back in his chair and placed his feet on the ottoman in front of him. He put his fingertips together, forming a tent, and sat that way for a long time, scrutinizing me. I was beginning to wonder if I needed to ask my question again when he finally spoke. "Before Paula passed away, we discussed that at length. Eventually, we decided if he wants to meet her, it's up to him. I don't feel threatened if he does and I don't think Paula would have either. We gave him the best home we knew how. And I feel he appreciated it and loves both of us. My main worry is what it might do to his wellbeing. He is comfortable with the way things are now. I'd prefer everything be left as is."

"Where is he now?"

Elwood settled deeper into his chair, folded his hands over his chest now, and smiled. "Callum is a cowboy." I must have had a look of doubt on my face. "I'm serious. A real, honest to God, cowboy. He lives up in the mountains of Northwest Colorado on a ranch. His next door neighbor has a breed of horses he developed, and Callum purchased two mares from the gentleman and then paid for stud fees to have the two mares bred. One mare produced twins and the other one a single stallion. The two of them actively breed the horses they have and keep careful records so there'll be no breeding problems later. His neighbor also has a guide service where he takes people out in the wilderness for a few days, and they live in tents and hunt. Callum helps often with the excursions. I've been out there twice and where he lives is beautiful. He loves it and I can see why."

"What's his neighbor's name?"

"Gates. Kip Gates. Mr. Gates went all the way to Australia to get the first stallion about twenty years ago and then carefully selected the brood mare he wanted to use when he got the stallion back to Colorado. I understand the horses they produce are very much in demand. When they sell one, the animal commands a hefty sum. I find it all very amusing my son is a cowboy. I'm very proud of him mind you, but it's amusing."

"Would you mind it if I went to Colorado and met him?"

"No. I think it might be a good idea. As an outsider, perhaps you're better able to decide how much you want to disclose to him about his mother. I take it you know where his mother is living now?"

I nodded. "Yes. She's dealing cards at a hotel casino in Vegas. Actually, I believe she's more than just a dealer. I've met the top man at the casino, and he acted like she was an important employee to his organization. When I asked her about meeting her son, she said she'd like to meet him, but only if he wanted to meet her too."

"I would say if the two of them will meet, he would have to go to her. Callum lives at the end of the world. Burns, the settlement where he gets mail, is accessible only by dirt and gravel county roads from Interstate 70, and then from a state road. The community is located in an arroyo along the Colorado River. Burns consists of a U.S. Post Office and a ranch. If you go, you will need to make arrangements with his neighbor Mr. Gates for a place to stay. Callum doesn't really have any room for guests."

The professor pulled out one of the desk drawers and removed a business card. He wrote on the back of the card and handed it to me. It had Callum's complete name and an address out in Colorado. I noticed the ranch was near the settlement of Burns, Colorado. I'd never heard of Burns. I needed to get to a computer and find out more.

I was looking forward to possibly meeting Bickerstaff's son. This would be a first for me since I'd never met a real cowboy. From what the professor had told me, his son made a living out of ranching and the guide service. It also sounded like the kind of place one didn't just show up at. I wanted to see this place. "Thank you for being so forthright with me. I appreciate all the information you've shared."

"I doubt if anybody would ever find him. If someone were to come snooping around, I wouldn't tell them a thing. The records of Callum's birth parents are sealed. In order for anyone to get more information, they'd have to do what you did. They'd have to come and talk to me, and what happened thirty years ago is none of their business. In a way, I don't want to know who the father was. I've always felt he was my son. I'm proud of the way he turned out. Not many fathers can say that about their children. Tell your boss, or your friend or whoever you're working for, there is nothing here to worry about. My lips are sealed, and I know Callum won't talk to anybody about his adoption either."

"Thank you, sir, I wish you a good day." I stood and shook the old man's hand. It was soft, but there was still a firmness in the shake. That made two professors from the University's English department I liked.

When I got to the car, I sat for a moment and enjoyed the feeling of accomplishment. I'd found out the information Mouse and Albert had asked me to find out. It had taken a while, but at least I had something to report back to them.

I called Henry. "Anything in my area?"

"How far are you from Denver?"

"I dunno, maybe eight to ten hours or so. Why?"

"I have a charter going into Denver. Then we have one leaving Portland a day later. Get to Denver and I'll take you to Seattle. I assume that's where you want to go."

"Yeah, I guess so."

"Call me from Denver."

"Done."

The next ten hours were a total bore. I'd driven across Kansas before many times, and I'm sure that the Chamber of

Commerce of Kansas won't like my comments, but the drive through Kansas had to rank as one of the most boring in the nation. I'm sure there are others, but you can put ol' Kansas right up there near the top. On the way, I called Mouse. The phone went to voice mail, and I asked him to call me when he had a chance. He called me back two hours later. "Matt, what's up?"

"Is Albert still around?"

"Yeah. Why?"

"I'm on my way back to Seattle and I'd like to chat with the two of you. I'd like to share with you what I've learned about Linda Ferrara and her son. Henry's picking me up in Denver and I'll be on my way in a few hours. I'll call you when I'm leaving Denver."

"Sounds good."

~ ~ ~ ~ ~ ~

I stood looking out across the bay from Mouse's condo, watching the ferries pass in the night. The lights danced on the water and in the distance, I could see the glow in the sky from one of the towns over on the peninsula. Far below, I could see the lights from the harbor of Seattle. The whole scene was very peaceful, reminding me of a Seattle I knew long ago. I could hear Mouse and Albert enter the room behind me and I turned. Mouse had two drinks in his hands, and he motioned for me to sit as he handed me one of the drinks. I took the drink and sat where he had indicated. Albert also had a drink in hand.

We settled into comfortable chairs and Mouse tented his fingers in front of his face in his usual position. Albert spoke first. "If I may?" Mouse nodded. "Senator Markel has disappeared again. And I think I have a line on this McKnight fellow. I had Admiral Orchard run McKnight's name through their computer system and we came up with a credit card trail. Right now, we think he's in the D.C. area. His photo is being circulated and we hope to pick him up. There is concern now that Markel has disappeared. Thought you might like to know."

"Thanks. When we're done here, I'll call Chief Davenport and let him know what's happening. Even though no one can prove that Wislond killed the two Seattle officers, Jeff would like some kind of closure."

I smiled at Mouse. He nodded. "So, Matt, what have you learned?" I told my tale, starting with Dr. Bueler in Arkansas and ending with my visit to Dr. Bickerstaff. "From what I've learned, it would be almost impossible for anybody to discover Albert might've had a child out of wedlock. I have the boy's address in Colorado, but from the sounds of it, getting to him is next to impossible."

"What do you mean?" Mouse asked.

"The young man's name is Callum, and he is a bona fide cowboy. He and his neighbor raise horses and they have a business where they take city slickers back into the toolies where they sleep in tents and fish from the backs of their horses in lakes and shoot wild animals with crossbows and guns. The professor who adopted Callum has no desire for anyone to find out about the adoption or anything else about the entire affair. The secret is safe."

Albert sat quietly for a long time. He took a deep breath. "But if I wanted to, I could see the young man?"

"Yes. Dr. Bickerstaff told him he was adopted. The young man was also told that the actual identity of his father was unknown. I guess if you wanted to speak to the man, you could. I take it you still want to know if he's your son or not?"

"Yes."

"May I point out something else?"

"What?"

"As far as Callum is concerned, he has a father. A man he loves. The professor. You would stir up things, pushing this even further. If you're not the father, and that seems to be the opinion of most people including the mother, then you would have disturbed Callum for nothing. He's happy right now. Since it is such a big *if*, why not just leave it alone?

"As far as running for office, you are safe. The chances of anybody ever finding out what happened thirty years ago are remote. Like almost zero chance. What good would it do to seek him out? Are you hoping the results would be positive so you could somehow make up for not being there all these years? My advice, Albert, is to leave it be. However, you know I'll do whatever you want me to do."

Albert stood and wandered over to the window. He stood there for a long time, looking intently out over the Sound and the lights in the distance. I watched him take a deep breath and let it out. Finally, he turned and looked at me. "Thank you for your efforts. I also thank you for your advice. You've done a lot. I owe you." I waved my hand to show it was no big thing. "Now, I guess I need to make my peace with Maggie. I know how she feels about me running, but I don't know how I feel about her feelings regarding this. Does that make sense?" Mouse and I grunted in agreement. "Let me sleep on all of this and I'll be in touch."

Mouse stood and walked Albert to the door. I'd stood up to leave as well, but Mouse motioned for me to stay. I could see he wanted to talk more without Albert present. After Mouse shut the door behind him, he called out, "Jade? Jade, you can come out now. Albert's gone."

I asked, "What's going on? What's happening now?"

Mouse explained, "I didn't know what you would report. I didn't want to embarrass Albert any more than necessary. I don't know how he feels regarding how much Jade knows of his past. I thought it best if it was only the three of us. Jade still listened in and heard your report."

Jade smiled at me. "Matt, you have been a very busy person. You have discovered a lot in a short time. The cowboy thing sounds interesting. I'd love to go there."

Mouse piped off. "What? Are you serious?"

"Yes! What's wrong with that?"

"Nothing, it's just that I can't see you on a horse. And for sure I cannot see you sleeping in a tent."

For the first time, I was seeing a new side of Jade and she frowned at Mouse. "Steve, there are a lot of things you don't know about me. I know I was young when I was given to you, and you think I hadn't lived much. But there are things about me you don't know. Now is not the time to talk about it, but I have slept in a tent. More times than I care to remember."

Mouse looked over at me. "Whoops! Looks like I stepped on my twanger." He turned back to Jade. "You know I love you and if I hurt your feelings, I'm sorry. You are so important to me. I'd love for you to share your stories about sleeping in a tent. And if you want to go to Colorado and ride horses and sleep in tents, then I'm with you."

Jade shook her head. "Darling, I can't see you sleeping in a tent. Ever! But thank you for the offer."

I'd slept in lots of tents over the years, and I had no desire to do it again if I didn't have to do so. The old body was getting soft, and I wished to treat it as gently as possible. "If you two don't mind, I'll stay back at the bunkhouse and keep the fires burning, waiting for your return. I've done horses, and not too long ago, and I really have no desire ever to do it again."

"Matt, to change the subject, how did things turn out with Zampuchini? You know who he is?"

"At first, I didn't know exactly who he was, but then I remembered things I'd read about him. Didn't he take out a couple of members of the Dragna crime family?"

"Yeah. You know he called me?"

"He left a message on my room phone after he spoke to you and asked me to call him. When I called him, he sounded frightened. What the hell did you say to him?"

Mouse smiled. "I told him I couldn't believe he was messing with you. I told him it was my understanding you were an assassin for some top secret government agency. I told him one time, you and I had a small disagreement, and I later found out I was lucky to still be alive. I said I'd tried to find out information on you and was approached in the middle of the night by some frightening people and told to leave things alone, and it would be my one and final warning. I told him it scared the shit out of me."

"You didn't do that."

"Yep. It was fun. I doubt if you will have any problems with ol' Sal again."

"Well, thanks. I hope you are correct, but he didn't seem like the type to back off that easily. I know he didn't like me asking Linda questions. I tried to assure him I was no threat to him."

"Again, to change the subject, you told me there was something you wanted to discuss with me the last time you were here. Things got out of control and you never asked me what you wanted."

"Yeah, you know I'm selling stuff here in Seattle." Mouse showed he was aware. "I have a buyer for the apartment building as well—"

Mouse interrupted. "I knew you were selling, but I didn't know you were getting rid of your apartment building. I'd hate to see you leave town."

I held up a hand. "Once that's sold, I have nothing left here in town. I would like to keep a few of my old cars, but other than that, I'm ready to leave Seattle behind. However, I find I don't want to completely check out of my life in Seattle. I think I'd like to have a place here at The Olympus. You told me you own some of the condos here on the top floors. And you said if I was ever interested in leasing one from you, you'd do it. So, what's ya got that I could rent, borrow, buy, or whatever from you?"

"Are you kidding?"

"Does this face look like it's joking?"

"No! I guess not. The unit just below me is empty. It has three bedrooms, a kitchen, dining area and three baths. The master suite is on the front of the building and has the same view you get from this room. I'll sell it to you, if you wish."

"Would you consider leasing it?"

"Yeah. Why don't you wish to purchase?"

"I need to speak to my accountant. I don't know which is the best way for me to go. And what about my request about some space down in your basement?"

"You saw how few cars are down on the very bottom floor. I'll let you have two spaces in that basement floor and there are two spaces higher up that go with your unit. Can you get by with just four parking spots?" Mouse was grinning, so I knew he was busting my chops.

"Well, it'll be tough. But I'll try."

"What are you going to do now?"

"I've told you I need to sell the bike. I'm getting to a point where it's not as enjoyable as it once was. Too much traffic and most of all, if I get hurt now, it would take too long to heal. That, I don't need!"

Mouse nodded. "Understood. When you are leaving on your trip?"

"As soon as I can. Right now, I need to make a few phone calls and then I'll see how free I am to go. I think in about two or three days, I'll head out if I can."

"Please be careful. Let me know as soon as you can how you want to handle the condo." I told him there was no problem.

CHAPTER FOURTEEN

I rode the elevator down and when I stepped under the portico from the lobby, I noticed my truck was waiting for me, as usual. I smiled at Marshall, the fellow who usually brought my vehicle around. "Thanks, Marshall."

"No problem, Mr. Preston. Mr. Fox tells me you'll be moving into our building."

"Matt! Remember? And yes, I'll be moving in soon. How did you find out so quickly?"

Marshall laughed. "Sorry, Matt, I should just tell you I know everything that goes on here, but one of my main duties at The Olympus is head of security. I sometimes park cars so people don't notice I'm checking things out. When you look like the hired help, people ignore you and this offers an excellent way of keeping track of who comes and who goes."

Marshall pointed across the street. "For instance, the two dudes across the street, over by the front door of that building..." I looked over and saw the two men standing there. Marshall continued. "They don't belong around here. They don't fit. They look totally out of place."

I glanced again across the street and when I realized one of the two men was Guido, one of Zampuchini's goons,

I was astonished. I thought I'd seen the last of Guido, but obviously I was wrong. The other fellow with Guido looked like he could have been Louie, his former partner, except Louie would be in no condition to travel for a long time. I wondered what the two of them were doing, standing across from The Olympus.

Instead of getting into the driver's side of my truck, I opened the passenger door, reached under the seat, and removed the pistol I carried there. I slipped it into the holster built into my jacket. "Marshall, do me a favor, please re-park my vehicle. I remembered something I need to take care of."

"Of course, Matt." He nodded towards the two hoods across the street. "And if you're going over there, be careful." I re-entered the lobby and exited from a side door where they couldn't see me from across the street.

I walked to the end of the alley, then turned left and continued to walk around the block. Entering the building across the street, I came through the back door then stepped through the lobby and behind the two assailants. I waited until both were looking away from the doors and exited directly behind them. Removing my pistol from the jacket's holster, I hid it under the edge of my jacket and stepped up behind Guido's partner. I poked the barrel hard into the small of his back, causing him to jump. "Don't move. Do not move an inch. Has Guido ever told you what happened to his last partner?"

"No…" He stammered.

Guido turned slightly.

"Guido, if you turn around, I'll shoot both of you right here, right now, and you know I'll do it. I know you're both armed, and I'm positive you don't have a carry permit for Seattle. Also, the Commissioner of Police is a childhood friend of mine and he'll back anything I do to you."

Finally, Guido timidly asked, "What are you going to do with me?"

"Hang on." I waited a moment for Marshall to come out of The Olympus' lobby. Once he was standing in front of the building, I whistled and called out. "Marshall. Marshall." He turned, and I waved. He looked at me, a look of surprise on his face. "Can you come over here, please?" I hollered.

Marshall waited for a break in traffic then ran over. "What's up?" He noticed the pistol in my hand. "Matt, what the hell is going on?"

"Are you armed?"

"Of course."

"I want to relieve these clowns of their pistols. Can you cover them while I disarm them? I'll warn you, sometimes they do stupid things. If either of them moves, shoot him. I'll square it with the police. Chief Davenport is an old friend."

"No problem." After Marshall had them covered, I took away both of their pistols. Marshall asked, "Okay, Matt, now what?"

"Can you help me get these two up to Mr. Fox's condo?"

"Mouse? Yes, no problem."

We got the two across the street and into the lobby of The Olympus with no issues, then ushered them into Mouse's express elevator. As the door of the elevator closed, I pulled out my cell and dialed Mouse. "Matt, what's up?"

"In about ten seconds, I'll be getting off your elevator with two of Zampuchini's hoods who were waiting across the street from your condo building."

"What?"

"Mouse, come to the elevator door now." The door opened, and Mouse was standing there with the largest pistol I'd ever seen in his hand. Part of the reason why it looked huge was the size of the gun itself, and part of it was how small Mouse looked holding it. He stepped back and motioned for the two thugs to step out of the elevator. They took three steps. Mouse told them, "Stop. Now get down on the floor, on your face." They hesitated for a moment, but

Mouse said, "Now." He pulled back the hammer on his pistol. "I've never shot this thing and I don't know how hard I have to pull on the trigger." Both dropped to their knees and fell forward. "Marshall, can you stay a moment?"

"Yes, sir. What do you need?"

"If either of them moves, and I mean any movement at all, I want you to shoot them. I don't care where you shoot them, just shoot them. They're mobsters from somebody I know down in Vegas. You'll not get into any trouble for shooting them since either Matt or I will take the blame. I'm so angry I really have no problem with shipping back a couple of dead bodies to ol' Sal right now."

"No problem, boss. I'd seen them earlier today, and I wondered about them."

Mouse stepped over to Guido. "Matt tells me your name is Guido." He made an affirmative grunt. "Good, now tell me why you were standing across the street watching my building."

"I can't tell you."

"Can't or won't?"

Guido explained, "Mr. Preston knows what Mr. Zampuchini will do to me if I tell you."

Mouse got down on the floor and put the barrel of his pistol against Guido's temple. "If you don't talk to me right now, you won't need to worry about ol' Sal."

"Look, I don't want to get involved," Guido pleaded.

Mouse's voice grew cold. "You stupid turd, you're already involved. Now start talking or I'll pull the trigger!"

"No! Stop! Zampuchini doesn't believe what Preston told him, or should I say what he didn't tell him. Mr. Z thinks the top secret stuff he was telling him is all bullshit. He never has trusted you either, and he thinks what you told him is a bunch of bullshit too. He thinks the two of you are up to something. Mr. Z instructed us to come up to Seattle and watch your building. If we saw Preston, we were to finish what we were supposed to have done back in Vegas. If we saw you, we were to just follow you and report what we found out."

Mouse's voice took on a tone I'd never heard before. "And what were you supposed to do to Mr. Preston back in Vegas?"

"I told you, Mr. Zampuchini feels Preston represents a problem regardless of what he says. He wants the problem removed. We were to take Preston out to the desert and take care of him."

"Take care of him? What the hell does that mean?" Mouse asked.

"What do you think it means?"

"I don't know. That's why I'm asking. What does it mean?"

"We were to kill him and bury the body out in the desert."

Mouse stood up and looked down at Guido. I could tell by his face when he'd made a decision. "Which hand do you shoot with."

"My right, why?" His voice was tinged with fear.

"I wanted to make sure I did this right the first time." Mouse stepped on Guido's right hand, then forcefully rocked his foot back and forth. I could hear bones breaking over Guido's screams. Mouse stepped back, jumped in the air, and came down hard with his heel once more on the back of the same hand. Guido screamed again and fainted.

The other fellow on the floor looked up at Mouse and begged, "Please, please, don't hurt me. What are you going to do to me?"

"Me? Why, nothing." Mouse pulled out his cell phone and dialed a number. After the person on the other end answered, Mouse spoke. "Zampuchini, this is Mouse. Wait a moment while I put you on speakerphone." Mouse touched the screen of his phone. "There, now you're on speakerphone."

"Mouse, why have you called me?" Sal didn't sound too sure of himself.

"Zampuchini, evidently you didn't understand our last conversation. I told you then I had no interest in your operation. Remember? I don't know where you got the idea I was trying to muscle in. I told you then that I represented no danger to you. Remember? I also warned you about Preston. I told you he wasn't to be fucked with. Now, what part of all that didn't you understand?"

Mouse waited a few seconds and when there was no reply, he continued, his voice raising in volume. "I see you didn't understand because now you've sent two of your clowns up here to murder him and I don't know what they would have done with me." His voice went up a notch. "And you're so stupid, you sent up one goombah who already screwed up the original hit. You are so stupid, you send the person who screwed things up in Vegas to screw them up again." Mouse's voice was now shouting into the phone. "And guess what, you prick? He did screw it up. I can't believe you sent Guido up here to murder someone in my back yard. Who the hell do you think you are?"

"That's a lie. Who told you that?" Sal retorted.

"Guido just did. You know Guido, the person who is now lying on my floor, unconscious with a busted right hand. And just to make sure you understand I mean it when I tell you to leave things alone, I will break your other thug's hand."

The man on the floor screamed, "You promised, you told me you wouldn't do anything to me!"

"True, but I never told you Matt wouldn't." Mouse looked at me. "Break his right hand." With no warning, I jumped in the air and landed directly on the back of the prone man's hand. Normally, I'm not such a violent person, but after hearing Guido calmly tell us he was to take me out to the desert and murder me, my peaceful nature seemed to

160

have disappeared. Since this goon had come to kill me, I had no problem with breaking his hand. The man on the floor screamed. Mouse told me to make sure the hand was broken so he'd never be able to shoot a gun again. Once more, I stomped on his hand.

Mouse stepped over to the man and tapped his head with the toe of his shoe. "Be still now. If you keep making noise, I'll have to do something so you can't make noise." The man was a little more still; he just whimpered.

"Okay, Zampuchini. Did you hear all that?" There was a moment of silence. Mouse asked again, "Hey, *pisano*, I asked you a question. Did you hear what happened?"

A frightened voice whispered, "Yes."

"Good, because I'm done playing games with you. Listen up and listen closely. I was not going to use this, but I know all about the Parisi massacre. Surly you remember that? I'm asking you, do you remember?" Silence. Mouse screamed into the phone, "Hey, asshole, do you remember?"

A timid reply came back, "Yes."

"I thought so. You really thought by capping him it would make you boss. You thought it made you The Don. However, Sal, I know where all the bodies are buried. I've kept my peace and allowed you to take on that mantle and you are only Don because I allowed it. I know where you thought you stashed the weapons used in the hit, but they are no longer there. I know who did the deed and I also have a recording of you telling them to take out the whole Parisi family."

"Bull shit. You don't know a damn thing." I could tell Sal was trying to sound tough, but actually he didn't sound as sure of himself as he tried.

"Really? How come I know all about Grasso and Carbone? I even have a video-taped, signed confession by Carbone. And how come I know how many people were in-volved in the hit? Do you want me to name more names who were involved in the clip? Do you want me to tell you where you thought the weapons were hidden? Do you want me to tell you what kind of car was used to take old man Parisi out to the swamp? Do you want me to tell you where that swamp is? You know, you really have some lame ass people working for you."

A long silence passed, then in a soft voice, "What do you want, Fox?"

"Good. I knew you could see reason. So, if anything ever happens to Matt Preston—I mean if he gets hit crossing a street, if he has an automobile accident, if he happens to fall in the shower and hurt himself, if he even gets a paper cut, if he is off on a secret mission and some harm comes to him—a lot of law enforcement people will get a shit ton of evidence regarding your involvement with the Parisi hit. I have enough on you so you'll burn, my friend. Listen to me, leave Preston alone. And that includes me too. I never want to hear your name. If I do, I will fall on you like a ton of bricks. Do you understand me?"

The voice on the other end of the phone was very weak. "Yes."

"What? I didn't hear you."

"Yes." This time, it was a lot louder.

"You also need to thank me for not turning Preston loose on you. I'd give you a phone number of a clandestine organization back in D.C. and they'd tell you exactly who and what Preston is, but it seems you're too stupid to understand what they'd tell you.

"I'll send your two clowns back to you. They're coming down by private plane. We'll call you when the plane lands and tell you where you can pick them up. And in case you try to take out your anger on those two sorry excuses for soldiers, the same deal applies to them. They get a pass on this screw-up. After all, it was your stupidity not to deal with Parisi yourself that got you into this situation and it was your stupidity in not calling me and making sure I had no designs on your operation. Zampuchini, I thought you knew never send a boy to do a man's job. So, Sal baby, are we clear on everything?"

"Yes."

Mouse screamed into the phone, "Yes what, asshole?"

"Yes, sir."

"That's better. You know you've really pissed me off. You think now that you're Don, life is good for you. Sal, you now have an enemy for life, and it was not a wise move on your part. You'd best make sure you keep me happy. Very happy."

Mouse hung up. I'd heard about this side of Mouse, but I'd never seen it before. His anger was tangible. It truly was a sight to behold. I never wanted it aimed at me.

I glanced at Marshall and when he saw me looking at him, he blanched. I think what he overheard Mouse telling ol' Sal must have frightened him. Mouse turned to Marshall. "Are you okay with all this? Are you still with me?"

I noticed his hands were trembling a little. "You bet, boss. Tell me what you want and it's a done deal."

"Good! Use the old station wagon on the fifth floor, you know the one?" Marshall said he did. "Take these two idiots down to Boeing Field. I'll make arrangements to have them flown to Vegas and make sure Sal knows when to pick them up."

Guido was trying to sit up on the floor while holding his damaged hand. He continued to moan as Marshall and I got the two up and headed off to the elevator.

Mouse stopped us. He stepped in front of Guido and his partner. "I'm letting you go. I've told Zampuchini he is not to harm either of you. However, if I were you, I'd be looking for a new boss. The way this has turned out, I don't see him keeping his position as Don for long. Please make sure

I never see either of you again. It will not turn out well for you, I promise. Now, go!"

I rode down to the parking garage with Marshall. After we got the goons into the wagon, he turned and said, "Thanks for your help, Mr. Preston."

"Marshall, after what we just went through, how about we make it Matt and Marshall? For good? Oh, and I know you're worried about what you heard Mouse telling Zampuchini on the phone about me. I'm not the bad ass he made me out to be. You have nothing to fear. We're friends." Marshall grinned at me as he stuck out his fist. We fist bumped.

"It's been a pleasure doing business with you, Matt."

"Drive carefully. I'm sure Sal wants his boys back in good shape."

I rode back up to Mouse's condo and found him standing in front of his large window looking out over the sound. When Mouse heard me, he turned and shook his head as he looked at me. "Matt, I'm sorry you had to see me like that. But Zampuchini has been getting too big for his britches for some time. He needed to be taken down a peg."

I smiled at him. "Remind me never to piss you off."

"After what you did for Jade and me, you have a few favors stored away." He winked. "What are you going to do now?"

"Not sure just yet. I wonder if I'll need to go play cowboy for a while. If not, I still want to go on one last motorcycle trip."

As I turned to leave, my pocket vibrated. Recognizing the number, I answered, "Funny you should call. I was curious to know when I would hear from you. So, Albert, have you decided about Callum?"

"Yes, we've decided that I should find out once and for all whether or not he is my son."

"Okay… I guess that means you want me to go soon and get this all wrapped up?" I turned to Mouse. "You heard?"

"Yes, any idea how this will turn out?"

"After I chat with Callum, I think I'll come back here. I want to discuss with you what I find out. You can give me some idea what you think we should do with what I find out. I need to see if Callum wants to meet his birth mother. And if he's willing to provide me with a DNA sample."

"I'd tell you good luck, but you always seem to have good luck."

"If you had been with me over in Azerbaijan, you wouldn't say that. I really thought my luck had run out."

"I didn't want you to go get involved in that deal, but I knew you felt honor bound to do it. And that's one thing I admire about you. You, Matt Preston, are an honorable man." Mouse extended his hand, and I took it.

It was time to visit Colorado.

I wondered what that would be like.

CHAPTER FIFTEEN

Henry landed the plane at the Eagle County Regional Airport, located East of Vail, Colorado, between the towns of Gypsum and Eagle on State Highway 6. I'd been in contact twice with a fellow named Kip Gates from River's Bend Outfitting. Since Callum didn't have a place for me to stay, I'd made arrangements to stay with Gates, who owned and operated a dude ranch up in the Colorado mountains, and asked him to pick me up.

I'd no idea what to bring to wear. I took two pairs of Levi's, two warm shirts, several pairs of socks, a warm coat, and tennis shoes. I know tennis shoes don't really paint a good cowboy picture, but this was my first time visiting anything like Kip's place and I was trying to make a good guess.

I'd made arrangements to stay for five days at Kip's ranch, River's Bend. Kip told me his family had owned and operated the ranch for seven generations, and that it was a working cattle ranch too. He didn't just breed horses. Normally, guests who stayed with him would be there to hunt the various wild animals found in the mountains around his ranch. Since I wasn't interested in hunting, but instead wanted to meet Callum Bickerstaff and the Gates Family, I didn't bring a rifle.

I'd jokingly told Kip since I wasn't bringing a weapon, I wouldn't be able to shoot my dinner. Gates assured me I wouldn't go hungry. There'd be three hot meals a day, and I'd stay in the comfort of their ranch house. That was two more hot meals than I normally got.

Because the ranch covered about 1,200 acres and was home to many resident elk and deer, most guests were hunters, and all a guest needed to bring were personal items, their hunting gear, a rifle, and a hunting license. After our phone conversations, I was really excited to see his place.

Walking towards the airport terminal from the plane, I didn't need anybody to point out Kip Gates. There are those wanna-be's in life, then there's the real McCoy, those who are genuine. Just because a person wears a cowboy hat and boots doesn't make them a cowboy. Yes, Kip was wearing a big black cowboy hat, black cowboy boots, Levi's with a belt buckle the size of a VW bug, and a bright red cowboy shirt; however, you could tell, this cowboy was authentic. Looking at him, I thought to myself, *Talk about your Marlboro Man moment.* I was having one.

All it took was for him to take one step and it erased any doubt, this dude was unquestionably the real deal. I can't describe his walk, but he appeared to have studied a few John Wayne films. It wasn't a walk, but more of a rolling stroll. His face—well-tanned from countless hours riding over his ranch—sported a moustache almost as full as mine, but his was still black, or should I say salt and pepper; heavy on the pepper while mine was totally white.

Ambling up to me, he stuck out his hand with a big grin. "Mr. Preston?"

"Matt, please." I extended my hand.

"Pleased to meet you, sir." The man exuded warmth, and I knew instantly I would like this person.

We were walking out to the parking lot when a stranger stepped directly in front of Kip, stopping him. Looking

Kip up and down, he sneered. "Are you a real cowboy?" He stuck out his hand for Kip to shake it.

Gates smiled. "By your question, I assume you mean do I have horses, and cows, and do I live on a ranch?"

Obviously, the answer the fellow got was not what he expected. He nodded, still holding his hand out.

"Naw," Kip retorted, "I drive an eighteen-wheel semi-truck. If I was a real cowboy, I'd be wearing tennis shoes."

Kip still hadn't taken the man's hand and I could see by the look on the man's face, he was working out what Kip had just told him. Finally, the guy said, "Oh! Well, I always wanted to be a cowboy. I'd love to ride bulls."

"Really? Do you ride many bulls?" Kip asked.

"I've never been on a bull, but I have ridden a calf," the man explained proudly.

Kip looked at the fellow for a few seconds. "Humm, somehow 'calfboy' doesn't have the same ring to it as cowboy. But you never know, there is always the horse ride in front of the grocery store. Perhaps someday."

We stepped around the fellow standing there with his hand outstretched and walked towards Kip's truck. I tossed my bag into the back and we climbed into a newer, four-wheel drive truck in desperate need of a bath. It looked like it had been down more than a few trails in its brief life.

"Sorry about that back in the parking lot," Kip said. "I get that occasionally. Because of the way I dress, people make stupid comments. Most of the time, I ignore them, but I wanted to screw with that guy's head."

"And you did a great job, I might add." We chortled.

After a short drive on the freeway, Kip turned off on a forest road and we headed north. Within a few miles, the road had turned to gravel and dirt. In parts, the road turned to something resembling a giant washboard and I wondered how he kept springs on the truck. We only went twenty-five miles per hour for most of the trip because of the condition of the road, and it felt like we'd been driving forever. Now I understood why the truck needed a bath. There really wasn't much point.

On the way to Burns, I asked Kip, "Do you mind if I ask, can you tell me about the belt buckle?"

He looked down at his lap and pointed. "This? I earned this at a rodeo. I got first place."

"Really?"

"Yeah. I'd heard about a rodeo down in Australia and I'd always wanted to see the place. I went down there, entered, and took first. That's where I first saw the horses I'm breeding now. I was awestruck at the Australian stock horse. I could just imagine crossing a stock horse with one of my quarter horse mares. Look Matt, you really don't want to get me talking about my horses. I'll talk your ear off."

"It's cool. I like to see a man passionate about what he does. I can see you're excited about your horses and what you're doing with them."

We were coming up to a bend in the road, and Kip looked over and remarked, "Get ready, we're coming up shortly on downtown Burns. It'll be on your left."

I didn't know what to expect and as we came around the bend, on the left was a tan and brown building constructed out of T-111 plywood with a three-tab shingle roof. The little building had a dirt parking lot in front, a large microwave dish mounted on the side, and a flagpole on the other side of the building. In front of the building was a sign: United States Postal Service, Burns, Colorado, 80426.

I looked around the rest of the area and saw nothing else. "What am I missing?" I asked.

"Nothing. This is it, downtown Burns, Colorado. For a while, Walmart and McDonalds were fighting to see who'd get to put in a store, but when they found out Burns has a population of eighty-nine people, they both bailed." Kip looked over at me and winked, and I knew I was being had.

"So, not much happening on Saturday night?" I asked.

"Oh no, ol' Elmer has a harmonica, and his brother has a washtub he beats on and we have a big hoedown every Saturday night. Usually around midnight, we have to have the police come and break it up 'cause Elmer flirts with all the women and it upsets the wife. She always carries her frying pan around with her."

By now, I was laughing so hard, it was difficult to speak. "Do you always give new people this much crap or am I special?"

"Oh no, this is just for you." The two of us were still laughing when we turned onto the dirt road leading up to his ranch. I'd have never believed it, but this road was even more primitive than the last. I wondered if a mountain goat could even use the road. After a few more bone jarring miles, we pulled into a large field in front of a bunkhouse.

Getting out of the truck felt great. My first couple of steps hurt, but finally the muscles loosened up and I could move without whimpering. We climbed up the front steps to the house and I turned around. The view in front of me was breathtaking. We were at the high end of a valley and in the distance, mountains surrounded it. I could see down to the bottom of the valley where the Colorado river flowed into the distance. I turned to Kip. "I'm sure that after a while, you get jaded and don't see the beauty of where you live. But this is stunning."

"You're right, after a while, I don't notice it as much as I should. But then we get a new guest like yourself who is impressed by the vista and I'm reminded how this really is God's Country."

We spent the rest of the afternoon and evening looking over his ranch and viewing his horses. I asked about Callum and Kip told me he would be at dinner that evening. I was eager to meet him. "How do you know Callum?" Kip asked.

"I met his father through KU one time. He told me about both of you and the horses you two are developing."

"Callum doesn't talk much about his family. I know his mother has passed away and I remember him telling me one time that they adopted him."

"That's what I understand too." This conversation was getting difficult. I didn't feel comfortable sharing too many intimate details of Callum's life, but Gates had been nothing but open with me. Thankfully, somebody who needed Kip to take care of a problem out in the barn came into the room.

They offered me a drink before dinner, and I met Callum. He dressed a lot like Kip but without the big belt buckle. Callum was almost as tall as me but a lot thinner. Blue eyes were set in a well-tanned face, and he was fighting a losing battle with his quickly receding hairline. I was pleased to see he had accepted it and wasn't trying to do a comb-over to hide his bald spot.

The woman he introduced as his wife appeared to be much younger than him and was attractive. As we chatted, I discovered she was a widow whose husband was killed over in the Middle East. I thought about making a comment regarding my last visit over there, but decided she might not appreciate having her memories of her dead husband revived. Callum told me he'd helped her around her farm and they'd dated. They seemed to be happy with one another and it pleased me that she could move on with life.

Just before dinner, I got to meet Kip's wife, Leslie. I'd been told she was a former rodeo queen and as far as I was concerned, she was still a queen. Lovely! If she was a representation of the women one met at a rodeo, sign me up. I don't know what I could do at a rodeo except pick up after the horses with a shovel and wagon, but if I got to meet ladies who looked like Kip's wife, I was ready. She extended her hand and asked, "Has my husband been treating you well?"

"He has, ma'am. Why, he even made sure I got to see all of downtown Burns."

She looked over at her husband with a puzzled look on her face. "What?"

I interrupted. "You had to be there. Kip was trying to give me a hard time. I think a Home Depot would do well in Burns, however."

Leslie looked at both of us and shook her head. "I can't believe it. I always thought my husband was one of a kind. Heaven help us, but there seems to be two of you." She gave my hand a gentle squeeze, and we all stepped to the table.

Dinner was interesting. I'd never had venison before. The dish was like a stroganoff but instead of beef, it was cooked with game. I thought everything tasted fantastic. There was a choice of three different vegetables and for dessert, there was a berry pie. There were two different red wines or beer served with dinner. One beer was on tap and Kip's son had brewed it. I took the beer and after the second glass, Kip told me I needed to be careful. Being so high in the mountains, it was easy to over imbibe. I thanked him for his concern. I still wanted another beer, but I declined.

As the others chatted for a while after dinner, I quietly told Callum if he had time during my stay, there was something I'd like to chat with him about. He nodded. He asked me if I had plans for the next day. I told him I didn't. "How about you and I take a couple of the horses and go up to a lake I know and do a little fly fishing?"

"That sounds great."

"We should find a few moments when you can tell me what you wanted to talk about," he said.

I agreed.

That night, I think I had the best night's sleep I'd had in several years. I remember lying down and the next thing I knew, the sun was shining through a window and it was time to get up. I stepped out onto the front deck, and down in the valley, I noticed the river was partially shrouded in a light fog. The vista was breathtaking. I thought Gates was one lucky man to see this every day.

After breakfast, Callum showed up on horseback, leading a large white horse with a black head and a black spot across the chest. He told me it would be my horse for the day. He was leading a third horse with various things strapped to it. I climbed aboard, and we were off. Now, I'm in no way a horse person, and as far as my adventures that day go, somebody who knows horses would probably tell it differently. The horse was gentle, considering its size. The animal seemed to tune in to my brain. I'd think of something I wanted and the next thing I knew, the horse was doing it. I knew Kip had brought a stallion from Australia and created this special breed. I thought the horse was very special.

We rode for about an hour until we came upon a large lake. Callum dismounted and took a box off the pack-horse. Inside the package were fishing poles. He assembled two poles, tied flies to the ends of the lines, and handed me one of them. "Follow me," he said. He mounted his horse and the two of them waded into the lake. My horse and I followed until the horse was almost chest deep in the water. Callum explained we would fish from horseback and he pointed to an area of the lake that looked a little darker than the surrounding area. "The idea is to put your fly right in the middle of the dark spot. It's deep there and the fish like to gather in the hole."

It took several tries for me to get the fly to land exactly where I wanted it, but finally, it settled perfectly where I'd aimed. With no warning, a fish came up and snatched my fly out of the air and took off. For several minutes, I was fighting a fish I was sure weighed over fifty pounds. I don't think I'd ever had a fish with so much fight on my line before. Finally, I got the fish close enough so Callum could net the thing. It stunned me to see how small it was. I wondered how a fish that size could put up such a fight.

For the next two hours, we sat on our horses, casting our lines into the lake and, from time to time, reeling in a fish. Since it was all catch and release, I didn't feel bad about seeing how many fish I could catch. At one point, Callum looked over at me and asked, "Are you getting hungry yet?"

I realized breakfast had been a long time ago, and I really was hungry. "Now you mention it, yeah. I'm starved."

Callum took my pole and disassembled it, then tied it back up on the packhorse. "Follow me," he instructed. We rode for about fifteen minutes up what appeared to be a trail worn into the grass. Rounding a bend in the trail, the vista before me made me rein in my horse and just sit there, dumbfounded. I was looking across a large bowl formed by a ring of mountains and in the valley below, I could see the river wandering along. The sight was spectacular. Looking ahead next to the trail, I noticed a tent set up on a wooden floor. Callum pointed at the tent. "That's where we get lunch."

We rode up to the tent and dismounted. When I moved, it was painfully obvious I'd been on a horse for several hours. My butt and my thighs were sore and the first couple of steps were more of a stagger than a walk. Callum laughed at me. I saw nothing funny. It hurt to move.

A young woman came out of the tent and invited us to sit. She served us our meal. Lunch was fabulous. I don't know if the food was really that good, or if it was a combination of fresh air, hours fishing, and time spent in the saddle, but I gobbled my lunch like I hadn't eaten for days. It was all I could do not to lick my plate. When we finished, Callum leaned back in his camp chair and looked at me for a while. "You know we didn't just come here to fish. You told me last night there was something you wanted to talk to me about. What did you want to discuss?"

"Callum, this is difficult. I don't know you well enough to just blurt things out, but because of the delicate nature of things, I guess being direct is the best way to go about it."

"Well, you have my attention now. What's up?"

"Let me start by telling you I've met your father, Elwood."

"Really? Where?"

"I went to the university to see him and the woman in the main office I talked to didn't know what happened to your father. She knew he retired, but that was all. The lady thought a professor named Dr. Audrey Billings might know where Dr. Bickerstaff was nowadays. Did you know Dr. Billings, she was a professor who worked with your father?"

"I know Audrey. I adore her, but Father isn't impressed by her. I think because she sees through his bullshit, and that bothers him."

"From some of her comments, I'd agree. I thoroughly enjoyed meeting the woman. Anyway, she told me where to find your dad and I went out and saw him. During our conversation, he told me you were aware you're adopted."

"Humm, that's not something Father shares with many people. Why would he tell you that? Who are you?"

"Allow me to tell you a story to answer your question."

"Fine."

"Several years ago, there was a young woman who was attending the university. Most people would consider this woman a free spirit, especially when it came to sexual matters. She had her own ideas of how to live life. She was ah…"

Callum interrupted, "She slept around? She enjoyed sex?"

"Well put. Yes. She had a steady boyfriend, but she also had a number of lovers. She ended up pregnant. Her problem then was she wasn't sure who the father might be.

She told one guy she'd slept with that he was the father, but he was aware she was promiscuous, and he told her it wasn't possible for him to be the father."

"Why didn't she have a DNA test done?"

"This was 1977. DNA testing was a new science, very expensive, and it took a long time to get results."

"Oh. So, what happened then?"

"Even though the fellow maintained it wasn't his child, he gave her money for an abortion, but she couldn't go through with it."

"If this story is going where I think it is, I'm glad she didn't. I assume you're talking about my birth mother?"

"Yes. However, the gentleman who gave your ahh… birth mother the money for the abortion asked me to see if I could find you."

"Why?"

"Well, I will ask the rest of this conversation go no further than between us for the time being. This is very important. I should get a signed legal paper from you that prohibits you from discussing this, but if you tell me you won't discuss this with anyone, that's good enough for me. I trust you."

"You have my curiosity piqued now. But I won't tell anyone about our conversation."

"One gentleman who was sleeping with your birth mother was Washington State Senator Albert Bradson. Obviously, he wasn't a senator when he and your birth mother were having their affair."

"I've heard of him, but I know little about him. Living out here, I really don't care for politics and stuff like that. One reason I became partners with Kip was to get away from things like that. I like this life. It's simple and makes for a good life."

"I can see why. Anyway, to finish with the story, they have approached Senator Bradson to run for President of the United States."

Callum blurted out, "You're kidding. Really?"

"No, I'm not kidding. He doesn't think the fling he had back in college would ever get out and bite him on the ass down the road, but he wanted to be sure. My purpose for meeting with you is twofold. I've recently spoken with your birth mother and she would be interested in meeting you, but only if you were interested as well, and I was wondering if you'd allow me to take a DNA sample and see if the senator might be your father."

Callum sat for a long time, looking out across the valley. Without looking at me, he spoke. "When Father told me about the adoption, I thought I'd like to meet my birth mother, but then over time, I got angry she'd given me up. How can a mother give up her child? She didn't even love me enough to raise me?"

"May I say something?"

Callum nodded.

"Your mother was in school. She had no employable skills that would provide her with sufficient income to raise you properly. She could barely afford to care for herself. She loved you so much, she wanted the best possible life for you. She wanted you to have a good life, and she gave you to people who could give you that good life, a good education, and help you succeed in life. She loved you so much, she sacrificed her happiness for yours."

"I see your point. But I still don't know if I want to meet her or not. You say she wants to meet me?"

"Yes, on the condition that you want to meet her too. I'll never tell her where you are. I got this information from your father, who is very proud of you. Anyway, it's totally up to you. Your decision and you can tell me if you want her information."

"What's her name?"

"Linda Ferrara."

"How do you spell that?"

I told him then asked, "How do you feel about providing me with a DNA sample?"

"I guess that's okay. What do I have to do?"

"Back at the ranch, I have a kit that has a swab in it. I take salvia from your cheek, put it in a bottle and send it to the lab. The lab has a sample from the Senator and once they have your sample, in six to eight weeks, we'll have the report and know for sure."

"Will you tell me?"

"Of course. I'll make sure they send a copy of the report to you."

"Thank you."

"If the results come back positive, do you want to meet the senator?"

"Wow. I don't know. From what you've told me, he sounds like a stand-up kind of guy. I really need to think about this. I don't know what to do about either of them."

"I'm sorry to complicate your life."

"No! Please don't feel that way. I am glad to know everything you've told me. But meeting them is a totally different issue."

We helped clean up the camp and headed back. Once we were back at the ranch, Callum gave a DNA sample then took the horses and left. As we shook hands, he thanked me again for coming out and finding him. "I know how to get in touch with you. I'll let you know what I decide."

The rest of my stay at River's Bend was delightful, and when the time came for Kip to take me back to the airport, I hated to leave. I'd told Leslie a bit about Lois and before I left the ranch, she found me and shook my hand. "Please come back sometime. And make sure you bring Lois with you. I'd love to meet her. She sounds like quite a lady."

"She is, and I'll be sure we get back here someday."

Standing in front of the terminal, I told Kip, "I didn't know what to expect when I came to visit you, but I have to tell you, I've had one of the best times of my life. I'll never forget this. Actually, I have a dear friend from the service, and I know he'd love to fly fish from the back of a horse. I'll tell him all about my trip and I'm betting we'll be back."

"You're always welcome Matt. Bring Lois next time. I hope your conversation with Callum turned out okay."

"It did, I'm just concerned about him. I laid a lot of new information on him about his past. Watch him. I think he may need a friend right now."

"Will do. You take care now."

I extended my hand, but he pushed it aside and wrapped his arms around me. "Come back and see us some time."

"Done!"

Walking out to the tarmac, I found Henry standing in front of the plane. I climbed on board and settled into a chair in the cabin. Henry could tell I had a lot on my mind. I wasn't being anti-social; I didn't know how I'd feel about what I'd shared with Callum. I had no idea how I'd react if somebody showed up one day and told me everything I'd just told him.

Once I got back to Seattle, I sent in the DNA kit. I had dinner with Mouse and Albert to cover the past few days. We decided on eating at one of my favorite places, Hanney's Hideaway. Hanney's is a throwback to a lost era. The restaurant looks like something out of the fifties. A true chophouse with thick, char-boiled steaks, fluffy baked potatoes with all the fixens, and a salad prepared at your table. White table clothes, candles and intimate lighting gives the place a feeling you don't find anymore. As you have your dinner, you keep looking over at the door expecting to see Frank, Dino, and Sammy with the rest of the Rat Pack come strolling in. Needless to say, I love the place.

I gave my report to Mouse and Albert, finishing with, "Now we have to wait for the DNA report. I don't know if Callum wants to see his birth mother. I told him to get in touch with me if he was interested and I'd give him her address where he can contact her. Until we get the results back from the test, I didn't think there was any reason for either of you two to contact him. Are the two of you satisfied with way things are?"

Albert sat quietly as Mouse responded. "Thanks Matt. As always, you've done a fantastic job. All we can do now is wait. If Callum decides to see his mother, will you let me know?"

"Yes. Albert, I'll let you decide what you want to share with Mouse." I paused a moment, "Albert, have you decided about running for office or not?"

"Maggie and I are still talking about it. I know it will be tough on her, and me too, but if it will cost me a marriage, then running for office isn't something I'm interested in pursuing. I thank you for the information on Callum. Sometimes, I feel you are a far better friend than me. I owe you for this one."

"Not really. It's what friends do. I'm just as curious as you regarding the results of the DNA test. As for Callum seeing his mother, I hope he does the best thing for him. I thought he was a very nice man." The two men nodded in agreement.

"So, if there's nothing else, I have a motorcycle I need to say farewell to."

Mouse smiled at me. "Go, but please be very careful. I also need for you to let me know how you want to handle the condo. It's yours. I can either sell it to you or lease it to you. I'm just pleased to have you for a neighbor."

After dinner, as we said our goodbyes in the parking lot, I mentioned, "If either one of you ever want an experience of a lifetime, I've just returned from one. You have not lived until you spend a few days with a gentleman I met named Kip Gates. He has a ranch and an outfitting company. He takes you on horseback into the backcountry, up into the mountains of Northwest Colorado. I rode horses until I could hardly walk, and I even got to fly fish from the back of one. I've never had such a good time. You both need to go sometime. Let me know and I'll get in touch with Kip. Let me tell you, there is one interesting dude. Okay, I'm out of here."

I got into my vehicle and sat for a moment before starting the motor. I could think of nothing else I had to do. I was free to start my farewell motorcycle trip. I can promise you I was planning on making it a good one.

I returned to my apartment and packed. The next morning, I closed my place, set the burglar alarm and headed down to the bike.

As I got to the bike, I thought, "Open road, look out— here I come…"

CHAPTER SIXTEEN

I savored the moment as I pulled on my helmet. This was my last road trip on a motorcycle and I was making sure I relished every second. I knew there would be times later in my life I would relive this trip and I wanted to sear every memory into my brain.

I reached down and moved the switch on the gas tank over to Start. Moving the kickstand up with my foot, I touched the starter, and thought how much I'd wanted this road trip. I planned it for a long time and the memories would last a lifetime. One of my poker buddies was killed while riding his bike, and I'd heard so many horror stories about people getting killed on their motorcycles, even when they were totally in the right, I knew it was time to sell. I know when I ride, I'm always aware of what's happening around me and I feel I ride safe, but there is always the freak accident and the older one gets, if you get hurt, the longer it takes to heal… provided you're still alive.

One part of riding I dislike is meeting someone new, and once I mention I ride a motorcycle, they feel it is their duty to tell you all the dreadful stories they know about people getting killed on bikes. Hey, news flash here, I know riding is dangerous. I don't need to be scared into giving up my bike. I will sell! Now, please shut up and let me get on with my ride... thank you!

I'd blocked out the next few weeks on my schedule with no particular place to be. I'd heard from Elora and Ramiro Tronscoso and told them I wanted to take part in their venture and I'd finance the floor for them. I called my bank and explained to them what was going on and told them that whenever the Tronscosos needed a draw, they were to give it to them.

With every detail I could think of taken care of, it was time for me and the open road. It was time to say my farewells to what had been a major part of my life. I'd been riding since I was fourteen and so far, I'd never had an accident. I always thought I'd never grow up... I sure hope this doesn't count!

I've discovered so many important things happen in our lives because of a simple matter of a choice made somewhere along the line. Like, back in our school days, it might have been the choice of going to class or skipping out for the day. It seems that those who chose the latter found themselves at the bottom end of the employment ladder, but it was a matter of choice. Their choice. The outcome of those choices might have resulted in a good quality of life or not. Had they gone to class, they might have learned enough to get a better job, or even be able to stay employed. As time passed, what was seen as an unimportant choice turned out to be a fairly major choice. One never has the chance to go back and change the decisions made without thought to the consequences. There are no do-overs in life.

Or sometimes the choice can be as simple as either taking the freeway or wandering down back roads and still ending up at the same destination, except I'd have more of my sanity by taking the back roads. So for me, that was how things turned out.

It was a splendid day, just the right temperature and with amazing blue skies. I'd fueled up the bike, purchased two large bottles of water, and I was ready to ride. I headed back towards the freeway and when I arrived at the junction, I found myself faced with a choice. One way was down the 'on ramp' and onto the freeway, or the other way which wandered through the countryside. I'd still end up where I wanted to be at the end of the day. I decided I'd seen enough endless concrete ribbons and because I was in no rush to be anywhere, I turned towards the long way to my destination. Some people refer to it as a secondary road and many maps show it as the blue road, but it's still the back way.

Once headed down the small blacktopped road, I kicked back and put my feet up on the high pegs and relaxed. Feeling the wind in my face, I knew I had a grin from ear to ear. The gas tank was full, there was no schedule to keep, it wasn't raining and looked to stay that way... Could things get any better?

I'd been riding for about twenty minutes when I realized I hadn't seen a single house, barn or any sign of civilization since I had turned onto this back road. It didn't worry me, though. According to the map, the road would eventually take me where I wanted to be. Up ahead, I saw a figure walking down the side of the road headed in my direction. The closer I got to the person on foot, the better I could see her. She was limping, badly. I passed by slowly on the far left and when I looked over, I realized one reason why she was limping: she wasn't wearing any shoes.

The woman's shorts came below the cheeks of what looked like a well-shaped, mature bottom, and her top struggled to hold her generous breasts in check. Her body was mature but looked well kept. The way she dressed and limped, I got the feeling she wasn't out there by choice. My guess was she'd been walking for a long time.

It bothered me to find somebody out here in the boonies on foot and limping badly. I pulled over then turned around. When I was beside her, I stopped and since I had seen no traffic since I started down this road, I suspected I was safe to turn off the motor. I could see her face was dirty and even though she kept her head down, I noticed she'd been crying because of the streaks her tears left behind. From the look of the body and what I could see of her face, I judged her to be somewhere in her forties. She seemed attractive, but being as hot and sweaty as she was, and with dirt covering her long, insect bitten legs, arms, and face, it was difficult to guess how she really looked.

She lifted her head a little and her streaked blond hair covered a lot of her face. She peered out at me with what I thought was a fearful look. I gave her my best boyish smile. "Hi. My name is Matt. May I offer you a lift?"

She mumbled something, and I noticed she had dried blood on one cheek and on the side of her mouth and chin. Through her hair, I could see her left eye was swollen almost shut and was changing color. When I saw what her face looked like, I blurted out, "Were you in an accident? Are you okay?"

She bowed her head and mumbled something. I told her I didn't hear her what she said and asked her to repeat it. A little louder, she replied, "Yes, I'm okay. No, I didn't have an accident. Thanks, but no, I don't need a lift." She lifted her head slightly and peered at me from behind her bangs. "Look, mister, it's best you keep going."

I pointed at her feet and commented, "You aren't going to get much further like that. Please let me give you a lift… at least to the next gas station or something."

She looked at me for a moment then looked ahead as she continued walking. I turned my bike around and used my feet to paddle my bike along, trying to keep abreast of her. She glanced over at me and because she wasn't looking down, she stepped on a rock and her ankle rolled. She fell to the pavement, and I quickly pushed the kickstand down on the bike and moved to her side.

Tears were flowing again down her cheeks and I could tell she was in pain. I picked her up and, as I helped move her to the side of the road, I explained that I wanted to get her off the highway in case a car came along. I placed her on a soft mound of grass and returned to my bike to move it out of the way.

I returned and knelt beside her. She looked up at me and I noticed her eyes were an interesting green color. Or I should say her eye, since now I could see how badly swollen one eye was. She was still crying but not as hard as when I had picked her up and moved her.

"Look, what are you going to do? You can't walk on that ankle or that foot. Please let me give you a lift." I could see she was trying to decide if she wanted to go with me or not and I waited. I tried again. "At least let me give you a lift to the next settlement or general store. You can't stay out here like this."

Finally, she spoke. It was still more of a mumble because of her damaged mouth, though. "Please, mister, I don't need any more trouble. You look like a nice guy and I don't want you to get hurt. You really need to keep going."

Even though she believed she probably was telling me the truth, I hated to see her stranded out in the middle of nowhere. There was no way I would leave her there. I put on my best, disarming smile and said, "There is no way I'm gonna leave you out here in the middle of nowhere. 'Sides, who's going to hurt me? You?"

That got me a little grin, and she quickly put her hand to her mouth. "Ouch! It hurts when I smile."

"What happened?"

"It's part of the reason you need to keep going." She looked down at the ground.

I'm not really that macho, but you know I'm not defenseless either. Looking at this beat up woman had riled my anger, and I wanted to protect her if I could. With slightly more macho than I was feeling, I responded, "I'm a big boy. I can take care of myself. I can see you need help and from the way you look, I guess there might be a little danger involved. Since you're stuck out here in the middle of nowhere, I'm willing to take that chance." I paused then lowered my voice a little. "Let me give you a ride... please?"

She looked at me and I knew she was seeing the silver hair and was probably trying to decide if I was a safe old man. "You don't understand. You could get really hurt by helping me."

I should have fired the old hog up and rode off. But you know me, I ain't wired that way. This wasn't something I could ride away from and go to sleep tonight. "And you don't understand," I countered. "You think you are looking at some helpless old dude. Miss, I've been to a lot of scary places in my life and I'm not as defenseless as you may think. You need help. It's plain to see you're not able to go on by yourself. You must admit, you really need help. Now, please let me help you. Okay?"

The nod of her head was almost imperceptible. I reached down and helped her limp to the bike. I picked her up as best I could then carefully set her down on the passenger seat. After she was comfortable, I opened one saddlebag and rummaged around until I found an old pair of Crocs I had. I pulled them out and asked her to hold out one of her feet. I explained, "Here, I need to put these on you. I can't have you riding without some foot protection. These aren't the best, but they're better than nothing."

She let me put the shoes on her and she could see how her feet were swimming in them. Finally, when she looked at me, once more I saw a brief touch of the cute grin and again she quickly put her hand to her mouth, grimacing in pain.

"What happened?" I asked as I pointed towards her lip.

"A disagreement… I told him I was leaving, he disagreed."

"And you're concerned he might find you with me and try to make things difficult for me?"

She nodded. "Yeah… in fact, for both of us. He's mean, and you don't say no to Jerry. He's put men in the hospital from fights in the past. You might say Jerry is kind of a law unto himself around here."

"Jerry? That's your old boyfriend's name?" I asked.

She shook her head. "Soon to be ex-husband if I ever get away," she mumbled.

Before I got on the bike, I found an old shirt in one saddlebag and I helped her slip it on. I noticed her wince as she lifted one of her arms. I keep a spare bucket in my saddlebag and I pulled it out. As I clipped the strap around her chin, I got a good look at her face. There were other signs besides the black eye that someone had beaten her. After my last adventure in the Middle East, I was a real expert on getting beat up. I wanted to ask her about it, but I thought it might be too soon to pry.

As I slipped my leg over the tank, I asked her if she'd ever ridden on a motorcycle. There are certain things you do not do as a passenger, and I wanted to make sure she understood what those things were. On the off chance she didn't understand what I wanted, I warned her about taking her feet off the pegs because her shoes were loose on her feet. Again, the movement of her head was almost undetectable, but at least I knew she had been on a bike before and understood what I'd told her.

I fired the ol' beast up. "Are you ready?" She motioned she was ready and her arms gently wrapped around my body.

And we headed off.

Have you ever noticed I tend to collect people?

And usually of the female variety?

I turned my head and spoke to her over my shoulder. "I told you my name was Matt. What's yours?"

Her voice was soft, and I had to strain to hear her over the wind. "My name is Heather, but my friends call me Skip."

"What did Jerry call you?"

"Depends if he was mad at me or not. When he was mad, it was bitch or fatty or something crude. Otherwise, it's Skip."

"I'm pleased to meet you, Heather. I refuse to call you Skip." We rode for a while and I called back over my shoulder, "How long have you been with your husband?"

"A little over four years. Why, ya writing a book or something?" There was a period of silence then I felt her forehead against my back. When she lifted her head, I heard her say, "I'm sorry, that was shitty on my part. That's not the attitude I should have after you've been so sweet. It's been a long time since a guy treated me with any respect. Jerry has been telling me what a fat ol' pig I am for so long, I'm not used to a man being nice. Usually, if a guy is nice, he's trying to hit on me and Jerry sets them straight. I know you were concerned about me." We rode for a few minutes before I heard her say, "Forgive me, please."

I called back over my shoulder, "Look, Heather, I don't care what the deal is, or who you are. I understand things haven't been going well for you lately. I can appreciate why you want to get away from Jerry because I have a problem with any guy who thumps on a woman. Am I correct in assuming this was not the first time he hit you?" I felt her nod her head against my back. "Where were you going when you took off?"

"Dunno."

"Any place you can go?"

"Naw, parents are both dead. No brothers or sisters. I was running away. I have no place to go." Heather was still for a while and I had to strain to hear her over the noise of the passing wind when she spoke, "This wasn't planned. It got to the point where I'd had enough. He hit me hard enough this time I passed out. When I woke up, I found myself on the floor and he was gone. I decided I'd had enough, so I took off. I don't know how far I got before I realized I forgot to put on shoes. But I sure as hell wasn't going back for them."

As I rode along, I wondered what I had gotten myself into. I didn't seek this bird out, and the last thing I wanted to do was try to take on any of her problems. But because I'd stopped and picked her up, now she was a part of my life and I couldn't walk off and leave her. Could I? When am I going to learn to stay out of other people's business?

We rode along for about half an hour when we burst out of the trees and came into a large clearing. Set back well off the road was a large rundown building which had a flashing neon sign on top that said Bar. Surrounding the building was a massive dirt parking lot. I was thirsty, and I wanted to stretch my legs. I pulled into the lot and stopped under a tree at the back of the unpaved lot. I held the bike steady for Heather as she climbed off. Once she was off, I pushed down the kickstand. Standing next to her, I noticed I was only a little taller than her. I'm two inches over six feet and she must have been about four inches shorter.

I asked her to please wait by the bike for a moment and I went off in search of the men's room. I found it and pulled off several sheets of paper towels from a dispenser and soaked several of them. I took them back to Heather, and offered her the wet ones first. "I thought you might like to clean up before we go in." I didn't want to tell her it concerned me somebody in the bar might think I was the one who gave her the fat lip.

She adjusted one of my mirrors so she could see herself then carefully placed the wet towel against her lip and held it there. When the towel first touched her face, she winced in pain. She tried to wipe as much of the dried blood as she could but missed few places. I held out my hand and asked, "May I?"

She held out the wet towel and looked up at me. As carefully as I could, I wiped at her face, removing as much of the blood as possible. She flinched occasionally, but she was a real trooper and let me clean up her face the best that was possible considering where we were.

There was nothing I could do about her eye. Time would have to heal that with no help from me. Aside from the cuts and bruises, I thought she was an attractive woman. I thought Jerry was stupid to mess this cute gal up so badly. I'll admit until you have lived with somebody, you never really know what they're like; but so far, this lady had been sweet and hadn't complained while I tried to clean her up. Finally, I looked at her and deemed she was cleaned up as well as I was able to do with a couple of paper towels. "There, it looks better. I really need a warm washcloth to do a better job."

I got a little smile along with a slight grimace as she murmured, "Thanks."

We walked into the bar and as I looked around, I noticed it was nothing out of the ordinary. Just a country watering hole out in the middle of nowhere. There were posters promoting upcoming bands and at the far end of the room was a bandstand with cyclone fencing surrounding it to protect the band from flying beer bottles. In the middle of the place was a large dance floor, with chairs and tables surrounding it. One side of the room had a slightly raised floor with tables and booths. Across the back of the bar were several pool tables and two of them were being used. I'd seen a lot of bars like this out in the sticks over the years and there was a certain sameness to them.

I noticed they had a basic menu, and I asked Heather if she'd like something to eat. I first got a slight nod then she shook her head no. I asked her which one she meant, and she mumbled, "I haven't got any money."

"How about you let it be my treat?" I asked.

She shook her head, and I had to lean close to hear her reply. "You've been nice enough already. I really shouldn't."

"Please let me feed you. Look at it this way. I picked you up, now I have to feed you. It's called the rules of the road."

She looked at me with her good eye as she shook her head. "That doesn't make any sense." Then she bowed her head and even though her head hung down, I heard her admit she was hungry. We both ordered hamburgers, and she asked for a beer and I had a soda. You know I won't drink or smoke weed or anything and ride… not even a beer. There had been one time I broke that rule, and it was when I was finally rid of two guys who thought I knew where a bunch of gold was hidden. There were a lot of reasons that night I smoked a little. Basically, the rule is for my safety. I couldn't care less about the other guy. Did you buy that? Yeah, I know. I care about the other guy too.

Heather excused herself to go to the ladies' room and see if she could repair any more of the damage. When she returned, the food had arrived. The burgers were good, considering where we were. We were finishing our meals when four men strolled in through the main door. Heather's eye got wide when she saw them, and she quickly tried to duck her head behind me. Obviously, she knew the four men, and I was curious. I looked each of them over carefully. The man standing in front of the group was larger than the other three. He was both taller and a lot heavier built and the way the others held back, I knew he was the alpha male of this motley crew.

I looked over my shoulder where Heather was trying to hide and I asked, "Is that Jerry?"

She nodded slightly. Jerry had long dirty brown hair sticking out from a baseball hat which he wore backward. He was graying at the temples, and gray stubble covered his greasy face. I thought his weak, dark brown eyes were set too close together and his heavily stained two front teeth protruded so much, his mouth didn't close properly. The overall effect made him look like a mean, retarded rodent.

He had a good-sized beer gut hanging over a large belt buckle and the sleeves of his shirt were gone, showing what at one time had been muscular arms but now were just large and heavily tattooed. Nevertheless, there was still a presence about the man. He seemed to exude an animal quality I couldn't identify. If I were a woman, I know I wouldn't be attracted to him, but I could see where some women might be interested. As far as I was concerned, I knew at first glance this fellow and I had nothing in common. When he spotted Heather trying to hide behind me, he came barreling over to the two of us.

Considering his size, his voice was rather high-pitched and very whiney. "What are you doing here, fat pig? I never gave you permission to leave the house. Get outta here and go wait in the truck." His attention now turned to me as he asked, "What are you doing here with my wife? You want me to kick the shit out of you, old man?"

There was no doubt this was Jerry. Normally, I wouldn't interfere, but I'd seen firsthand the effects of the beating Jerry had given Heather, and if I had any say in the matter, it was something that wouldn't happen again. I looked up at him and in the coldest tone of voice I could muster, I told him, "Jerry, you need to go away. Leave us alone. Heather and I are having lunch."

He looked at me with a stupid vacant expression on his face. "Who's Heather?"

I couldn't help myself and I snorted. "Heather is the lady I'm having lunch with. Now, you're bothering us. Go away, son. You're upsetting us."

I could see he wasn't used to being spoken to in the tone of voice I'd used. He stared at me for a moment and asked, "Hey, grandpa, the home know you're missing?" He looked at his friends who were chuckling at his little joke. I guess he assumed because my hair was speckled with silver, I was an old man.

I leaned back as I looked up at him. "Boy, you make me sad when you talk like that. Now go away so I won't have to hurt you."

I knew for sure nobody had ever spoken to him like that before. "What did you say, dick weed?"

Still looking at up him, I asked, "What's the matter, Bubba, are you hard of hearing and retarded?" I raised my voice to almost a shout. "I said for you to go away and leave us alone. You bother me. Did you hear me this time? Now go away," I paused before I said the next word, "boy!"

Jerry made a stupid move and reached out to grab me. I surprised him by using his forward momentum, grabbing his wrist, and yanking him towards me. As he fell onto the table, I slipped out of my seat and brought my elbow down with as much force as possible on his back, right over a kidney. I stood and moved away from him and heard him grunt and moan. One of the other three men took a step towards me and I pointed and looked at him. "Stay!" I commanded.

By now, Heather's husband had pushed himself off the table and slowly turned to face me, slightly bent from my hit. "Asswipe..." he growled at me, "that was the biggest mistake you ever made. I hope you have a wallet with your address in it so we know where to ship your dead body."

This clown's crap tired me out. "Bubba, I'm giving you one chance to take your sweethearts and leave." I motioned towards his three buddies. "If you don't leave now, I'll assume you wish to do me bodily harm and I will defend myself. I have warned you and if you continue, you are doing so at your own risk."

Jerry turned to his friends and in a little boy's voice, said, "Did you hear? We've been warned." As he turned back, I was prepared for what I knew would be his next move. He thought he was being sneaky, and he was so used to grabbing his opponent and hitting them with his massive fists, he had no other plans.

I watched one of his shoulders drop as he turned and prepared to swing at me. Once the shoulder dropped, I'd already started my move, and I quickly lashed out with my right boot at his kneecap. His knee bent backwards with a snapping sound when I connected. Jerry dropped to the floor like a fallen tree, screaming all the way down.

He lay on the floor, rocking back and forth on his back, holding his damaged knee amongst the litter, old cigarette butts and discarded peanut shells. I stepped up to him and stomped once on his chest as hard as I could. Jerry lay there gasping for air and I turned to face the other three. "Stay!" I told them. "And you too, Jerry."

One of the three ignored me and pulled out a knife, dropping into what he must have thought was a fighting stance. I chuckled. You know what I did over in Nam and, as they say, "I've seen the world." I've done some interesting things for the military and learned a lot of nasty things I can do to people who wish to mess with me. I'm not trying to sound conceited or like a tough guy, it's just I've had to fight men for other reasons than stupid male vanity in a backwater bar. These three were laughable in their stance, their attitude and the look in their eyes. They were all talk, and it was plain to see they didn't understand how to walk the walk. This one didn't even know how to properly hold a knife in a fight.

The fellow with the knife lunged at me and I stepped past him as I pulled on his arm. One of my feet seemed to get in his way as I pulled him past me and he found himself on his hands and knees on the floor. The knife was gone, and he now had a sore arm and two scuffed knees. I stepped up behind him and kicked him soundly between the legs, causing him to scream as he somersaulted forward. The other two put up their hands and backed away. Both kept repeating it wasn't their fight, and they were leaving.

I noticed Jerry had rolled over and was now trying to push his way off the floor. I kicked one of his arms away and after he crashed back down to the floor, I kicked him in the side. I know, I'm not a nice person sometimes. "Hey, stupid, you really have a hard time hearing. I told you to stay."

I saw the front doors darken, and I watched two county sheriffs come striding through the swinging doors, stopping just inside the room. Standing side by side in the doorway, they looked like two hanging sides of beef. Both were large and looked fit in their well-tailored uniforms. They reminded me of Sargent Polk, except Polk had a look of intelligence about him that these two lacked.

They continued to stand shoulder to shoulder in the doorway, leather belts all shined and wearing matching Canadian style Mountie hats as they slowly scanned the room. They glanced down at the two men lying on the floor and one county-mountie finally looked over towards the bar and hollered, "Harvey!" He paused, then in an even louder voice, he yelled, "Harvey! Where the hell are you? Get your scrawny ass out here and tell us what happened!"

For the first time since the fight had started, I noticed somebody back behind the bar with a baseball bat in his hands. Because the man with the baseball bat answered the sheriff's question, I assumed this was Harvey. When Harvey answered the sheriff's questions, I noticed he was lacking several of his teeth. The absence of his two front teeth especially made him lisp.

Harvey explained to the two sheriffs, "Thisss older feller and the gal came in and were having a burger. Thisss one," Harvey motioned towards Heather's husband lying on the floor, "came in here and ssstarted the fight. Called the woman a lot of vulgar sssstuff and then tried to hit the older dude. Damn, you should have sssseen it. This older dude beat the crap out of ol' Jerry." I was getting a little tired of being referred to as "the older dude."

Harvey continued, "I called ya'll asss ssssoon asss I could ssssee what wasss gonna happen. The other guy there on the floor pulled a knife. He lossst it durin' the fight. Anyway, the other two were jussst leaving," Harvey pointed at Jerry's two buddies who were still standing. "And the gal and the old man alssso need to leave."

I didn't know what relationship ol' Harvey had with the sheriffs, but I could plainly see he wanted me to leave... and now. He was providing me with the opportunity to go without any more problems with the law. I pulled two twenties from my pocket and dropped them on the table and thanked Harvey for two good burgers.

Heather's husband was trying to get up again and one sheriff told him to lie back down, or there would be more trouble. The large man dropped back to the floor. Walking past ol' Jerry, I drew back one of my boots and, looking at both sheriffs, I kicked Jerry in the ribs the same place I'd kicked him before, as hard as I could.

"Damn," I said to the sheriffs, "looks like I stumbled." One sheriff started to move towards me. I held up my hand. "Stop!" I commanded. I turned Heather to face the sheriffs then reached over and carefully lifted her hair off her face. They could see the one eye that was swollen shut, and how her cheek was a dark purple, and that she had a very noticeable fat lip. I pointed at Jerry lying on the ground, nodding my head to signify it was Jerry who had beaten her up.

Both sheriff's eyes grew wide and one of them seemed to pucker his lips in disgust. I continued to point at ol' Jerry as I explained to the cops, "This is some of Bubba's handiwork and it isn't the first time he's done this. So far, Heather will not press charges. However, if you want to push this any further either, she may change her mind. That will take you two a long time to sort out. You don't really want to do that, do you?" Both sheriffs shook their heads. "Good. We're leaving, and Heather will file for divorce as soon as she finds a lawyer. You need to thank her since she saved you a lot of paperwork. Am I correct?" Both nodded in agreement.

I turned, took Heather by the hand, and walked towards the door. As we passed by Jerry again, I stepped firmly on the fingers of one hand, rocking back and forth with my boot. I thought I heard a crack as Jerry cried out. He looked up at me, hate smoldering in his eyes. I stood with my boot still on the back of his hand and stared down at him. "That's for busting up the lady. And, so you know, she won't be back."

I continued to look down at him on the floor. "Oh, one other thing, if I ever see you again, I'll give you a lot more than a busted rib, a fat lip, a ruined hand and a messed-up knee. You disgust me!" I slipped my arm around Heather and as we approached the door, the two sheriffs stepped aside and let us walk out of the bar. One sheriff lifted his hand to the rim of his hat as we passed and nodded at Heather. "Ma'am," he said.

I helped Heather climb up on the back of the bike then I swung my leg over the tank. The bike came to life as soon as I touched the start button and we began slowly riding across the parking lot. I noticed both sheriffs now standing on the porch of the saloon, watching me as I pulled up to the main road. I bowed my head towards them and they nodded back. I stopped at the road hoping they would see the gold 'V' on my license plate signaling I was a military veteran. I know police looked favorably on veterans. I slipped out onto the asphalt and sped away. I was willing to bet that wasn't the first time the two officers had been summoned to that saloon to deal with a problem.

After we had gone a short distance away from the parking lot, I became aware Heather was laughing. I looked over my shoulder and called back, "What's so funny?"

She leaned forward and spoke into my ear. "The way you dropped Jerry! I swear, nobody has ever kicked the shit out of him like you did. Where the hell did you learn to fight like that?"

"It's a long story. I'll tell you later."

After we had gone a mile or two, I noticed Heather had settled against my back and I could feel her womanly shape against me. My mind wandered, and I recalled how sexy I thought she looked, and she felt great against my back. She reminded me how lonely I was feeling without Lois. We rode in silence for several minutes and finally, I looked back over my shoulder and asked. "Is there a place I can take you?" She greeted my question with silence.

We continued to ride in silence until finally, I noticed a small country park ahead. I pulled into the park and stopped next to a picnic table. Heather slipped off the bike and I put down the kickstand. When I was off the bike, I had her sit on the top of the table. Heather looked up at me and asked, "How come we stopped?"

"Heather, I don't want to assume anything here. You have had enough shit to deal with to last a long time and the last thing I want to do is make things difficult for you. It would appear you are rid of Bubba. You are free to get your divorce. You get to choose what you want now. I can take you to an airport or a train station and I'll get you a ticket to wherever you want to go. Tell me, what would you like to do?"

From the look on her face, I could tell she was still trying to process the idea she was finally out of her abusive relationship. I continued, "I asked you before if you wanted to go anywhere and I didn't get an answer. I don't want to be a pest, but I believe we need to come to some a decision. Do you have someplace to go?" She shook her head. "How about parents?" She shook her head again, and I remembered she'd told me before they were dead.

I was still. I had a thought, but I wondered if she was ready for my suggestion. I thought about the next move. "Okay, I'll make an offer. There is nothing expected from you and you don't have to do a thing. But would you like to stay with me for a while?" I motioned towards the bike. "I'm on a small trip. I'm working on trying to figure out where I want a relationship to go with somebody I care about. When I get back, I plan on selling the bike. I have no plans but if you would like to tag along while you sort things out, you're welcome to come. Would you like that?" This time I got a small nod from her. "Can we talk more about this a little later?" I asked.

Tears had flowed down her face and her chin was quivering. It was difficult to hear her words through her crying. "I've been so afraid for so long. I had no money and Jerry made sure I never had any. He kept beatin' me up." She sobbed and hiccupped. It was still difficult to hear her as she continued. "I wanted to leave. Oh, god, I wanted to leave so bad. But I couldn't. Finally," she motioned towards her face, "finally I'd had enough. This time, when he hit me, I didn't even remember falling down. When I woke up, the house was dark. I was cold and in so much pain. I decided right then I was leaving no matter what, since Jerry wasn't there."

I stood there in the little park, wishing I could go back and kick the shit out of Jerry all over again. What is it with men like Jerry? Why did they do things like they did to the women in their lives? What did they get out of being that way? It's a mystery and it sure makes me angry to see so many ladies abused like I'd seen lately.

I waited for her to finish whatever it was she wanted to tell me. I could tell she was having a difficult time digesting the idea she was free. She could—had to, in fact—decide what to do next. The idea must have been frightening. Finally, she gave a deep sigh and continued. "I ran with this," she motioned towards the clothing she had on. "You've seen I didn't even grab shoes, I was in such a rush." Heather looked me directly in the face. "I was so scared when he came into the bar… and you… and you…"

She sobbed as her shoulders moved up and down. I reached out and as she stood up, I gently pulled her against me. She burrowed against my chest and her body shook as she wept. She cried so hard, and all I could do was stand there and hold her. It surprised me to discover I had tears in my eyes and rolling down my cheeks too.

From the sounds she was making, I figured it had been a long time since she'd had a really good cry. Holding her in my arms, I also got the feeling this was the first time in a long, long time she felt safe enough to let go. I understood there was nothing I could do for her except let her cry, so I stood there holding her, rubbing her back. I tried to keep my touch as casual as I could… the last thing I wanted to do was frighten her even more.

CHAPTER SEVENTEEN

I've no idea how long we stood there with Heather crying against my chest. We stood there so long, when a park
ranger drove by, he stopped. As he backed up, he rolled down
the window to his truck and called out, "You okay ma'am?"

Heather pulled her head away enough to nod.

I smiled at the ranger and told him, "She had a bad
day. A friend of hers got badly hurt and she's feeling sorry
for him. We'll be moving on soon."

I couldn't tell if the ranger had seen her face or not,
but I could see he wasn't real wild about leaving the two of
us. Finally, he drove away, looking back in his mirror several
times before he turned the corner. She pulled her head away
from my chest as I looked down at her. A little grin pulled at
the sides of her mouth and she whispered, "Sorry. You must
think you have a fruit loop on your hands."

"No, Heather, I think what I have on my hands is a
woman who made a bad decision at one time and now wants
to see how she can undo it. If it helps, you're welcome to
come with me for as long as you want. I'll help you all I can.
How does that sound?"

She leaned her head back and looked up at me with a
look of suspicion on her face. "And what do you want in

return?" I could tell she was getting concerned about what I might be thinking.

I made a point of slowly and carefully checking her out. I released her and stepped back. I bobbed my head as I explained. "I'd be lying if I told you I didn't think you were kinda cute. I love your body type, all nice and curvy, and I can feel you curled up back there behind me and I like that. Other than the beating you show on your face, you really are eye-catching." I could see Heather was trying to grin, but it hurt her lips to smile.

"But you aren't ready for me or any other man to show you any kind of physical attention." I waited for her to show me she understood what I meant before I continued. Heather smiled, and I continued. "I think sometime in the future you might want to be with a man again, but for now, you need to work through your feelings about Jerry and perhaps men in general. You need time to heal—both physically and men-tally." Heather put her hand on my chest and I smiled at her. I added, "I don't want a thing from you. Actually, I have a friend that I'm very fond of and I'm working on deciding what I want with her. And, last but not least, looking at you makes me feel good. I want to protect you."

She was silent for a while, then her hand left my chest and she reached up and touched the side of my face. "Thanks. Thank you for not putting pressure on me. Thank you for seeing I need some time to get over what happened. Now, I'm pleased to hear even looking like shit, even being an old fat pig, I'm pleased to hear I make you feel good. I'm not saying we'll be intimate and I'm not saying we won't, but if I decided I wanna, then we will."

"Really? And I have nothing to say about this? I also have a friend that would have something to say about it. Actually, I'm not sure I'm ready to have an intimate rela-tionship with anyone other than Lois, my friend, right now."

The cute grin came and went again as she bowed her head. "Of course you do. I was trying to tell you I see you as a sexy man. I know Jerry made stupid comments about age and I don't even want to know how old you are, but there are damn few men who could do what you did to ol' Jerry back there. 'Sides, I think your friend is very lucky."

I didn't have the heart to tell her that old oaf Jerry really wasn't much of a problem. He was big and kind of stupid. His luck ran out when he ran across someone who knew how to take him down. She gave a little hiccup and continued. "I like the way you've made me feel so far. I feel safe with you, both physically and mentally, and it's been a long time since I felt that way. Is that good enough for now?"

"Like I said earlier, I have a lady friend and I'm trying to figure out where that relationship is going. She lives in D.C. and I... well, as of right now, I haven't decided where I want to live. I'm selling off a lot of my stuff. I live in Seattle, but more and more, it doesn't seem like home anymore."

"I'm grateful. Thanks for helping me escape from Jerry."

"Yeah. Come on squirt, let's ride."

"Where?"

"Well, like I said, I was making a farewell trip. I had several buddies I was planning to stop and see, and I need to get back home eventually. You're welcome to tag along as long as you want. When we get back home, if you're still with me, we can discuss what needs to happen. Okay?"

Heather smiled at me. I helped her climb onto the back of the bike and we headed off. As I rode, I couldn't help ponder how things worked out in life. I wanted to examine exactly my feelings towards Lois and I wanted to be as up front with Heather as I could be. Now, I seemed to have picked up a new challenge. And all I'd done was decided to take the back roads instead of the freeway. Along the way, I'd picked up a waif, a waif who needed to mend. I seem to have a penchant for waifs who need help. Some things in life are sure strange.

~ ~ ~ ~ ~

The first night, we stopped in a small town and she asked me if she could borrow enough money to stop at Walmart and get some clothing. I told her I had no problem loaning her some money, but I wouldn't let her shop at Walmart. When she asked me why, I explained. "Their business model is to go into a small town and run all the little businesses out of business. They want to drive all the mom and pop businesses away. Then you're left with a small town that totally depends on this big giant to provide the town with goods and jobs. In addition, they don't pay their employees enough to make a living wage and the employees have to get food stamps, get subsidized housing and seek free medical.

"Did you know that each Walmart costs the community where they are located over a million dollars a year in burdens on their welfare system? You have a bunch of businesses gone that used to pay taxes and therefore a community that has lost its tax base. Businesses that have been in town for decades and the town has to come up with more in taxes to support the employees who work for Walmart. I refuse to shop there. I know my little amount of shopping ain't gonna hurt them, but I sleep better at night."

"Wow, I had no idea. Is this true?"

"You can read several reports on what those stores are costing Americans."

"Wow ... I'll go naked before I shop at Walmart again." I grinned at her as she slapped me gently on the chest. "You are a pig!" She giggled.

"Well, you were the one who mentioned going naked."

"And here I thought you were an old man and couldn't get 'er up anymore."

"Yeah, well, I try." Heather laughed, and I blushed.

~ ~ ~ ~ ~

Over the next couple of weeks, we visited several places. Every evening, I offered to get her a room of her own, but she said she was fine being with me. I assumed it was because of fear left over from Jerry. She told me a room with two queens was comfortable. Heather said she really didn't want to sleep in a separate room yet.

I explained the purpose of my trip and why I decided to sell the bike. I wanted to give it up before I got hurt or killed. "You know, when you get to be an older person like me, it takes longer to heal if you get hurt."

"Knock it off with the old person shit, would you?" she snapped at me.

Days passed on the road and her attitude improved. The last few days, I'd discovered what a fun, lively person she really was. I hated to admit it, but during our travels, I'd become fond of my little waif. She wasn't Lois, but this was one very nice lady.

Nevertheless, I was true to my word! I didn't lay a hand on her. Whenever I thought about Lois, it wasn't too difficult to not touch her. I'll admit I did a lot of looking because there was a lot to look at. Her body was mature, full and lush, and she had kept herself in good shape. She was sexy, and that didn't help me keep my promise. But I kept thinking of Lois and I, and what that relationship meant to me.

I didn't know what Heather's past had been like and I didn't want to open any bad memories for her, so I didn't pry. I remembered another young woman, Nicki, and the floodgate I'd inadvertently opened once with her. I decided that unless Heather wanted to share something with me, I'd leave things as they were. Since there didn't seem to be anything coy about her actions, I figured she was feeling more comfortable around me.

We'd been on the road long enough and I decided it was time to end my wandering ways, so we finally pulled into the apartment garage. Heather's face had healed well, as had several other bruises I hadn't noticed when I'd first picked her up. Even though it had been only a few weeks, it seemed like we had known each other a long time.

When we pulled into the garage at my apartment, I heard her over the motor when she asked, "Who lives here?"

"This is my apartment building."

"Are you for real? Seriously, this is your place?"

"Yeah, what's wrong?"

"Wrong? Nothing's wrong. But this is, like… um… like luxury condos or something..."

"I take it you approve?"

Her fists softly hit my back as she exclaimed, "You are a goof. You never told me you owned an apartment building."

"You never asked."

Again, she struck my back. By now, we were at the end of the garage where I always parked my bike. I turned off the motor and after she had dismounted, I put the kickstand down. I lifted my saddlebags off the bike and placed my hand on the gas tank. Mentally, I said my goodbyes and turned away with a heavy heart. I knew I was doing the right thing, but it didn't make it any easier. I felt being able to walk away from the bike instead of being carried away on a stretcher was a good thing. However ……

I stepped over to the elevator, inserted my key in the slot, and the door opened. We stepped into the elevator and I put my key in the slot for my floor and the door shut. When the door opened again and Heather saw my place, I heard her say, "Holy shit! This is amazing." She quickly put her hand over her mouth and apologized. "I'm sorry. Sometimes, I have a potty mouth." I snickered.

Heather followed me as I went towards the back of the apartment. I tossed the two bags onto the laundry room floor and I heard her going from room to room, making comments along the way.

Eventually, she found the front room. "Oh, my god! This is crazy." When I came into the room, she turned and with her fists on both hips, asked, "Are you like rich or something?"

"I've had a certain amount of success in my life… so I guess you might call me well off." I was becoming slightly unsettled by the way she showed so much interest in any money I might have.

"Well, I know you've been super the past few weeks… paying for my meals and getting me some new clothes and all. I figured you were being nice and well… I thought once I had a job, I'd pay you back. I still want to do that, but I mean like you never told me you had money… and like that."

Now that embarrassed me. "Look, can we please get off the money thing? I have enough so it's not an issue. I wanted to take care of you. I enjoyed getting your clothes and feeding you. You made my trip a lot more interesting than it would have been if I was alone. I have the money to take care of us and I saw no reason to make a big deal of it. If there was any chance we might become interested in one another, it wouldn't be for what I had."

"Oh, crap… Is that what you're thinking? That I don't care about you… it's the money?"

I replied, "It crossed my mind."

She turned and walked back towards the elevator. I chased after her and when I could reach her shoulder, I gently turned her around. "Where are you going?" I asked.

"I'll go now."

"Why? I'm sorry if I said the wrong thing. Besides, where are you going to go?"

"I'm embarrassed now. I think I need to…"

"Heather, I kept my word. I've kept my hands off you… precisely as I told you I would when we first started our trip together. I've told you about my friend in D.C. I felt I needed to take care of you until you decided what you want to do. I've said nothing about money because I saw no reason to and I also didn't want it to get in the way. I figured you'd realize I had enough since I could take care of us. But I'll tell you, I've grown very attached to you… as a friend." I paused for a moment as I considered how I wanted to cover my other issue.

"Umm, I don't really know how to say this, but I want to be upfront with you. Actually, I don't think I want to have an intimate encounter with anybody for now because I'm still working on how to make things work with the lady back in Washington D.C. I need to figure that out. But, as soon as I figure it out, I'll let you know."

I paused, considering what I wanted to say next. "The best part of our time together has been you've made me feel young again. I find I really don't care about the difference in our ages. You make me feel good and I know I'm happier having you around me than if you went away. You've turned into a good friend."

"So, what are we gonna do?"

"What do you wanna do? Do you want to stay here for a while? I know you have no place to go right now. I think you need to take some time to figure out what you want to do with the rest of your life. I have a spare bedroom and until either of us decides differently, you're free to use it."

"Are you asking me to live with you?"

"Well… yes… in a way. But you'll have your own room!"

"Yes, Matt, I want to stay here with you for a while."

I knew I was making things difficult for myself. I was still trying to decide how to work things out with Lois. The longer we were apart, the more I missed her. I was discovering I didn't like to be alone. Actually, it was more than that; I didn't want to live without Lois being part of my life. Nicki had been fun to be around, and Heather was fun too, but I wanted something more. Like I said, when Nicki was living with me, I found I really liked having somebody in the place with me. Knowing there was another person around was comforting.

CHAPTER EIGHTEEN

I was curled up in my favorite chair, mulling over the many changes I'd seen so far in my life. I thought about how quickly things had happened. It didn't bother me having Heather living in my apartment since I didn't feel she was much temptation, I really thought of her as a good friend. And those thoughts brought me to Lois. When I thought of her, there was actually a pain inside me, I was so lonely. I knew I was dealing with the inner anger which was new for me and I also knew when I was with Lois, it was easier to come to grips with the anger.

I was lost in deep thought and I almost missed the vibration in my shirt pocket. For a moment, I couldn't figure out what was going on. When I realized what was happening, I pulled my phone out of my pocket. I looked at the display and didn't recognize who was calling me. As a rule, if my cell phone rings and I don't recognize the number, I don't answer. I figure if it's important enough, they'll leave a message and I can decide later if I want, or if I need, to return the call. This time, even though I didn't recognize the number, something told me I needed to answer it. As it turned out, it was a good thing I took the call.

"Hi, this is Matt."

"Hello, is this Mr. Matt Preston?"

"Yes. Who is this, please?"

"Good morning sir. My name is Douglas Brower. I'm the managing partner at the law firm of Brower, Brower, Smith and Hodel here in Fort Myers, Florida."

"Yes."

"We represent the estate of Tom Frost. I don't know if you were aware, but Mr. Frost passed away a few days ago and I've been trying to get ahold of you. Mr. Frost specifically mentioned you in his will."

I was glad I was seated. This news saddened and touched me deeply. For a long time, I sat there thinking about the old man. Snooker was gone! It hardly seemed possible. I recalled how recently we'd sat on his lanai, reminiscing about our days in a war so much of America had hated. Another veteran gone. I had no idea he was that ill. I wondered what I would have done differently if I had known time was so short. Somehow his passing seemed to fit with what I felt were a multitude of changes happening in my life. Who would blow the conch shell now that he was gone? Another change to deal with. I heard the voice on the phone. "Hello. Hello, are you still there? Mr. Preston?"

"Yes, I'm still here. Sorry. I didn't know he was gone." I took a deep breath. "The news caught me unprepared. He was a friend." Was anyone ever really prepared to hear about the death of a friend or loved one? "The last time I saw Tom, he mentioned the doctors had a concern about things that were growing inside him, but he didn't act like he was that ill or in danger of passing away so quickly. He'd spent several tours in Vietnam. I knew Mr. Frost was getting older, but to look at him, you wouldn't know he was that close to dying. No, I didn't know of his passing and I am saddened. I don't know how well you knew him, but he was a real gentleman. I'm so sorry to hear this. I considered him a good friend. I

…" I realized I was blathering and finally came to the point. "Sorry for rambling, how am I mentioned?"

"I'm sorry, but I'm not at liberty to discuss this over the phone. There will be a reading of his will this coming Friday at my office. Can you be there… say at ten a.m.?"

I thought about it for a moment then told him yes and he provided me with his address. It dumbfounded me that Snooker would mention me in his will. I knew he was happy because I'd helped with Zoe and the difficulties with her boyfriend; and our last chat had been one of nostalgia and reminiscing. But were we close enough for him to mention me in his will? Then I remembered he'd asked me to help Zoe with his little car collection and wondered if it had something to do with that. I could see no reason not to help her get rid of a couple of cars if that was the case.

I went looking around the apartment for Heather and found her in the kitchen. "Hey, kid, I need to fly back down to Fort Myers, Florida. Are you interested in coming with me?"

"Where in Florida is Fort Myers located?"

"It's on the west side, near the Gulf of Mexico. There is a river named the Caloosahatchee that runs through town and continues until it empties into the Gulf."

"I'd love to go, but I have no money for the airfare."

"Not to worry, I have access to a plane."

"Really?"

"Really. Does this mean you would like to go?"

"Yes," she shouted as she ran out of the room. I called Henry and asked him if he had a plane near me that was available to go to Florida on Thursday and able to take two passengers. He told me what time to be down at Boeing Field on Thursday, and I thanked him.

~ ~ ~ ~ ~

When we got to the airport Thursday morning, there was a plane waiting, but this one was different from the plane Henry usually flew. If I thought our old planes were nice, this one was over the top, like the difference between an old Cadillac and a new Cadillac. The plane even smelled new.

Henry mentioned whose plane it had been, but the name meant nothing to me and I promptly forgot. It turned out when the fellow's company went bankrupt, the bank repossessed the plane. Somehow, Henry had found out about it and got a great deal. Our little company was growing fast, and Henry was making plans for more. The best part of all this was the company was booked continually and was already in the black.

I parked the car in the long-term lot, then Heather and I boarded the plane. As soon as we were buckled in, the plane began taxiing. Heather looked over at me with a big grin. "This is nice. This is the only way to fly. How did you score a ride on this thing?"

I debated my answer. "I helped the owner of the flight service get started and in return, I get the use of a plane occasionally." It wasn't quite the truth, but it wasn't a total fabrication either.

A few hours later, we were made our landing at Page Field and I saw the Hertz lady with a car ready to roll. If I kept coming down to Florida, I needed to consider getting a car and storing it somewhere close to the airport. We checked into the hotel where Lois and I had stayed, except Heather and I had individual rooms. I enjoyed Heather's company, but she wasn't Lois. Damn, I missed that woman. I was beginning to see I needed to do something about it too.

The next morning, I asked Heather if she could keep herself amused for a few hours since I was positive she didn't want to hang around some lawyer's office. She told me to do what I had to do, then call her on her cell when I was free.

I located Brower's office in downtown Fort Myers in a new modern building on the top floor. I introduced myself at the front desk and was immediately shown to a conference room looking out over the river. Martha, Zoe, and Stephen— Zoe's boyfriend— were already there. Zoe squealed when she saw me. She ran over, wrapped her arms around me, and gave me a big hug. I told her how sorry I was to hear of Snooker's passing and I noticed her eyes were glistening. I shook hands with Stephen.

Stephan held onto my hand with both of his. "Sir, I know I've said this before, but I'm so grateful for what you did for me. Thank you."

"Yes, I know. You've told me before, and now you need to stop. It was as much for Snooker as it was for you."

I stepped up and gave Martha a big hug. She also had a tear in her eye as she hugged me back and I kissed her cheek. I whispered in her ear, "I miss him already."

As she moved her head, I heard her murmur, "Me too. A lot!"

We all took a seat, and we chatted for a few moments. Martha mentioned my last visit with ol' Snook and how happy he'd been to have me spend so much time with him. It hurt me that I hadn't tried to spend more time with the old fellow. It was too late now, but it still made me sad.

In few minutes, a gentleman in his mid-forties with a substantial girth strode into the room and extend his hand towards me. "Hello, my name is Doug Brower. Matt Preston, I presume?" I nodded. "Good, we will need to make a photocopy of your driver's license to keep everything proper. You know Zoe and Stephen and Martha?" He motioned to the three people in the room. Again, I assented. "Okay, let's get down to business. Can I get any of you water, coffee or a soft drink?" I told him I'd appreciate water.

After we were all seated around a sizeable round table, Brower opened a large folder and extracted a few papers which he spread in front of him. He read. Basically, Snooker left everything to his granddaughter. The will included a huge bequest to Martha which brought fresh tears to her eyes. It was obvious she had expected nothing from Snooker and was taken aback at something that large. It didn't surprise me in the least. As the meeting dragged on, I was wondering what the hell I was doing here. Finally, Doug got to the part where he read about Snooker's car collection.

Brower stopped reading the will and looked at Zoe and Stephan as he explained. "Mr. Frost had been purchasing cars for many years and I understand many them are now considered antiques. He started his collection when he first entered military service. Military personnel could purchase new cars at a large discount through the PX service."

"Yes, you could save a lot of money by purchasing a car through the PX." I knew firsthand the savings could be substantial.

Brower continued. "My father knew of the collection, but I don't think he ever saw it. Until Mr. Frost passed away, I'd never even heard about it, let alone seen it."

Zoe interrupted, "I was aware he had a few cars in storage somewhere. And, please call him either Tom or Snooker. Mr. Frost doesn't fit him at all."

Doug smiled and continued. "I understand what you mean. Anyway, back when Snooker was in the service, he used almost all his winnings from pool games to buy cars, and he even won cars in pool games, then he stored them all."

When Brower returned back to reading the will, it turned out Snooker asked that I handle the sale of his car collection, as I suspected, and for doing it, I was to pick three cars, any three cars regardless of their value, and they would be mine. It made me wonder just how many cars ol' Snook had. When the collection was gone, I was to make the arrangements to sell the building that housed the collection. In addition, for doing all the things he had asked of me, Snooker left me the deed to his condo.

I was shocked.

I looked over at Zoe and asked if she knew, and she told me she knew about the condo.

"Because of what you did for Stephen and me. He told me about the condo shortly before he died. I've got my own place and as nice as his condo is, well… it isn't really... how shall I say… suitable for my age group."

I smiled knowingly.

"I knew my grandfather had a few old cars, but I didn't know what would happen to those or the building they're in."

Brower interjected. "Buildings, not building. Your grandpa owned the entire business park."

Zoe told us it was okay with her for me to dispose of the cars. "Grandpa thought the world of you. He was so impressed when you got Stephen out of his difficulties, and I guess you did something back in Nam he wouldn't tell me about, but you found out something he wanted to know, and you told him all about it. Grandpa was very pleased and impressed you took the time and trouble to tell him everything."

Brower handed me an envelope with the address where the collection was stored along with a set of keys to unlock the doors. I was flabbergasted. I asked Brower what he knew about the collection and he replied again, other than the addresses where Tom stored the cars, he knew nothing. I asked him about the business park and Doug told us Brower and Sons was the leasing agent and took care of the management of all the buildings. Brower told us the company that owned the buildings was Snooker Management, LLC. I had to laugh. "Since you are the leasing agent, why can't Zoe hold on to the property and you manage it for her? It sounds like a nice investment for her."

"There's no reason we can't do that," Brower responded.

I turned to Zoe. "You don't have to sell the buildings. With Brower managing the properties for you, you have a nice steady cash flow and you don't have to deal with the day-to-day operation of the business. Isn't that a better way to handle things?"

"This is all so new. Do you really think it's the best way to handle it?"

"Yes. As you get older, Zoe, you realize that having property is always a good thing. If you don't have to, never sell property. Especially commercial property, and even more so if it's free and clear. Zoe, you need to keep the business park. Do you want to come out with me and see the car collection?"

"No. I don't think so. It would be way too sad for me and reminds me too much of grandpa. And sorry, but I'm really not interested in looking at a bunch of old cars. They smell, and I don't understand why grandpa found them so interesting. That was grandpa's hobby, and that's fine with me.

"I did see one of his old cars once and I thought it looked like a boat, it was so long. I mean the car was a nice, shiny convertible, but it was way too big. Nobody wants or needs a car that large. As I remember, the car was from either the late fifties or early sixties and I also think it was a brand they don't make anymore, but grandpa was so proud of the car. It was white with an interesting reddish interior. But I thought the whole thing was stupid. Mr. Preston, if grandpa trusted you to sell his cars, then I trust you too."

I explained to Zoe since I would be selling the collection, she needed to call me Matt. I joked about my pop being in his nineties when he passed, and he was Mr. Preston. She said she'd try.

As I turned away from Zoe, it made me sad to realize there were more millennials like Zoe than not. Her attitude was not that uncommon. This group didn't grow up with our cars or have the chance to indulge in our culture. Like Zoe said, they smell. They are big, take a lot of gas to run and are very expensive. She didn't understand and neither do a lot of others her age.

I didn't know how many cars I'd have to deal with, but I wondered how much longer prices would increase for the cars from our youth. As the Baby Boomers pass away, or get to be like Snooker who, at the end, couldn't drive, those collectables will turn into worthless pieces of junk. So many things are changing so fast. Our towns are losing their character; the clubs our parents used to belong to, like golf, country, and yacht clubs, are going under. Too many changes too fast. Having to deal with Snooker's collection was making me feel like the chaplain on the Titanic. About the only thing I would be able to do is watch it sink. With no warning, I found myself depressed. Oh, Snooker, what have you done?

But in another way, I was still excited about my task. I asked Doug, "Do you have any idea how many cars we're talking about?" I knew I'd asked that question already but I was getting the feeling because of where Snooker stored the cars, and the way the talk was going there was more than just a few cars like Snook had told me.

"Like I said earlier, I didn't even know Tom had a collection until I read through the will. I knew what we were doing for Snooker Management because my father had served with him in the army back in the day. Father was the one who drew up the original documents, and he told me about it. It was only a few days ago Snooker had called me and had the part about the condo put into the will, and told me how he wanted you to handle the sale of his cars.

"Oh, and then he also wanted the disposal of the buildings added because he was afraid it might be too much for her, but I see no reason Zoe can't keep the properties since she wants to, and we can continue to manage them. Her grandfather left them to her and they're hers to do with as she wishes."

I thanked Doug and as I prepared to leave, I asked Martha if she had a moment. We stepped over to a corner of the room. "What you need, Mr. Matt?"

"I know this is kind of sudden, but do you have any plans for the future?"

"No. I have no plans. Why you ask?"

"I can't be down here all the time and now I have the condo, I haven't decided what to do with it. Would you be interested in working for me?"

"I thinking about the retirement. What you need from me?"

"When I'm in town, I would like for you to be at the condo for a few hours during the day. We can discuss later what your duties would be. When I'm not there, perhaps you can stop by twice a week and check on the condo and make sure people know it isn't vacant."

"Okay, Mr. Matt, I do that for you." We exchanged phone numbers, and I told her I'd get her a new cell phone since I didn't feel it was fair for her to have to pay for a phone in order for us to stay in touch. I could see she liked the idea of a new phone. After we finished, she came up and hugged me around the waist. I hadn't really noticed how short she was. "You a tall man, Mr. Matt."

I laughed. I didn't think she would appreciate it if I told her she was a short woman. And you think I can't be taught new things!

I called Heather and asked where she was. She was only two blocks away, so I picked her up on the way back to the hotel. I told her about the collection and the condo I'd inherited. "What kind of cars are they?"

"I don't know. Not only that, I don't even know how many cars we're talking about."

"Are you curious?"

"Are you serious? You bet! Do you want to ride out there with me and see what I'm in for?"

"I'd love to."

I entered the business park's address into my Garmin and followed the directions. The address led me to a large building nestled in the middle of a business park across the Caloosahatchee River in North Fort Myers near the freeway. I had to smile. Snooker kept his car collection close to his condo. I wondered if anybody in the business park knew there was a car collection in one building. I found the building I was looking for and was surprised at the size. The building was so large, I wondered what else was inside. It was way too large for only small collection of cars.

I unlocked the door and Heather and I stepped into a reception area with a small office on one side. The reception area had a desk and a chair, with two additional chairs against the wall. If you came in off the street and didn't know what to expect, it looked like the office for some kind of small business. I looked around the small office and on the desk was a computer monitor. I stepped behind the desk and I noticed a computer tower in the hollow place in the desk designed for the computer. When I glanced at the name on the tower, I recognized it as a high-end brand. When I had time, I knew I needed to fire it up and see what was on the PC.

We went back into the reception area and at the back of the office, I discovered a steel door made to look like it was wood. The door was locked but after carefully searching through the ring of keys Doug had provided, I found the key for the door. I opened the door and stepped into a huge, long room. By counting the panels between the supports and multiplying by eight feet between each support, the room appeared to be about eighty feet wide and about twice as deep. Damn, over twelve thousand square feet of space. That explained why I thought there must have been something else inside the building. The room was dim, lit only by a few, very dusty, screen covered windows located high on top of the walls.

I was sure there had to be lights, which would mean there should be a switch somewhere. Looking around the door area, I eventually found a bank of switches and I flipped them all on. When I turned back to look over the room, I was shocked at the sight which greeted me. Before me were lines of vehicles all covered with protective covers. I counted six rows of cars across and there were eight cars in each row. In some rows, cars were stacked two high on lifts. Counting at least eight lifts, I did quick arithmetic and came up with somewhere around fifty-six or more cars in the building.

Fifty-six fricken cars! No wonder the building was so big. I said the number out loud. Oh my god! How the hell was I ever going to get rid of over fifty-six antique cars? Heather asked what kind of cars they were, and I had to admit, I wondered that too.

I stepped up to a large covered lump directly in front of me and carefully pulled off the cover. Once the cover was off, there sat an early fifties Buick convertible in absolutely pristine condition. The lights shone off the spotless paint, and the chrome was perfect. The big grill looked like a grinning teenager with braces. The old car was massive.

I checked under the tarp of the car alongside the Buick, which looked like a very early Corvette. One of the first ever built. I believed it to be a 1954, but not knowing much about old Corvettes, I wasn't sure.

As I stood there looking over all the cars, I wondered how I would ever deal with liquidating such a massive number of cars. Trying to get an inventory on them would be a chore in itself. Snooker had said he had a car collection, but when he'd told me about it, he'd called it a small car collection. Small my ass! I'd no idea he had a collection this size.

What the hell was I going to do now? Where do you even start on something like this? I wondered to myself.

I covered up the Corvette and as I pulled the cover back over the old Buick, I stopped. It took a moment then I remembered why the car had seemed so familiar. The car re-minded me of an old friend from my school days.

Driggs. Driggs Bertram.

Driggs was even more of a car nut than me, if that was even possible. I wondered if he could help me? I'd heard he'd sold his business and was enjoying retirement, but the big question was, could I even find him again after all this time? It must be at least twenty years since I'd seen him.

Well, it didn't matter; I had to find him.

Somehow…

CHAPTER NINETEEN

I met Driggs in the seventh grade when we were entering junior high school. We had two classes together and we got along well. His whole name is Fredrick Driggs Bertram, and when he had to give someone his name, he used his middle name as his first, but all of his friends called him Digger. Somewhere during the early part of his life, Driggs had developed a fascination with dump trucks, road graders, large bulldozers, and any type of enormous, earth moving equipment. Any kind of sizeable road equipment caught his attention.

If he saw a backhoe on the way to school, you knew he would be late. If he saw a tractor on the way home, we usually left him standing there because it might be dark before he headed home. The joke was if he had the choice of having sex with the most desirable girl in the school or driving a Caterpillar D6, the girl would come in second every time. Digger always told us when he grew up, he'd be in the construction business. His ambition was to own his own construction company. Because of his fascination with digging and dumping, it seemed natural to call him Digger.

In high school, we traveled in different factions—or cliques, if you will—but we shared an occasional class together, and we knew each other from band. When we passed in the hallways, we'd wave or say hi. In high school, Digger started his growth spurt and ended up growing to around six feet tall. There was nothing notable about his appearance; he was handsome but not stunningly or movie star handsome. But what he had was a personality that made him exceptionally likable. Other than a couple of girls he dumped, I never met anybody who didn't like Digger. He seemed to be able to make friends with members of all the little cliques so prevalent in junior and senior high.

Digger wasn't a great student, but his grades were decent enough to keep him off the vice-principal's list of poor students. He wasn't fast, but he ran in Track and Field events and earned a letterman jacket, a very important accoutrement when one is in high school. Basically, Driggs was like every one of us, trying to get through those difficult years of growing from a child to an adult, dealing with all the peer pressure that went along with those difficult years, and somehow coming out at the end with some form of sanity.

The one thing about Digger that stood out even more than his love for large equipment was his attitude regarding cars. Like most boys, Digger loved automobiles. His father Carl liked to play poker, and it was an obsession. Over the years, Carl had won, and lost, several automobile dealerships among other things. Yes, you read that correctly. Complete dealerships. Needless to say, that was hard on Digger's parents' marriage. Because of his father's easy access to automobiles, on Digger's sixteenth birthday, he received a car. I've forgotten what kind of car it was, but because of the way Digger drove, the car lasted less than a week before he totaled it.

Over the next eighteen months, ol' Digger cost his father somewhere around 65,000 dollars in cars, speeding tickets, court costs, attorney fees, and bribes to keep Digger out of reform schools. Keep in mind we're talking early sixties dollars, here. Plain and simple, Digger loved to go fast as much as he loved cars, he had no regard for the law, and when it came to driving, he didn't give a shit.

During those crazy months, one of Digger's cars was a late fifties Thunderbird. On his way back from a skiing trip at Steven's Pass up in the Cascade Mountains, he blew through a radar trap. The state patrol officer tried to give chase, but Digger outran the police. However, you cannot outrun Motorola, as the saying goes, and two towns later, the highway patrol blocked the road and forced Digger to stop. Some of the sixty-five grand Mr. Bertram spent went to getting him out of that adventure.

The Thunderbird eventually met its demise as it slid off a slick, twisted road in North Seattle while Digger was being chased by a motorcycle cop. What Digger didn't know until later was the cycle cop had already lost control of his bike and crashed—but wasn't hurt—and Digger would have been home free if he'd only slowed down.

He was going way too fast, and he lost control. The car rolled down a hill before landing on its top. Digger kicked out the back window and extracted himself from the car just before it burst into flames. Eventually, the police showed up and he denied he was being chased by the motorcycle cop, and since the officer on the bike never got the license plate number, there was nothing to charge Digger with, except for burning without a license, and he received a citation for that.

Running the 'Bird off the hill and having it catch on fire was the last straw for Digger's father. Carl Bertram decided he had to somehow clip Digger's wings. Looking over the inventory at the dealership, he found a car that he thought would settle Digger down and keep him out of trouble. Carl had a new Falcon they just couldn't seem to sell. So, Digger ended up in a brand-new, early sixties, white, four-door Ford Falcon with a 6-cylinder motor and a Ford-O-Matic automatic transmission. It was the least expensive model that Falcon offered, and the most gutless car on the road. Basically, it was your grandpa's car. Other than the AM radio and a heater, it had no bells and no whistles. A plain Jane white car with crappy red plastic interior and the smallest motor Ford offered. To say Digger was unhappy is an understatement—devastated was more like it.

Driggs drove the Falcon for a few weeks and around the start of August, a turn of events changed the poor gutless little Falcon. That summer, Ford came out with a fancy Ford XL that came equipped with a 390-cubic inch V-8 motor. One of Mr. Bertram's poker buddies bought one and then had an accident while intoxicated which totaled the big Ford. The wreck ended up in the back row in one lot of Digger's father's dealership.

During the summer, Digger had been working as a lot boy at the dealership. The term 'lot boy' is a fancy way of saying he was a gofer—if they needed anything, he'd 'go fer' it. He washed cars, moved cars around, if there was a dealer trade, Digger would take one car over to another dealership and bring back the new car. Any piddly job that needed doing, Digger got stuck doing it. And as always, Digger had made friends along the way. He was friends with the salespeople and with every mechanic in every shop within a twenty-mile radius. His friendships even included the management of several dealerships.

When the totaled Ford showed up in the back lot, one mechanic asked Digger if he would like to have the motor installed in his little Falcon. Basically, the mechanics just wanted to see if they could pull it off, and of course Digger thought the idea was grand. The mechanics shoe-horned that big old motor into the little engine compartment and two weeks later, Digger had the ultimate sleeper. The four-door Falcon still looked like a grandpa's car, but it flew like a bird. In less than two weeks, Digger burned through one set of back tires. Also, because of the fast starts, something broke in the rear suspension and the little Falcon ended up back in the shop for repairs.

Mr. Bertram didn't know that what he thought had been the answer to Digger's wild ways with cars had been slightly modified. When Papa Carl walked through the service bay one morning and noticed Digger's Falcon up on a hoist, it surprised him since the car was basically brand new.

"Why is that car already in the shop being repaired?" he asked the mechanic. "Drop it down!"

When they lowered the car, and Pop saw a motor now completely filling the small engine compartment, he exploded. "Who the hell did this?" Carl's scream was heard throughout the entire service bay. Of course, nobody would fess up.

Digger had the misfortune to be walking past the large entrance door to the service area and his father saw him. "Driggs," Papa screamed, "get your ass over here… now!"

Digger strolled over and greeted his dad, "What's up, Pop?"

"Don't, 'What's up, Pop,' me, you little shit. Who put this motor in this car?"

"Dunno. I never got his name and besides, he don't work here no more."

"Bullshit. Nobody has quit or been fired from the service department this entire past year. I watch those things. Tell me, who did this?"

Digger paused. "Okay, do you remember the Ferris twins?" Carl nodded. "Well, them and two other guys and me got the motor out of that totaled XL in the back row over from your other lot. We put it in."

Carl knew Digger was lying through his teeth. Nevertheless, Pop Bertram was also proud that his boy would take the rap and not rat out any of his workers who had done all the work. "Son, you can consider yourself 'de-horsed' as of this minute. I'm taking that car away from you. Now!"

"Pop, you can't do that. College starts real soon and I'll need a car."

"Do not tell me what I can do and can't do. I'm taking the Falcon away from you and I'm immediately placing it on the showroom floor. I know some idiot will come in and want that car and perhaps the dealership just might make a little money on the deal." Papa Carl sold the car later that same day, and the dealership made a shit ton of money on the sale.

Mr. Bertram understood that Driggs needed a car for school, but what kind of car would keep his boy out of trouble? Totally frustrated with Digger, Pop went out to the used car lots looking for another car for Digger to use at college.

When Mr. Bertram got to the lot where they stored old beaters, in the last row he spotted a 1952 Buick convertible up against the fence. Carl had been the one who made the deal for the old car to be taken in trade for one hundred dollars. The car had belonged to an elderly doctor who was now retired, and the doctor had traded it for a brand-new Thunderbird.

In 1952, the Buick Roadmaster was the top of the line. The old convertible had every option available that year from power windows to air conditioning. The car was huge, and painted a dark slate gray with a black convertible top. It had red leather interior and even though the car looked like a whale, there was something graceful about it. It took forever to get up to sixty miles per hour, then it would float down the freeway in a ghastly silence all day long; the car, in its own way, was delightful.

For some reason, Digger fell in love with it. Of all the cars Digger had owned and destroyed up to that point, this one struck the right chord. He washed it and waxed it, drove it like a sane person; in one defining moment, Digger had changed. For the next two quarters at college before he dropped out, he never got another ticket or was even stopped for any infraction.

During his short college career, Digger also had a girl-friend. Because we'd known each other throughout junior and senior high, even though we'd not been good friends back then, since we were the only two from our high school, we bonded and got to know each other well. Both of us had girlfriends, and we ended up double dating a few times. I remember fondly curled up in the back seat of that old Buick, making out with my date. As I recall, her name was Lenora, and I thought she would be The One. I can't recall what Digger's girlfriend's name was, but I remember she was a knockout. Cute and a great body. Digger's name for her was Super Virgin. At the end of almost every date, her favorite thing was to get into bed with Digger and take off all her clothes while they made out. She loved to have Digger touch and fondle her, but he was forbidden to enter. She "helped" him out, but she would never go all the way.

Digger and I both had the same problem when we went off to junior college, we were too busy having fun to deal with mundane things like school and studying or going to class. After two quarters, both of us saw the writing on the wall: we needed to either drop out or they would expel us. We dropped out. Lenora and I were no longer an item, and I joined the army. A few months later, Digger got drafted and we lost touch with each other for a while.

I have no idea what made Digger change so much regarding his attitude about cars so quickly after he got the Buick. Some of the cars he had in the sixties were spectacular, but for whatever reason, he never seemed to bond with them the way he did with that old Buick. I've always meant to ask him what ever happened to that car.

It was several years after we were both out of the service before our paths crossed again. In the intervening years, Digger had lived up to his name. He started a construction company specializing in excavation, concrete and asphalt work, and cutting holes in existing concrete and asphalt. His company was incredibly successful. As his company made money, he started buying old cars. Eventually, he sold the business but kept the land the business was on and leased it out.

When Driggs decided to retire, he sold everything in Seattle and moved to Idaho. He invested well and between the payments on the business, money from his investments, and the rent money from the land, Driggs was doing well. He retired and could now concentrate on his cars. Over the years, on the rare occasions when our paths crossed, he'd tell me about various cars he either had or wanted to get; he was very knowledgeable about antique automobiles. Some of my collection had been purchased with his blessing after he had looked them over and told me I was getting a good deal.

Seeing Snooker's old Buick and all the cars sitting covered up in the building reminded me of Digger. I tried to remember the names of some of our mutual friends. I recalled an old girlfriend of his from high school, a gal named Sherral. I knew Sherral and I had a mutual friend, but that name escaped me at the moment. I asked Heather if she was hungry and she said she was. I was opening the door to the restaurant when a name popped into my brain: Becky. Becky Lawyer.

Becky would be considered a free spirit. Over the years, she'd had several male friends, but had never married. As an artist, she was famous, and I was sure one of the local art galleries located around Seattle would have information on how to contact her. I called a couple of them and finally lucked out. The gallery provided me with a business number, and I called her studio. She answered and we chatted for a little while before I asked her if she remembered a friend of hers from high school named Sherral.

"Do you mean Sherral Kotter?"

"Yeah, that's it. She went with Digger Bertram for a while."

"Oh my god, you remember Digger?"

"Yeah, actually I'm trying to get ahold of him, and I was hoping Sherral might have an idea how to find him and can help me."

"You're living dangerously Matt. You do know she can't stand him?"

"Seriously?"

"Seriously! She hates the man. I don't know the exact details, but he did something at the senior prom and she never forgave him."

"Senior prom? Sherral, that was a long time ago. That's a long time to hold a grudge. She can't still be that mad at him."

"In a way, you are in luck. The funny thing is as much as she hates him, she has kept track of him. However, if you do call her, you're going to find out just how angry she is."

"Well, if you have a number for her, I'm going to take a chance and see if she knows how to get a hold of him."

"Just a sec…" A moment later, she came back on the line and gave me a phone number.

I called the number and when the woman answered, I said, "Hi. Sherral?"

"Yes. Who is this?"

"This is Matt Preston. Do you remember me from high school?"

"Of course I do. Wow, what a lovely surprise to hear from you. How are you, Matt?" For the next few minutes we played the *Do You Remember* game and caught up on who had left us for the big study hall in the sky and who was still with us. We both remembered a lot of the guys who had lost their lives over in Nam.

Finally, I screwed up the courage to ask her, "Do you remember Driggs? Digger?"

Her voice exploded over the phone. "What? That asshole! You bet I remember him."

"Wow, girl, there's a lot of hostility there. Even after all this time, you seem pretty pissed with the lad."

"Did you know he took me to the senior prom?"

"Yeah, and I heard something happened that night and he ended up in the dog house with you."

"That was supposed to be the night we were going to make love for the first time. We talked about it and I was ready. I had been on the pill for a while. He'd rented a really nice motel room and we were headed there after the prom. About halfway to the room, he turned around and took me home. He chickened out. After all of our make-out sessions where he was prodding me to go all the way with him, when I was finally ready, he bailed on me. I was so hurt and angry. He wouldn't even talk to me about it. He just pulled up in front of the house, leaned over, opened the door, and told me to get out. I cried all weekend."

I felt bad. I didn't mean to open old wounds. "I'm sorry, Sherral. I wouldn't have brought it up had I known you were still so upset."

"It was a real blow to the old ego. For years I wondered what it was about me that turned him off. Actually, I've never really gotten over it. Anyway, why did you ask about him?"

"Well, I kinda need to find him."

"I can't help you much. I did keep track of him for a few years but then I lost track. He really hurt me. About the only help I can give you is I know one of his friends, Steve Learner. Do you remember Steve?"

"Yeah. In junior high, we called him Inch because he was so short. Then in high school, he hit a growth spurt and ended up like six foot something. That stopped everybody from calling him Inch. Do you know how to get a hold of Steve?"

She gave me a phone number and an address. She finished the call with, "If you do find Digger, tell him thanks for nothing. Oh, and tell Steve hi for me."

"Will do." We hung up and I called the number for Steve. His voicemail picked up the call and I told him who I was and what I wanted and gave him my number. Heather and I were halfway through lunch when my cell phone went off. It was Steve. "Inch! How the hell are you?"

"Damn, Matt, nobody has called me Inch for years. I'm doing well. How are you? Great to hear your voice. But how did you get this number?"

"I called Sherral Kotter. I asked her about Digger and she told me to call you."

"Are you serious? You asked Sherral about Digger? You've got more balls than I do. I'm surprised you're still alive. She hates that man. I was always surprised she didn't hire some mafia hit man to rub him out."

"Yeah, I kinda figured that out after my last phone call with her when I asked if she remembered Driggs and got my butt chewed off. Anyway, she told me to call you, that you might know how to find Digger."

Steve didn't know exactly how to get a hold of Digger, but he managed to remember somebody else who might be able to help. It still took a couple more calls to mutual friends before I ended up with Digger's number. I called him as soon as I had it. "Digger, this is Matt Preston."

"Matt! How the hell are you? What's up?" He sounded very pleased to hear from me.

We bullshitted for a while and I did mention Sherral. "Matt, not a day goes by I don't regret that night. But I had no idea what to do. I'd never had sex with a woman, and I was scared shitless I was going to make a fool of myself and totally mess up. I was afraid that once I saw her naked, I'd lose it and embarrass myself. I thought it was better to take her home and have her unhappy with me rather than pissed that I fumbled through the experience. Who knows? I might have wrecked sex for her, like forever."

"Digger, I'm not the one to give advice. You did what you felt was the right thing to do that night, but you might call her and tell her what you just told me. To this day, she has no idea why you took her home and didn't go through with your plans."

"You really think I should call her?"

"Yeah. It would mean a lot to her. I think you should for both of your sakes. It will make her feel a lot better about herself and it will finally put the whole thing to rest in your mind. You do what you want, but you really might consider giving her a call. Hey, who knows? Maybe she might still want to do the big nasty with you."

"Yeah right. That ain't ever gonna happen."

"Anyway, the point for me calling you, Digger, is I need your expertise. A fellow I knew passed away, and in his will, I've been asked to deal with the liquidation of his collection of old cars. I've uncovered a couple of them and when I saw the first one, I thought of you at once. It's an early 1950's Buick Convertible."

For a moment, the phone was silent, then I heard a whisper, "No shit?"

"No shit. Can you get away for a few days and come down to Fort Myers and go through these cars and help me come up with some kind of value? And some advice on what to do with them."

"Fort Myers? You mean like Fort Myers, Florida?"

"Yeah. Like there's any other."

"Isn't it hot there right now?"

"Actually, it's not too bad today. Somewhere in the low 80's, I think."

I heard his voice explode out of my cell phone I waited for him to calm down. When he ran out of gas, I spoke.

"Digger, nobody I know has as much knowledge about old cars as you do."

"Matt, you are so full of shit, I can smell the stink all the way up here in Idaho. But yeah, I'll come down. I'll let you know when I'm getting in."

"If you can give me the name of the closest airport to you, I'll have my pilot call you when he's getting close and you can fly down in my plane."

It took Digger a few tries to get it out, but he finally said, "Your plane. You have a plane? What are you, like fucking rich?"

I couldn't resist. "Yeah, Digger. Remember all of the holes you were digging over the years all over Seattle? Well, I usually owned the land where you dug those holes! I got twice what you got paid for digging the holes and then I upped the price on the land because of the holes." I could hear him laughing on the other end. Finally, I told him, "Actually the plane isn't exactly mine. It's like a timeshare, and I can call and have it go wherever I need and pick up what I want and then bring it to me."

I gave him Henry's phone number so he recognize it when the call came to tell him the time he could expect to be picked up at the airport. As we hung up, I reminded him again to give Sherral a call. I could hear him in the background. "Fucking dude has a plane. He owns an airplane."

Since Digger was getting such a big bang out of the whole thing, I could see no reason to try and straighten him out...

Again.

CHAPTER TWENTY

Heather and I were already waiting on the tarmac when Digger's plane touched down. I'd pulled the Buick out of storage, had it washed and re-filled with fresh gas. The paint was in amazing condition considering the age of the vehicle, and all the chrome sparkled in the sun. The grill was massive and the four ports on the front fenders glistened. The old convertible top showed no signs of rot when I put it down. When the car went into storage, Snooker disconnected the battery and, once I made sure it had a charge, I reattached it. To my amazement, when I turned the key to the start position, the motor turned over a couple of times and caught. I was aware this was the first year Buick had gone to a 12-volt system from a 6 volt, and I was sure that helped get the car started.

Snooker stored the car with care. He'd added a fuel stabilizer to the gas tank, however, I still had the tank drained and re-filled. Because it had been resting on foam pads, the tires were still round, holding air and in good shape. After we got it out on the road, the ride was amazing. The Buick's motor was still as quiet as I remembered, and it was still as slow.

Digger stepped off the plane and when he saw the car, he stopped and stared. I swear there were tears in his eyes. When I'd first seen the car in storage, I had paid little attention to the color, but after I got it cleaned up, I noticed it was dark gray with red leather interior and a black roof. It looked exactly like the car Digger had back in college. He grinned at me as he said, "You know, you really are an asshole. How can you live with yourself? You show up with a car like that and ask for a favor, how am I going to say no? You know that's the same year as my old Buick. You have a 1952 there."

"I kinda thought so, or at least I was sure hoping. I'm giving you that car. For helping me, I'm giving you the car."

The look on his face was priceless. "No shit?"

"No shit! The deal is, I get any three of the cars I want for handling the sale of the collection and this one is yours. We can have it shipped back to Idaho when you're ready."

"Three cars! And you're going to give me this one? Okay! And now I suppose I have to look at the rest of the fucking cars?"

"Yep!"

"How many are there?"

"I'm not telling you. I'll let you find out precisely like I did." Digger had a totally confused look on his face. "Trust me, you'll love it!" I assured him.

As we put Digger's stuff in the trunk, he asked me, "Who's the young lady? Girlfriend?"

"No, this is Heather. She's a friend. I'm selling my bike, but I wanted to do one more motorcycle trip. I was out in the middle of nowhere when I found her alongside the road, barefoot and limping. I stopped to see what the problem was, and I... well, let's say I rescued her." I motioned towards Heather. "This is my old friend, Digger. Digger, this is Heather." I could see steam coming out of ol' Diggers ears, and I thought Heather seemed to be interested in him too.

Since Heather was wearing a tube top with a rather skimpy pair of shorts, she looked sexy as hell. I wondered if I might have solved my *What to Do with Heather* situation.

I had Digger drive the old Buick out to the warehouse after I gave him directions. I swear, the smile never left his face. Heather sat in the middle of the car next to Digger, close to him. I don't know if it was the car or Heather which pleased him the most. Digger parked the car, and as he turned to walk away, he stopped for a moment and gently patted the hood. He was smitten. And yes, I know I was an ass for doing that. Hey, I was desperate.

I unlocked the warehouse door, and we stepped into the waiting area. I'd been by the shop earlier and left the lights on in the main warehouse. Digger stepped into the room and stopped. The look on his face was priceless. I don't think I'd ever heard a grown man whimper until that moment but Digger whimpered as he stood there rubbernecking. Eventually, I heard him mutter, "Fuck me! They go on forever." Finally, he turned and asked, "Dude, how many cars are there?"

"Fifty-six, I believe."

"Damn! Are you serious?"

"Yeah, and I've only uncovered the Buick and the car next to it which is an old Corvette."

"Old Corvette?" His voice rang with excitement. "How old?"

"I dunno, I think it's one of the early ones they made. It was white and…"

Digger interrupted, "That would be a 1953. Matt, do you really have a 1953 Corvette here? Show me!" He sounded like a kid at Christmas. I led him to the car I'd uncovered the first time I visited the warehouse. Carefully, we removed the cover and Digger slowly walked around it. The way he gawked at the car, you'd have thought it was the Crown Jewels. "Look at this," Digger said, still animated. "It has the original chrome screens covering the headlights. Have you looked at the VIN?"

The VIN, which stands for Vehicle Identification Number, besides identifying the vehicle, tells the way the manufacturer built the car and when they built it. I told him I hadn't looked since I didn't know where to locate the VIN tag. "It's on the post on the driver's side," Digger told me as he reached inside the cockpit to carefully pull the door lever and open the driver's door. He glanced at the mileage, then bent over and looked again. "Matt, this thing has less than 28,000 miles on it."

Digger found the VIN plate and discovered it was the twenty-seventh Corvette out of just 300 built that first year of production. Out of years and years of Corvettes, this was just the twenty-seventh Corvette ever built. The hairs on my arm stood up. Carefully, we opened the hood and Digger said the condition looked like at one time, someone might have restored it, but there were other things that made him think differently. Finally, he stepped back and just stood ogling the car. "Matt, this is a survivor. This baby is untouched and intact. It's just like it left the factory."

"What do you think the value is?"

"Well, I'm not sure, but I'd say this car alone is for sure over a hundred and fifty thousand, and possibly a lot more."

"What are we going to do? How are we going to sell all these cars?" I asked.

Digger took a step backwards, "Hold up there, Tonto, where the hell do you get this 'we' shit?"

"Kemo Sabe, when you drove your new Buick over here, it went from a 'me' and became a 'we.'" I beamed at him.

"You know, you really are a prick. A great big prick! But thanks for the car. You do know you play dirty?"

I smiled at him.

Oh yeah, I know I play dirty.

~ ~ ~ ~ ~

The three of us went to dinner and the more time Heather and Digger spent together, the more it was obvious there was a real fire developing between them. They were sitting next to each other, and I noticed her hand now rested on the top of his thigh. He seemed smitten and was treating her well. I already knew some of her past and I was sure she hadn't met a lot of gentlemen like Digger. He may be gruff—a man who speaks his mind—but he was still a gentleman and basically a very sweet man. If it worked out, Heather was a lucky woman.

About halfway through the meal, Digger set down his fork and grinned at me as he leaned back in his chair.

"What?" I asked.

He turned to Heather. "Excuse me for talking about an old girlfriend for a moment." Heather smiled and nodded. Digger turned to me. "I called Sherral. We had a really nice talk and she told me she was grateful I called her. She was still a little upset it took me so long to call, but she told me she was finally able to bury a lot of hurt and anger. She even confessed that she had also been frightened if we had gone ahead and finished what we'd planned, she might not have been very good and I would have been disappointed or angry. Anyway, thanks for encouraging me to call her, it was the right thing to do. We both feel so much better."

I noticed Heather gave Digger's thigh a squeeze and smiled at him. I think she was starting to see what a great guy he really was. I was starting to feel like a third wheel. Still grinning at me, he pointed at me as he proclaimed, "And I have the solution to our problem."

"Well come on, don't leave me in suspense here."

"Have you ever heard of Amelia Island?"

"Duh! Of course. This is Florida."

"And because it's in Florida, we don't have to pay an arm and a leg to ship the cars anywhere. I suggest we divide the cars into three lots. Let's get a third of them detailed, serviced and then send them directly over to the next auction at Amelia. We can look for another auction where we could send one of the remaining two lots and we make sure they heavily advertise the auction.

"Matt, there are rich fat cats from all over the world who fly in to buy stuff like that Corvette at the auction. If half of those cars in that warehouse are in the same condition as the Corvette, your friend's granddaughter is now a multi-millionaire."

"Perfect. I knew calling you was the right thing to do."

Digger and I discussed if we wanted the temptation we knew we'd encounter if we were to look over what was in the collection ourselves, but we decided even though we didn't need the temptation, we really had to inventory what was there.

We agreed what time to meet at the warehouse the next morning and got ready to part company. I could see that Heather seemed troubled about something. She motioned she wanted to chat with me, alone. When we were by ourselves, I asked her, "What's up kid?"

"Umm, would it upset you if I spent some more time with Digger?"

"You mean like the night?" She smiled as she looked up at me. "I don't own you," I said. "I feel protective of you, but I've known Digger a long time and I think he's exactly what you need right now in your life."

Heather had the good grace to at least blush a little as she nodded. I walked over to Digger. "Old friend, I think I need to explain something. Like I told you out at the airport, Heather's a good friend, she's not a love interest. She seems to like you and I didn't want you to feel you were intruding on something between us. I have a lady friend up in

246

Washington D.C. I need to see… soon! But I want you two to do as you see fit and not worry about me. I'm happy for both of you, you seem to appreciate each other. You have my blessings, children."

As I watched the two of them walk away holding hands, somehow seeing Digger and Heather that way made me feel lonely. I could guess what they would do this evening and it made me want to see Lois as soon as I could all that much more.

I realized I missed her…

A lot.

~ ~ ~ ~ ~

The next morning, the three of us worked on an inventory of the vehicles in the warehouse. As we uncovered the various cars, we discovered Snooker seemed to have had a real passion for late fifties, sixties and early seventies automobiles. Mopar products seemed to be a favorite, but he had several other brands as well.

I didn't know nearly as much as Digger did about older cars, but I was positive a few of them were rare. When we uncovered one Plymouth from the late sixties, Digger said he wasn't even aware they'd built one like it. He believed it might be a one of a kind special order thing, or at least it was ultra-rare. He knew somebody back on the West coast who had been a Mopar person all his life and could give us more details. When Digger got off the phone with him, he had a big smirk on his face.

"I'm such a bad person. I called him and he's coming here. When I first told him what we had, he called me a liar. I gave him the VIN number since I know he has access to all the codes and then I hung up on him. I knew he'd call me back. Once he realized what I'd told him was true, and

247

that I wasn't fooling with his head, he did call me right back and made me promise I wouldn't tell anybody else about the car. He said he'd call me with his flight number as soon as he could get a flight down here and I'm to go pick him up." Digger leered at me. "Help me get that car ready and I'll go pick him up. If you could fuck with my head with that damn Buick, I can do the same!" We both chortled.

Later, I came upon a 1962 Pontiac Bonneville convertible, which must have been the car Zoe saw when Snooker had it out. It was long, sexy and gorgeous. The white paint was in perfect condition and the red leather interior was in remarkable shape. The bucket seats seemed to call out for me to get in and drive the car. When I looked inside, I noticed it had a four-speed transmission shifter sticking out of the console between the bucket seats. The car had special factory rims that were finned with eight lug nuts. The badge on the fender told me the car was fuel injected. From everything I had learned, I knew this car was rare, and Digger confirmed my suspicions. I wanted this car, but I was also trying to get rid of my collection back in Seattle since the city would claim my buildings by the right of eminent domain. They weren't condemned yet, but I knew it was a matter of time before I had to move the cars, and it would be soon. I didn't need another car in Florida since I had no place to store it.

We'd been making a list of the cars we found and later that day, as we were going through one car, we found two large notebooks on the passenger seat. The notebooks contained both a CD and a printed list. It listed every car, when it was purchased, where it was purchased and how much Snooker had paid for the car. He'd kept a surprising amount of documentation on each car. We took the CD into the office and fired up the computer, and when we opened the files, we were amazed at the amount of detail Snooker included with the list of his collection. The provenance on so many of the cars was superb.

It turned out he was the second owner of the old Corvette. He had purchased the car from the original owner two years after he'd joined the service. It was his first purchase, and the car listed the mileage and over the years, he'd driven it fewer than 10,000 additional miles.

Snooker won the Buick in a pool game and I told Digger some stories about Snooker's prowess with a pool stick. Knowing how the car came to be in the collection seemed to make it even more special. Digger said he was going to name the car 8-Ball. I thought the name was perfect. The car was a very dark gray, almost black, and considering how Tom had ended up with it, 8-Ball was the perfect name. Digger said once he had the car back home, he would have the name painted on the dashboard. I hooted. He was like me, still a kid at heart.

Snooker had purchased several of the cars through the PX while he was on active duty, as I'd suspected. As we continued to uncover the cars, with no warning, Heather let out a squeal. "Matt! Digger! Come here." Digger and I ran over to her. I wondered if she'd found a spider or a snake.

"What happened?" Digger asked.

Heather pointed to the car she had just uncovered. "Is that what I think it is?"

All of us stood gawking at the dark red car. I knew it was a Shelby Cobra, or at least it looked like one. I wasn't sure if it might have been a kit car or the real thing. Digger looked carefully for the VIN tag. Finally, he found it on the passenger side foot box. "Matt, this is a 1967 427 Cobra. But it's even more special than that. You know I'm a Ford nut?" I nodded. Digger really was a true Ford nut.

"Some of the so-called 427 motors were actually 428-cubic-inch Police Interceptor engines—a cheaper motor. In an effort to earn more profit, Carroll Shelby saved a few a hundred dollars per car by installing the cheaper police engine, which had about thirty less horsepower. This car, however, was the real deal. One of the letters in the VIN tag indicates the car came with a real, 427-cubic-inch, special built, Shelby Cobra motor. That makes this puppy worth a lot more money."

"What do you think the car is worth?" I asked.

"My guess, at least a million bucks. I really don't know. I wonder where Snooker got it."

"There's still a lot of paperwork missing that we need," I remarked.

Heather pointed out in the office she'd seen a large safe bolted to the floor. I'd hadn't paid much attention to it because at first glance, it looked like a normal filing cabinet. However, none of the drawers opened, but when you pulled on one of the middle handles, it opened like a door to reveal a dial to enter the combination. It was brilliant. On one of the CD's we'd found was a file marked Safe Combination. Once we opened the safe, we found the titles to each of the cars and even more records on some of the vehicles. What a big relief!

After we finished our first list, we compared it to the list we found. There were two cars we wondered about because they didn't seem to fit Snooker's normal purchases, and there didn't seem to be much if any documentation on them. After we decided on which cars we would send to the auction, we emailed them the list. Then we made a list of some other cars and emailed that to people we thought might be interested in the cars.

After we emailed the list to the auction house at Amelia Island, we received a phone call within the hour. When the people at the auction house first saw the list, they thought it was a joke. Digger took several pictures with his cell and sent them off. After that, the people at the auction house were beside themselves with excitement over the cars. When we mentioned this was only about a third of the cars we had, they wanted to come over immediately and see the rest of what we had. However, we declined.

I made arrangements to get the cars in our first lot cleaned up and when they were ready, we would ship them over to the other side of the state for the Amelia auction. There were several cars I was interested in, but I had my collection to dispose of, so I only lusted after them.

I needed to get rid of most of the cars I currently owned. The hardest part would be to get rid of all the MGB's. There must have been enough pieces and parts to build a dozen cars, along with the few already assembled. I decided it was time to give Art a call and get the ball rolling. Dealing with all of Snooker's cars made me realize that I also had no one I knew who would do this for me, so I'd better get to it myself. Art is the older gentleman who works on my cars. "Hello Art. It's Matt."

"It's good to hear your voice. I'd heard through the grapevine you were someplace in the Middle East and you were injured."

"Yeah, but I'm okay now. I'll admit, it was dicey for a while."

"Well, I'm sure glad you're back. It worried me hearing about you. Having to finish up the rest of the MGB's on my own didn't excite me much."

We both laughed. "Funny you would bring that up, that's one reason I called you. You know you've been telling me you want to retire, full time." He grunted his agreement. "Well, I agree. It's time for you to retire and for me to sell off the cars."

"Oh, Matt, you don't have to do that."

"Actually, Art, I do. The city will condemn the buildings and I need to do something now so we don't get stuck with a bunch of parts we have to dump."

"Matt, I know a fellow down in Portland who's a big MGB lover. Let me call him and see if he is interested in any, some or all of the MGB stuff we have here."

"Would you mind? I don't know how much time we have."

"When will you be back?"

"Dunno, but if I get an interested party, I'll have them contact you to look at the vehicles. Do you mind?"

"Naw, I've spent so much time working on them, I feel they're partly mine, anyway."

"Sounds good, let's stay in touch. Goodbye." Selling the collection wasn't what I wanted to do, but I understood it was time.

As Digger and I went through Snooker's collection, I saw cars I knew I might never see again. The temptation to buy some of them for myself was huge!

Oh shit, decisions, decisions.

~ ~ ~ ~ ~

I couldn't help myself. That evening, I drove the old Pontiac back to Snooker's condo where I was staying. Driving down the street with the top down, I received countless thumbs up and honking horns telling me I wasn't the only one who appreciated a beautiful old car. As I pulled into my parking stall, I realized I'd done a stupid thing; I was falling in love with the darn car. I had cars I needed to sell, not adopt more. But the car was so cool!

Martha greeted me at the door and told me Zoe was trying to call me. Martha gave me Zoe's number, and I called. "Hi, Zoe. It's Matt."

"Hey, Matt! I was wondering how things were going," she responded.

I apologized for not getting back to her sooner, but once I told her how many cars were in the collection, she was quiet. "Hello! Hello, Zoe, are you there?"

"Did you say there were fifty-six cars?"

"Yes. There are several racks where the cars are stacked two high. We're still working on a complete inventory of the collection. But we know there are at least fifty cars in excellent condition from what we can tell, minus the three the will entitled me to. When everything is done, we'll have over fifty cars to be sold."

"Like, are the cars expensive?"

"What do you consider expensive? Some of them are worth a lot of money, some of them not so much. There's a very old Corvette there that's one of the first ones ever built and the car is in perfect condition. After we looked into it, we found out that car alone is worth over two hundred thousand dollars. There is also a car there we feel might be worth over a million dollars.

"I've got an old buddy from my school days helping me get them ready for sale. We divided the cars into roughly three lots so we don't dump a bunch of collector cars on the market at one time. Each lot will have some prime stuff and some nice but not as desirable cars. We've been arranging with the auction people over in Amelia Island for the first lot of twenty cars. A rough estimate right now for the first third of the collection headed for auction is as much as three million dollars."

She stuttered then finally blurted out, "Three million. You mean like American dollars?"

"Yeah, why?"

"I never knew there was so much money tied up in his cars."

"Remember, this is just for a third of the cars. Who really knows how much is there until we get them to auction?"

"How did this happen? How come there is so much money there?"

"Your grandfather purchased cars when he was in the army. He got excellent deals through the PX and things he purchased for perhaps three thousand dollars are now worth sometimes over one hundred thousand dollars. The car that's worth a million now, he bought for fifty-five thousand dollars. Your grandfather had great taste in cars, and he never drove a lot of them which makes them worth more money. Do you have any idea what a rare car from the late sixties with only a few miles is worth today? Plus, he was a fantastic pool player, and he earned a lot of money shooting pool. You know his nickname was Snooker. That was because if you played pool with him, you'd been snookered. He was amazing."

With sadness, she said, "I never saw him play, but I've heard stories about him. Was he really that good?"

"No, Zoe, he wasn't just good, he was fantastic. He was the stuff they make legends about. And it looks like he used a lot of the money he won over the years to purchase old cars."

"Matt, please excuse me. I need to talk to Stephen. I'll call you back." I told her to call me back on my cell number and explained it was better to call me that way. She thanked me, and we hung up.

While I had been chatting with Zoe, my phone vibrated. Later, when I checked, I noticed it had been Henry calling me. I called back. "Henry, Matt. What can I do for you?"

"Hey, partner. Are we having any luck with finding space for our business?"

"Well, I'm still waiting to hear if the old ladies have decided. Why?" I asked.

"Look, even though we only have just a few planes at the moment and you know I'm looking to secure a couple more and who knows what's waiting in the wings, we still need a home office, a base of operations, and especially hanger space for repairs. You thought you had a lead, I was wondering if you were having any luck with that?"

"I need to check on that. Let me contact them and I'll let you know what I find out."

"Great, talk at you later."

"Ciao."

~ ~ ~ ~ ~

I was still driving the Pontiac, and I knew the more I drove it, the harder it would be to sell, but I continued to drive it anyway. I drove down to Page Field and on the south end, I noticed the warehouse with a 'for lease' sign in the window was still empty. I called the number listed on the sign and a woman's voice answered. "Good afternoon, Tilkens Leasing. How may I help you?"

I explained who I was. "Hello, Mr. Preston."

"I'm in front of the empty buildings down here at Page Field. I see they are still available. Can I speak to Mr. Tilkens?"

"Gee, Mr. Preston, Mr. Tilkens is out right now showing a property, but if you'll give me your number, I'll have him call you back the minute he returns. I know he has been in contact with the sisters that own the hangar space across the road with airfield access and the warehouse property. I'll make sure he calls you at once."

"That's fantastic. It's exactly what I wanted to hear."

No sooner had I hung up when my phone rang again. The display screen told me it was Lois. "Hi, babe. I'm so pleased to hear from you." I told her. "I really miss you."

"Hi, lover. Really? Do you really miss me?"

"Yeah, like you can't believe. I think we need to see each other, soon. I miss you like crazy. I was thinking of coming up to see you as soon as I got back from my bike trip. But you know what happened when I got back."

"How'd that go?"

"I ended up collecting a woman."

"What! You did what?"

"I picked up this gal who was walking barefoot out in the middle of nowhere. Her husband had beaten her up, and she was running away. I've been taking care of her until she met my buddy Digger. They are now an item."

"Did you sleep with her?"

"You mean did I make love with her? No! Until we get things worked out between you and me, I'm not interested in any other women right now."

"Really? Like me, do you?"

"Damn straight. I don't just like you, I love you. I'm missing you so much. I'm finishing up with the part of the car collection we're selling and it's ready for shipping. How about coming down and spending the weekend with me?"

"For real? I'd love that. I've been missing you, too."

"Ditto. Let me check with Henry and see if there's anything close to bring you down."

"I'm waiting for your call."

When I called Henry, he was out. I left a message for him, letting him know I wanted to bring Lois down to Florida and asking if anything was coming this way. Now I had to wait and see what transpired.

My wait didn't last long. "Matt, got your message."

"Anything coming down here soon?"

"No, but I have a plane going up to D.C. from Miami that's empty. You want a ride up here?"

"Got to make a phone call. Give me a sec." I hung up and called Lois. "Hi, lover."

"What's up?"

"How would you feel if instead of you coming down here, I came up there for the weekend?"

"Yes! I'd love it. When can you get here?"

"Henry has a plane in Miami. Once I'm on board, I'll call you."

"Wonderful. I love you."

"And I love you."

There was a moment of silence, then in a whisper, she asked, "Do you realize you don't tell me often enough you love me."

"I'm sorry. I do love you and I promise to do better. We can talk about this when I get there."

"Hurry. I want you."

"Ditto!"

CHAPTER TWENTY-ONE

I still was driving around Page Field looking for an empty space to lease for our new company, since I hadn't heard from Tilkens, when I felt my phone vibrate in my pocket. "Hello, this is Matt. Hang on for a second while I pull over." Because the top was down, I couldn't hear, so I pulled over to the curb and placed the car in park. "Hi, this is Matt Preston."

"Hello, Mr. Preston, this is Tom Tilkens. My secretary tells me you're at the warehouse space near the airport?"

"Yes, sir. She mentioned you've been in contact with the sisters and they may have come up with an offer so I might be able to rent the properties? If it works out, you know I'd be interested in leasing both spaces. What can you tell me?"

"Mr. Preston, they will be the death of me. They're still bickering between a sale or leasing. But they agreed if you will make an offer, they'll consider it. For them, that is a major step forward. The hanger and warehouse are for sale, but so far, there's no action."

"Is it possible for you to show me the buildings now?"

"You bet. I'm on my way."

I turned around and drove back to the warehouse. Twenty minutes later, I was shaking hands with what appeared to be a movie extra. If there was such a thing as a person who looked like a true Floridian you wanted in a movie, Tilkens was your man. Short-sleeved silk shirt, gold chains around his neck and wrist, a big pinky ring, linen shorts and open-toes sandals, a perfect haircut and sporting a killer tan. He looked like he'd just stepped off the golf links and the only thing missing was a putter in his hand.

Walking through the warehouse, I thought it'd be perfect as a workshop for our planes, and I also noticed a corner which might handle the storage of a couple of cars. With some change in plans, the old Pontiac was looking a lot more and more like a keeper. I noticed a puddle of water in one corner and when I looked up, I could see blue sky. The building needed a new roof. Something to keep in mind.

After we finished with the warehouse, we walked across the street and inspected the hanger space. Other than having a few missing windows and needing some work on the large sliding doors, the space was perfect for our needs. The space was large enough to fit at least four planes and perhaps even a fifth with an ample amount of tarmac in front which went with the building. Combined with the warehouse space, in a pinch, we could store up to seven planes. In addition, there was a toilet and a sink in the hanger and an office the size of a broom closet, while the warehouse had two restrooms along with two reasonably sized office areas. I asked again what the asking price was for both and when Tilkens told me, I asked, "Are you in a rush to go anywhere? Do you have a little time right now?"

"No, I have a little time. Why?"

"I need to speak to my partner. Can you wait?"

"I'll call the office. You do what you have to do, I'll wait."

I excused myself and stepped outside. I called Henry. "Busy?" I asked.

"No, what do you need?"

"I've found a warehouse and hanger space and it's for sale." I told him how big they were and what the asking price was. I told him how the owners didn't know if they wanted to sell or what. "I thought I'd make an offer. Do you need to see the spaces, or will you trust me?"

"Matt, so far you have done nothing to alarm me. If you think this is a good deal, go for it."

"There are several factors why I think this is good for us right now. Down the road, we can always move. I'll be in touch. I wanted to get your blessings first."

"Consider it done. I bless you my son." We were both laughing as we hung up.

I went back inside to speak to Tilkens. "About the two spaces, we would like to purchase both." I made a counteroffer of considerably less money to the asking price.

"Are you serious? You mean you want to purchase both properties?"

"Yes sir. If you can convince the owners to sell and if my offer interests them, I can give you the phone number of two banks I do business with up in Seattle for credit references. As for local references, you can check with Sargent Brian Polk at the Fort Myers police station and I'm sure he'll give me a clean bill of health."

"How do you know Sargent Polk?" he asked with some skepticism.

I sniggered. "It's okay. I'm not a convict or anything. Some weeks ago, there was a murder, and I assisted him with part of the investigation."

"Do you mean that dance hall thing?"

"Yes, something like that." I really didn't want to get into any more explanation. Tilkens asked me to come to his office Monday morning, and he'd have the paperwork ready to sign allowing him to make an offer for me. I explained I'd call my banker as soon as we finished today and have arrangements made to wire the money by Monday afternoon to close the sale to cover my offering price if he could get the sisters to go for the deal. All that was necessary was for him was to send wiring instructions to my banks for the money.

My comments were surprising to him. "Wait a minute. I'm sorry, I didn't understand what you meant at first. Do you mean you want to pay cash for the properties... now? Don't you have to arrange financing?"

"No, sir. This is a straight cash deal, an all-cash offer. I am prepared to close the deal as soon as we can. Let's get this done as quickly as possible." The smile that came over Tilkens' face was priceless. I continued. "Mr. Tilkens, please let me explain. That's why I named the price I did. You told me the current owners want to sell, but so far have been unsuccessful. Additionally, there are some condition issues I will need to take care of and that also figured into my offer. You told me there are problems between the two sisters. With my offer, they'll be cashed out and since you say it's an estate sale, I'd think they'll appreciate it's not contingent on any financing going through. Also, would you also mind asking the sisters when I might get a set of keys?"

Tom excused himself a for a moment and stepped outside to make a phone call. A few minutes later, he came back. "I can't believe it, but they are actually interested in selling the place since you're making an all-cash offer." He continued to present me with a counteroffer.

I shook my head. "Mr. Tilkens, even though these buildings fit my needs, I'm sure there are other buildings around here which would do the same. Since I'm offering an all-cash offer, the sisters get their money immediately. In addition, I feel I'm making a fair offer considering how long the property has been on the market and building's current condition. You know about needing a new roof; so, I will stay with my original offer. There will be no counter offer. Now, sir, not to be rude, but you need to put on your salesman hat and make this deal happen! You know both buildings need work. Sitting empty is not good for the buildings or for the sisters. This is a good deal for everybody concerned and you know it!"

Tilkens lost a little of his tan. He looked at me for a moment, nodded, and excused himself again. I watched him pace back and forth in front of the building, talking on his cell phone. From time to time, he'd make a gesture or shake his fist. I knew he was talking to the owners of the buildings, but it was impossible to tell how the negotiations were going. Finally, he returned, smiling, and handed me a set of keys. "You have purchased yourself a building. Or should I say two buildings? The sisters said they thought they could let you have keys since you were paying cash for the buildings on Monday and you seemed to have provided a good reference down here."

We laughed as we shook hands and exchanged business cards, deciding when we would meet Monday afternoon. After Tilkens left, I called Henry. "Hello, do you have a moment to chat?" I asked.

"Yeah, what's up?"

"I purchased the hanger, and it's big enough for at least four and maybe five planes with a warehouse right across the street from the hanger. These are all on the south end of Page Field. I'll create a company you and I will own together, and this company will hold the title for the buildings and then lease the space back to our other company. Are you okay with that?"

"You never cease to amaze me, Matt. That's perfect."

"Oh, some of the warehouse space is mine. I need a place to store a couple of cars."

I could hear him laughing on the other end of the phone. "Okay. Tell me, what type of cars are they?"

"Collector cars. One of them is a 1962 Pontiac Bonneville convertible…"

His voice was almost a scream. "Where the hell did you find a car like that? I'm so jealous."

"Do you like old cars?"

"Does a bear make big do-do in the woods? Does he use a maple leaf to wipe? Damn straight I do."

"I'll make you a deal, if you can get down here in the next few days, I have a surprise for you."

"What is it?"

"Remember what you told me? If I tell you, it ain't a surprise, right?"

Henry was laughing. "Ya know, I knew when I said that to you in Vegas, it would come back and bite me in the ass. Matt, you really are a shit! Okay, I'm on my way to take you up to Lois."

The phone went dead.

~ ~ ~ ~ ~

My flight up to D.C. turned out perfect. The weather was just right for flying and visibility was excellent. I was getting used to flying in private jets and I was pleased to see our company was getting busier. We had a booking lined up and another one right after that for the plane I was on. Henry needed to get up to Washington, dump me off, and pick up the clients.

Walking through the small terminal towards the entrance, I noticed a woman dressed in a suit and tie holding a placard in her hands. It read Matt Preston. I stepped up to the driver. "I'm Matt Preston."

"I'm here to give you a ride. I have the address where I'm to drop you off. Do you have any luggage?"

"Nope, just what I have here in my briefcase." I didn't need to bring much since my suit was still in Lois' closet. Normally, we didn't need much in the way of clothing when I visited anyway.

The ride was fast and comfortable. We pulled up in front of Lois' condo and I got out. "Thanks for the ride," I told the driver.

When I turned, Lois was standing in the doorway to her lobby. She reached out a hand, and I took it. I pulled her to me and gave her a kiss.

"Did you like the limo I ordered for you?" I nodded. "Come on. I need you." She told me with a wicked grin on her face. I was correct about not needing much in the way of clothing. Our weekend was perfect.

~ ~ ~ ~ ~

On Monday, I hurried back to Fort Myers and helped Digger finish our project. One of our other pilots flew me back because Henry was off on some secret mission for John Orchard. When I left, I asked if Lois would come down for the next weekend. I explained it was the weekend of the auction over on Amelia Island and I wanted her to attend with me. She said she would. We planned for her to work half a day on Friday, come down that evening, then fly back to D.C. early Monday morning.

When my plane landed, the pilot took me over to the hanger area and dropped me off. By the time he was airborne, I had the Pontiac out of the warehouse and headed for my meeting with Tom Tilkens. The signing of the paperwork at Tilkens' office went off without a hitch.

I headed up to the business park to meet up with Digger. Coming over the rise on the bridge, I looked down at my speed odometer. Oh shit! I was almost twenty over the limit and I saw a black and white tucked away up ahead on the side of the road. I slowed down as quickly as possible, but I was sure I'd blown the radar trap. Sure enough, as I drove by, the lights on the police car came on and he pulled out behind me. I signaled to pull over at the first opportunity and parked. When I looked in the rear-view mirror, I saw it was Sargent Polk getting out of his squad car and heading up to my driver's side.

"Damn it, Matt. This is getting to be a habit with you." The smile on his face belied the tone of his voice.

"Sorry, sir. I wasn't paying attention."

"And where did you get this car?"

"I'm doing a favor for an old friend who passed away." I explained about Snooker's car collection and how I was helping his granddaughter by selling off the cars. "For my troubles, I get to pick three of the cars I want for myself. I think this will be one."

"Well, try to keep all four wheels on the ground, please." For the next few minutes we chatted, then his face got serious. "We got a report from some little town in Arizona. They found Ruth, Gilberto's ex-wife." A few weeks ago, Snooker had asked me to help solve a murder mystery because his future grandson-in-law was being charged with the murder. Gilberto, the previous owner of the Troncoso's dance studio, had been murdered by his ex-wife and she'd fled and never been caught, until now.

Polk continued. "They found her in some flea-bag motel where she'd committed suicide. There was a note telling how she had killed Gilberto. She ended the note by saying rotting away in a prison wasn't something she could deal with and the only thing she regretted was not killing the bastard sooner. She really seemed to hate that man."

I sat there for a moment feeling sorry for her. I'd learned so much about Gilberto during my investigation, so many bad things he had done, and I understood how hurt she must have been. I hoped she'd finally found peace. Speaking of peace... "How are things with you and the lovely Doris?"

I didn't think Brian could get any redder, but his face bloomed. "Also turns out that the physical part of things isn't as over as much I thought they were. I'd no idea... well, things like that could be so enjoyable. I never thought a woman could open so many new doors in that area." I couldn't believe how embarrassed he was. "Thanks for encouraging me to go talk to her and date her. It's... well, it's beyond description."

"I thought a lot of you when I met you. And I thought Doris was special too. I couldn't think of a couple who are better suited for each other."

"Your partner Digger tells me you're making a habit of setting up couples." He had the good graces to at least laugh as he said that. "I know for me, you did a nice job, and Digger seems to be happy. So, Cupid, what are your plans now?"

I resisted making a comment. "You know, Seattle is changing too fast for my taste. It's not the place I grew up. I feel it's sold its soul to the devil. It's all about the money now. I'm selling my car collection up there, and all my properties. Since the city will take my downtown buildings where my cars are stored anyway, they decided for me. I have a good friend who has offered to sell or lease me one of his condos if I want up in Seattle, and I accepted. Now I'll become a snow bird. I have the place here in North Fort Myers and I'll have a place in Seattle, but no holdings of any sort up there. I haven't spoken with Lois yet, but I think she would like for me to be on this side of the country more. Oh, and I promise to slow down... a little."

Polk guffawed and slapped my shoulder, "Yeah, that will be the day. Not if you keep driving this puppy."

I started again to head out and check on Digger and Heather at the business park when I got a call from Henry asking me where I was. I told him I was about five minutes from the airport, so he told me to come and get him.

"I thought you were on some mission somewhere."

"Just got back."

"Where were you?"

"Matt, you know better than that."

"Woops, sorry. I'll see you in five minutes."

When I got there, he was waiting next to one of our planes. When I rolled up in the Pontiac, he stood there grinning at me. I called out to him to come and get in. Instead, he slowly walked around the car. Finally, he stepped up to the passenger door and as he opened it, he proclaimed, "You're a dog. This car is amazing."

"Get in, I have a lot more to share with you." I took him over to the hangar space we now owned and then we crossed the street to the warehouse. I could tell our acquisition impressed him. He called somebody on his cell and instructed them to move the plane he'd flown in over from where it was on the tarmac in front of the terminal and park it in front of our hanger. Walking out to the Pontiac, Henry told me, "This will be perfect for us. We're not that far from D.C., and other places here on the east coast where most of our charters come from. Nice job, Matt."

We headed out to the freeway then north. I pulled into the business park's driveway and parked in front of the building containing Snooker's collection. Henry followed me in and I took him back to where the cars were stored. Digger had moved the cars we were to ship to Amelia Island off to one side, and they looked great sitting there all spiffed up. Henry stood there gaping at all the cars. Finally, I stepped up and took his arm and led him over. I watched as he tried to speak. I had to laugh.

I left Digger and Henry to chat about the cars and went over to speak to Heather. "How are things going with the two of you?"

"I feel kind of guilty."

"Why?"

"For one thing, I can't believe how happy I am with Digger. He treats me like no other man ever has. And I feel bad because you've been so nice and the way you helped me out with Jerry and all and now I'm…"

"Stop. I told you all along I have a friend who I've been trying to figure things out about. I know she is in love with me and I care for her. No, strike that. I *love* her. I know she's looking for a more permanent relationship than I thought I was, but now I don't know what I want except to spend more time with her. Anyway, I want you to do whatever you want with Digger. He's an old friend and I think the two of you are a good match. Basically, you two have my blessing and I'm so pleased to see you happy. I don't think I've ever seen Digger this happy and I don't know if it's you, the Buick or both."

Heather chuckled. "I think it's the Buick more than me."

"That's not true, and you know it."

As if on cue, Digger came wandering over with Henry. Digger was laughing as Henry told me he had spotted two cars he was lusting over. "How about the little 1962 red Porsche convertible over there? It's a model I've never seen. I thought the biggest one was the Super 90 Porsche shipped into the states and that one is a Super 120."

"Yeah, Digger tells me they didn't export those from Germany. I guess when Snooker was stationed there, he found that one and had it shipped back to the states. That puppy is very rare."

"Is it for sale?"

"No, it's not for sale. It's yours. I'm giving it to you. Since I have three cars coming and I've only picked two so far, that car is now yours. As for the second car you liked, I'll check with Hemmings and with Haggerty, and whatever the going price is, I'll take ten percent off of that and it's yours."

"That's not right, Matt. I should pay for both. Why are you giving me a car?"

"Henry, think about this. Without you, I'd be dead over somewhere in that god-forsaken sand box. At great risk, you came and rescued me. Come on, a car is a small payment for my life. Now shut up and take the Porsche. And as for the other car, I've changed my mind, I've decided I'm taking twenty-five percent off that car instead of ten."

Since I was handing Zoe several million dollars she had done no work for, she shouldn't mind if I sold one car at a slight discount. If she said anything, I'd cover the difference myself. Considering all the work Digger and I had put in on getting this first lot ready for shipment over to Amelia Island, Zoe was getting a hell of a good deal.

Henry stuck out his hand. Shaking hands, I mentioned again for him to remember I was taking one of the inside parking places in the new warehouse. Henry mentioned somehow now he needed to create three parking spots inside the building. I pointed out the large space behind the warehouse and how easily a large steel structure could be erected.

"Something to think about," he said.

~ ~ ~ ~ ~ ~

I was back in my condo by 4:30 p.m. and at five, I picked up the old conch shell. I'd never blown on one, but I figured it couldn't be too difficult. I blew on it with all my power and produced a loud, mournful tone. I blew it five times, as long as I could each time. When I put the shell down, I heard somebody at the other end of the canal answer me with five blasts from another shell.

I sat down in the old wicker chair, looking down the canal towards the river, and Martha brought me a drink. With tears in her eyes, she handed me the glass. "It would please Mr.

Tom that you play the shell. He did right thing when he give you this place. Welcome home, Mr. Matt."

"Martha, my friend Lois is coming down for the weekend. Can you make something for us for dinner Friday evening? It can be anything."

Martha grinned at me in the way of an answer. "Is this special one, Mr. Matt?"

"I think so, and the more I get to know her, the more I enjoy her. She's a very special lady." This coming weekend, I needed to have a long talk with Lois. I wanted her to understand why I wanted her to come and spend as much time with me as she wanted. For now, I understood I needed her more in my life than less. I needed her... period. It was important I share with her how I felt about things. Resting in the chair and thinking about her had stirred things up, and I really wished she was with me right now. I wanted her physically and Friday was a long way off. The prospect of several nights in an empty bed did not make me a happy camper.

I wondered about Heather and Digger and how things would work out for them. For now, they were like teenagers, they couldn't keep their hands off one another. They were currently heading back to Idaho. Together! I appreciated Digger for dropping everything he had going on and coming down to help me. Since there was time, I offered to fly the two of them back to Idaho for him to take care of things and asked him to return.

The first lot of cars Digger and I had fixed up were picked up and successfully shipped to Amelia Island where they would appear in the next auction. Digger promised me he'd return to Florida when it was necessary to get the next lot ready for consignment.

~ ~ ~ ~ ~

The next morning, my cell went off when I was in the shower and I missed it. I was dressed and headed out the door when I happened to notice that I'd missed a call from Mouse. I called him back, and he picked up on the second ring. "Matt. Thanks for calling me back."

"What's up, Mouse?"

"I wanted to let you know the DNA results came back. Albert is not Callum's father."

In a way, the news saddened me. I knew Albert wanted the kid to be his, in a way, and I know Callum wanted to know who his father was. "Does Albert know?"

"He was the one who called me and told me the results of the test."

"I assume Callum has to know by now. I set it up so that both Albert and Callum would receive the results. I wonder how Callum is taking the news?"

"Albert is relieved but also rather bummed. He was pretty down when I spoke to him. He's regretting his decision to run for office."

"Why?"

"All the memories this stirred up. He never really got over Linda. I know a lot of their relationship was only about sex, but he also had feelings for her. She wasn't his first, but she was his first really big deal. Jade and I feel the way it ended never gave him proper closure. He still carries a torch for her."

"I met Linda. Not to say she's a dog or anything, but I think Maggie is a much better match for him. I know I have no right to make this kind of judgement, but I can't help but feel that if he had married Linda, they wouldn't be together today. I adore Maggie and think the world of her, but I can see where Linda would have been a sexual partner one never really gets over. Maggie was the one you took home to meet your parents, but Linda was the one you checked in with at the local motel for the weekend. Do you think I should call Albert and talk to him?"

"No. We had a good talk yesterday and I expect him to call me today. Let me talk to him again and I'll let you know if I feel you should call him."

"Okay. Ciao! Oh, Mouse wait… the condo. I want to lease it from you."

"You've finally made a decision? I was wondering if you'd forgotten."

"I've been meaning to call you but when I finally remember and start to do it, something else always seems to interrupt my train of thought. Yes, I want to lease the condo please."

"Great, I'll get the lease prepared."

"Perfect. Thanks."

"Goodbye, Matt."

I sat for a long time staring at my cell phone. I don't know what I expected it to tell me. I was just really bummed the way things had turned out. When I'd was involved in the rescue operations over in the Middle East, once it was over, there was a certain amount of satisfaction regarding what I had done. I found I wasn't getting any satisfaction out of this outcome.

I went to my desk and rummaged around, looking for the business card that Callum had given me. It was at the bottom of a pile of papers I kept meaning to sort and file. I called the cell number listed on the card. "Hello, Callum here."

"Callum, Matt Preston. How ya doing?"

"Hello, Matt. I take it you heard how the DNA test turned out?"

"Yeah. How are you doing?"

"I've decided that it was for the best. At least this way I know one person for sure who isn't my father. I looked at it positively."

"I admire you. I would agree that's the best way to look at things. Are you interested in meeting your birth mother?"

"Yes, and no. I'm glad you called because I was going to call you. I know you have one of my business cards. On the bottom is my email address. Can you send me her address and phone number? That way I have it and if or when I decide I want to call her, I can do it without bothering you."

"It's no bother, but I'll send you the information I have. I would also like to add that you are free to call me anytime you want. I know we don't really know each other all that well, but considering what we shared, I feel a closeness to you. I'm here for you if you need to talk."

"Thanks, Matt. If nothing else, this has brought my wife and I a lot closer. We didn't have problems or anything, but this somehow has helped us share feelings we hadn't addressed before. Our relationship is in a great place because of all this. Thanks for coming out and telling me in person and thank you for calling just now and checking up on me. Remember, you have an invitation to come and visit anytime."

"Careful, I might hold you to that. Goodbye, Callum. Say hi to your wife for me."

"Take care, Matt."

"Will do."

We hung up.

I sat at my desk for a long time. I found I was still disenchanted. Callum had somebody to be with and help him deal with his disappointment. He had a loving person there to share his pain. As for me, my loving person was up in D.C. I knew she was coming for the weekend, but I didn't want to wait that long.

You know me, Mr. Patience.

~ ~ ~ ~ ~

I met Lois' plane late Friday afternoon. The way she kissed me, I don't know which one of us was more excited about seeing the other person. We got to the condo, and I was glad Martha had just left dinner ready to put into the oven and was absent for the rest of the evening. What happened between Lois and me over the next couple of hours would have warped the poor woman for sure.

Later, we ate dinner on the lanai. I had on a pair of shorts and she was wearing only a silk robe and when she moved, it was obvious there was nothing on underneath. We hardly finished dinner. We took our dishes and stacked them in the sink and headed for the bedroom. By the time we got there, I'd lost a pair of shorts and she lost a silk robe. Good lord, that woman was a delight when viewed from behind.

We spent the rest of the night wrapped in each other's arms. I'd told her what time I wanted to leave for the Amelia Island auction the next morning, and we almost didn't leave on time. I don't know what it is about that woman, but she's just like Chinese food. Half an hour later, and you want more.

Lucky for me she felt the same way.

CHAPTER TWENTY-TWO

When Lois and I pulled into the parking lot at the Amelia Island auction, we showed the attendant our passes. Since this was my first auction, I didn't know what to expect or where to go. When the attendant saw my pass and my name, he visibly stood more upright, coming almost to a position of attention. "Good morning, Mr. Preston. Is this your first time with us?" I told them it was, and he motioned for me to drive forward to the next parking area. As I pulled away, I heard him call after us, "Nice ride. Beautiful car."

I noticed as we drove up to the next parking lot, we were getting closer to the actual auction house. The next attendant stopped us and looked over my pass carefully. There was a stub at the bottom which he removed and slipped under my windshield wiper. "This is for your VIP parking," he informed me. I'd driven my old Pontiac over from Fort Myers and the attendant asked me if I would sell this car.

"No, this is my baby! I couldn't part with it," I told him.

"I understand." He pointed out a third attendant ahead who was showing people where to park. I parked the car and this attendant also asked me if I was interested in selling the car. I guess, when driving an early sixties Pontiac Bonneville convertible, one has to expect that it draws that kind of response. The attendant pointed out a large gold golf cart and told us that the cart would deliver us to our seats. Since this was our first event, and we wanted to look around, we declined.

The walk up to the main tent was a car whore's dream. I pointed out several cars to Lois, and she surprised me when she pointed out several old cars and made comments. She was more savvy about cars than I realized.

The collection of Snooker's cars were all grouped together, and I'd sent over a placard to be displayed on each window. It read From the Tom 'Snooker' Frost Collection. I swear I could hear ol' Tom above me chuckling. I sure wish he was here to see what his cars looked like, each one polished like a gem. I was excited to see how we would do today. This truly was Snooker's Legacy, and I felt privileged to be a part of it.

When we entered the main tent and showed our passes, we were escorted to a special area reserved for VIPs. I hadn't realized we would be treated like this. Evidently, having over a couple of million bucks worth of cars to auction had some perks. After they seated Lois and I, a waitress approached. "Hello, my name is Jennifer and I'm your server today. What would you like to drink"?

"Since it's a little early, how about two Bloody Mary's?"

"Coming right up, sir."

After Jennifer left, two gentlemen in suits approached us. One of them extended his hand and introduced himself. He was the Director, and the other was the CEO of the auction. When Digger and I sent the cars over, we didn't realize our cars would bring this kind of attention.

The Director informed us, "If there is anything you want or need, anything at all, just tell Jennifer and someone will see to it."

After they left, Lois leaned over and whispered in my ear, "You know, I could get really used to this kind of treatment."

"Baby, believe me, I didn't realize we'd receive this kind of treatment." I told her, "I guess if I'd thought about it, few people bring twenty cars worth several million dollars to an auction. This should be fun."

This was the last day of the auction and because of the value and rarity of some of our cars being offered today, there was a large crowd. Our drinks arrived, and I asked what I owed. Jennifer smiled and shook her head. "Nothing, sir. Your drinks and food are complementary. If you need anything, just tell me. You know my name is Jennifer and I'm your hostess today."

Damn, I thought to myself. This will be even more fun than I thought. I settled into my seat when I heard a voice behind me say, "Good, they haven't started yet." I turned, and Digger and Heather were standing there.

"You didn't think I'd bust my ass just to get all those cars ready and not watch the show. If you didn't want me here, you shouldn't have sent me the tickets. By the way, one of your planes was over in Seattle and headed this way, so one of Henry's pilots gave us a ride. I hope it was okay."

"Of course. I'm tickled you kids made it." I made the introductions between Lois and Heather since this was the first time they'd met.

Because of the value of some our cars, the earliest any of them would be up for bidding would be about mid-afternoon. Digger excused himself, telling me he and Heather wanted to look at some other cars. Heather put her hand on Digger's arm. "Just a minute, lover, I need to use the little girl's room. Lois, you want to come with me?"

As they left, I wondered about that. If I asked Digger to go to the can with me, he would have made some crude remark and embarrassed the hell out of me. Guys didn't ask guys to go to the bathroom with them. Makes you wonder what the ladies do in there, anyway, besides the obvious, of course.

When the two of them returned, Digger and Heather left to look at cars. I reminded him not to fall in love with something since neither of us needed to deal with another car for a long time. His response was to tell me to perform a physically impossible act. Heather elbowed him and told him to be nice.

After they'd left, Lois leaned over and kissed my cheek. "What's that for?"

"For being you. For you being such a good guy."

"And why are you telling me this now?"

"Heather and I had a little chat in the girl's room."

"And?"

"Did you know she would have made love with you? She wanted to have sex with you?"

"Yeah. I kinda knew. Why do you ask?"

"Heather was very impressed with you. You told her about me and even though she tried to tempt you, you resisted. I'm pleased you care that much about me."

"Baby, I won't tell you I wasn't tempted. I was. Actually, several times. You can only look at a cute little naked body go prancing through the room so many times without being tempted. But I'm still working on us. I know when we are together, it's like no other woman before. I love you. I love how you make me feel. I didn't want to do anything that might screw that up. I wanted to find out where we are heading."

"I kind of wish we were someplace more private. My talk with Heather made me see what a special man you are."

"No, babe, I'm not that special. I find there is an anger inside me that's new. I find I'm not such a nice person after all. I'm having a hard time putting away what happened over in the Middle East. You're helping, but there's still that rage within."

Lois leaned over and put her hand on my cheek, turning me to face her. Her kiss was gentle but full of passion. As we pulled apart, I read her lips. I love you. I want you.

I winked.

~ ~ ~ ~ ~ ~

Our first car went on the block just after 5:30 p.m. I thought the auctioneer did a great job of hyping the entire collection. The first car up was a 1957 Chevy Bel Air post with V-8, fuel injection and a factory floor shift. The combination was very rare. The auction guide Digger and I received listed the collection as Snooker's Legacy. The guide said the '57 was worth between twenty to thirty thousand dollars. I thought the estimate was way too high. Perhaps the high teens, but I found it difficult to believe it would go into the twenties. When the hammer fell, it had sold for thirty-three thousand dollars. Digger and I looked at each other and shook our heads. Digger mouthed the words, Holy shit! I agreed.

A few other cars went over the block and the next one of Snooker's was a cute 1966 Mercedes 230 SL with both tops, a hard top and a soft top folded up. In the information we'd found that Snooker had on the car, he said he had purchased it new at the factory while stationed in Germany. The car had a few extra things on it that most don't have because he had gone through the factory and watched it being built. The estimate on the car was for the high forties and when the hammer fell, the car had sold for fifty-nine thousand, five hundred dollars. Things were going really well.

Next up was a Lincoln Mark V that was a real cream puff, and because it wasn't that rare, I didn't expect it to do that well. It cleared the block at just over twenty grand, which I felt was respectable.

The next three cars were a 1966 Mustang Convertible, a 1968 Dodge Charger and a 1955 Chevy Convertible which drew, $48,250, $71,500 and $68,200 respectively.

When I'd seen the catalogue price for the 1956 Oldsmobile '88 convertible estimated between sixty and sixty-five thousand, I thought the auction people were crazy. Again, I was wrong. The car crossed the block for $74,800. The car was nice and all, but I thought it was a stupid price.

I was totally enthralled with the auction. I was like a little kid on his birthday with Christmas thrown in. I glanced over at Lois and noticed she was just as engrossed as I was. I saw that Heather and Digger were also spellbound with the activities. All of our hard work for Zoe was paying unexpected dividends. We were really enjoying ourselves. I mentally sent out a big thank you to Snooker. I hoped he was looking down on this event and was as mesmerized with it as we all were.

The next car brought the auction to a halt. The book for the 1965 Buick Riviera Grand Sport was listed between sixty-five and seventy thousand and I felt it was a fair price. Digger and I had both lusted over the car because this one was especially nice. It was heavily optioned and in excellent condition. The price blew past the seventy number with amazing speed and kept climbing in five-thousand increments until eventually the hammer fell. Digger and I almost fell out of our chairs. $117,700 for the car. The crowd cheered, and we shook our heads.

I was flabbergasted when the 1930 Ford Model A went over the block. It was a frame off restoration with a great color scheme and the interior was absolutely perfect. The book estimated the price was between twenty-five to thirty thousand and I thought it was a low price. When the bidding was over, the car sold for only $22,000. I felt somebody had stolen the car. Lois could tell it bummed me out, and she patted my leg. She leaned over and whispered, "Now, don't be greedy."

There were just three cars left when the Shelby Cobra came up on stage. The 1965 Cobra 427 had become an overnight sensation among both Shelby devotees and any car nut who was looking for a rare car. The low mileage and the provenance that Snooker had assembled helped the value of the car. From Snooker's documentation, we had determined that car was last driven somewhere around 1991. I thought the estimated value of nine hundred thousand was a little low and I was right. Bidding opened at half a million and took off. The hammer dropped at $1,245,000. Crazy. Absolutely crazy. I was positive I heard Snooker screaming up above. I doubt if he had any idea when he purchased the car in 1980 for $55,000 that someday, it would be worth over a million bucks.

The final cars from the collection to cross the block were two cars that were being sold as a set. One time when Snooker was stationed in Europe, he went over to England on leave and visited the Austin-Healey factory where he had two Healey 3000 MK III BJ8's built. Both were British Racing Green with tan leather seats and tan tops. The chrome spoke wheels sparkled as the cars passed before the bidding podium. The unique feature about the cars was that they were identical except that one was right-hand drive and the other was left-hand drive. The cars were only one serial number apart on the VIN and every bell and whistle Austin-Healey offered at the time was on each car. Both vehicles had fewer than two thousand miles on them. From some comments Snooker had left in his papers, the cars were some of his favorites. Normally, one car would have been worth somewhere in seventies. That would mean that two of them should bring around one hundred forty thousand dollars, right?

The bidding opened at one hundred thousand and jumped by ten thousand as fast as the auctioneer could speak. Every time the price jumped, Digger and I looked at each other and shook our heads. Finally, when the hammer fell, the two cars sold for over three hundred thousand dollars. It was insane. Totally unbelievable. I guess because they were the only twin cars in the world, it made them worth much more. The pair really were unique. All I knew was that even though I thought the cars were amazing, there was no way I would have paid that kind of money for them.

Two million, seven hundred eight thousand, three hundred fifty dollars was the day's total. Digger had been keeping score and after the pair of Healeys had sold, he leaned over and whispered in my ear, "What a shame we didn't break three million!" We both cackled, and I was so pleased for Zoe. I reminded him he still had to take off the 10% the auction house kept from our side of the sale.

He reminded me, "And the seller has to pony up an additional 10%. No wonder we're being treated so well. We put over two hundred and seventy grand in their pockets plus another two hundred seventy from the buyers. That's a hell of a deal."

"Yes, but Zoe just made two million, four hundred thirty-four and change. That young lady did very well today." The next time Jennifer came by, I asked her if we could have four glasses of single malt scotch. She grinned and told us normally, she'd have to check with management, but since we had put so much money into the auction's pockets with their commissions, she felt sure it was okay.

When we got our drinks, all four of us held our glasses up towards the sky and I looked up at the heavens. "Snook, you did good. I think this will help your granddaughter for some time to come. Nice job!" We clinked glasses and took a sip. Jennifer had done an excellent job selecting the Scotch.

Digger looked over at me. "How long before we have to have the next lot ready to go?"

"I have no idea. But knowing what kind of stuff we're dealing with, it makes it a lot easier to get them all ready to sell. I didn't know today would be this productive."

"If you had told me what kind of money we would have gotten for the Healeys or the Cobra, I'd have told you, you were crazy. Those numbers totally blew me away."

Lois and I headed back to my condo on the river, and Digger and Heather headed for the airport for their ride back to Idaho. We all gave each other hugs, and he gave me a parting shot. "How come you never come and visit me in Idaho?"

"Keep the spare bedroom ready. Lois and I will be along shortly," I promised.

For those who are interested, the final scorecard for the first third of Snooker's collection:

- 1957 Chev Bel Air post, with floor mounted 4-speed tranny, $33,000
- 1966 Mercedes Benz 230SL Roadster with two tops, $59,400
- 1977 Lincoln Mark V   Low mileage, $20,000
- 1966 Mustang Convertible 4-speed, $41,250
- 1968 Dodge Charger Hemi 4 speed, $71,500
- 1955 Chevy Convertible, $68,200
- 1956 Oldsmobile 88, Convertible, $70,400
- 1965 Buick Riviera Grand Sport, $117,700
- 1970 Barracuda ('Cuda) $69,700
- 1957 Chevy Bel Air Convertible $66,000
- 1969 Mustang Fastback $51,700
- 1961 Chevy Bubbletop with 4-speed 409 motor $77,000

- 1969 Chevy 396 SS Convertible, $74,800
- 1930 Ford Model A, Frame off restoration, $22,000
- 1957 Mercury Convertible, $40,700
- 1966 Buick Grand Sport Convertible, $79,200
- 1967 Corvette Sting Ray, big block with a stock 36 gallon gas tank, $175,500
- 1965 Shelby 427 Cobra with less than 18,000 miles, $1,245,000
- (2) 1967 Austin Healeys' Mark III, identical, $330,300

Digger felt we had a very respectable day. If you'd asked me, I was stunned.

That night in bed, Lois snuggled up to me and asked, "Do you wish you could have kept some of those cars, or that some of them had been yours?"

I kissed her and held her close. "No, baby. I have everything I could ever want right now in my arms."

She took one of my hands and placed it on her naked breast. Taking my face between her hands, she purred, "Good answer, lover. Good answer. And just for that, I'm going to... "

And she proceeded to...

Well, sorry, but you don't really need to know what happened next. Suffice it to say what I had told her was true. Lois made things so all I could ever want was truly right there in my arms.

Almost two and a half million dollars for Zoe then Lois did...

Wow!

What a day to remember!

~ ~ ~ ~ ~

The next evening, I was feeling a bit despondent. I leaned back in my chair in my new condo, put my feet up on the ottoman, and took a sip of my drink. Lois had returned to Washington D.C. and now that I was alone, I realized how important she'd become. I hated to admit it, but I wasn't sure if I could settle in and be happy and content living with just one woman. However, if it were possible for me, I felt it could be her. We'd planned it so that I'd go visit her in two weeks and spend more time with her again. I was already looking forward to that.

I continued sipping my Scotch, looking down the water-way and the river beyond in the distance. The old planter's chair wasn't as comfortable as the old leather chair I had back at my old place, but it would do. Everything was being moved from my old apartment to the new condo. My new pad. Well, actually it still belonged to Mouse since I was just leasing. Let's see, does that make it a mouse pad? Lois had been gone for only a few hours and my brain was turning to mush!

A friend of mine wanted to purchase the bike and if he hadn't already picked it up, he would in the next day or two. I was glad I wasn't there to watch it drive away. This way, in my head, the bike was still in the garage even though I knew it was gone. That was for the best.

I knew whatever I had left in Seattle, Scott was liquidating, and the more I thought about it, the more I realized it was the right thing to do. Having the condo was about all the attachment I wanted, or needed, in Seattle.

Digger and I still needed to get the next lot of cars ready for auction, I still had to help Henry get the warehouse and the hanger set up, but those were manageable things. For now, I needed to concentrate on Lois. I planned to call her in the morning and fly up and spend some more time with her.

This might work out….

And now, as I understood more of what was happening, I realized I'd done the right thing in Seattle. It had been a good run, but it was time. Seattle would always be home, in a way, since it was where I'd been born and raised, but I was bitter about the changes I'd seen. Having Mouse's condo at my disposal was the just the right amount of exposure I wanted in Seattle.

Gazing off towards the river, I found a peace settling over me. A peace that had been missing lately. I still had to get my dogs from Walter, but with access to a private plane, it would be easy to bring them down. I really missed the love and companionship they gave to me. I took another sip and reflected. "Yes, for now, I guess I'm home. I'm close to Lois and with the air business, I have easy access to her and she can visit me anytime she wants to."

Without realizing it, I'd been seeing for quite a while it was time for changes in my life and now they were happening.

And it felt good.

I was happy.

I was at peace.

THE END

(Well, not really; however, this is a good place to leave... for now.)

LIST OF CHARACTERS

Albert Bradson, Washington State Senator, running for President of the United States

Audrey Billings, Professor at KU in English

Callum Bickerstaff, Linda Ferrara's illegitimate child, see Elwood and Sarah

Elora Tronscoso, dance instructor, owner of E&R Dance Studio

Elwood Bickerstaff, head of the English dept at KU, adopted Linda's child

Guido, Zampuchini's capo

Henry Walbourn, pilot and business partner of Matt

Jade Fox, Mouse's wife

Jeff L. Davenport, Commissioner of Police in Seattle, childhood friend of Matt

Linda Ferrara, Albert Bradson's love interest at the university

Lois Tollifson, works for John Orchard, friend of Matt

Margaret 'Maggie' Bradson, Albert's wife

Ramiro Tronscoso, dance instructor, co-owner of E&R Dance Studio

Robyn Meenen Bueler, veterinarian and former roommate of Maggie and Linda

Salvatore Zampuchini, head of Das Berliner and other casinos, Linda's boss

Steve Fox, 'Mouse', Matt's mysterious friend

Thein McLaughlin, wife of Walter McLaughlin

Tom Frost, 'Snooker', buddy from Nam, grandfather of Zoe Frost

Walter McLaughlin, a buddy from Nam who saved Matt's life

ACKNOWLEDGMENTS

I think a cover without Kevin Summers being involved would be a disaster. For the fifth time Kevin has come up with what I feel is a killer book cover. And then there's his mastery over the little bytes and bits lurking in the depths of the computer which somehow through his magic, turn into this novel you hold in your hands. What a great job of formatting my manuscript he does so my novels appear in a readable format. A double thank you Kevin.

Thank you, Jessie, for taking my words and thoughts and making some semblance of sense out of them. A good editor is invaluable as I have found out. Thanks Jessie, for your help with this novel.

A continuing thank you to Dr. Dinesh Sharma for keeping me upright. Whatever amazing new piece of modern technology he did to my old ticker seems to be working since I'm still here and still writing. Thank you for all that you've done for me.

Another big thank you to Bill Crawford, owner of Gulf Coast Auto Repair for his expertise regarding automobiles and for sharing his immense knowledge of classic cars with me. To say that he would have liked to visit Snooker's collection is an understatement. His biggest regret is that this is a work of fiction. Thanks' Bill.

A personal note of gratitude, as well as thanks to my old friend Burt Fraley. Burt plays a most important part in this tale, but I won't exactly tell you who he is in this novel. Burt is a colorful person who has led a most interesting life and has provided me with some excellent anecdotes. Thank you, Mister Fraley. I hope I have done your tale justice.

A special thank you to Joe Spielman. Back in the day, Mr. Spielman was a VP with General Motors in charge of

North America production. There's a very interesting story regarding his saving the Corvette brand from extinction. In some circles, Mr. Spielman is known as Mr. Corvette. It's my understanding one of the streets at the Corvette Museum in Bowling Green Kentucky is named Spielman Street. Joe's knowledge of old Corvettes was invaluable. Thanks Joe. Joe has an interesting theory regarding driving a Corvette and the size of a man's masculinity which I'll not get into at this point.

There really is a person named Kip Gates, and he's a true cowboy in all senses of the word. (He really is seventh generation cowboy.) His stories of his ranch, and the breeding of a special breed of horses have been fascinating. Mr. Gates does live at the end of the world and you can go there and either fish or hunt just like I've outlined in this book. Thank you to Mr. Gates for sharing the stories of his life with me and his valued insight.

Thank you to my youngest daughter, Robyn. Besides being one of the driving forces behind my novels, she is one of my biggest fans. Without her constant, "Is it done yet? Is it done yet?", my novels might still be slumbering in the depths of my computer. Okay Robyn, here! It's done. Now give me a break and let me see if there is another story in my ol' brain.

Finally, I wish to express my gratitude to my wife, Sandy. You all know none of my novels would exist today without her support and encouragement. Thank you.

And this brings to close another Matt Preston adventure. There are plans for a book six, and some of it is written, other parts of it are floating around inside my head. The trick is to get it from my head and into the computer.

For now; I'm finished. This time I plan on resting the ol body for a while and let Dr. Sharma's device try and do its job…

Until the next novel…….

Good Night

ABOUT THE AUTHOR

Paul lives in North Fort Myers, Florida with his wife and biggest fan Sandy and their beautiful American Cocker Spaniel Samantha, better known as "Our Baby Girl."

Born and raised in Seattle and now transplanted to Florida, in addition to writing, Paul keeps busy learning to ballroom dance and working on an HO scale train layout. A graduate of Western Washington University in Education, Paul taught for four and a half years and became self-employed when he left teaching.

Over the years, Paul has owned and operated many businesses, where he met countless interesting people who always seem to confide astonishingly personal information to him, hence the varied knowledge of people, parts of which he massages to create his fictional characters.

To contact Paul Shadinger, please email him at pshadingerauthor@outlook.com. He enjoys hearing from his fans.

THANK YOU FOR READING

Thank you for reading this book. If you enjoyed it, please post a review on one or more of the websites listed below and tell your friends about this book. (If you didn't care for it just let Matt Preston know.)

Amazon:
www.amazon.com/author/paulshadinger

Goodreads:
www.goodreads.com/pshadingerauthor

Readers Favorite:
www.readersfavorite.com/book-review/snookers-legacy

To contact Paul Shadinger:
pshadingerauthor@outlook.com

Follow Paul Shadinger on:
www.facebook.com/pshadingerauthor
Twitter: @paulshadinger

Also Check for Events and Announcements on:
www.paulshadingerauthor.com

www.ingramcontent.com/pod-product-compliance
Lightning Source LLC
Chambersburg PA
CBHW070653180626
46817CB00006B/2344

9 7 8 1 7 3 3 7 2 1 5 0 9